Mostly Human, Mostly Cat

BOOK TWO

THE OMNIST SERIES

ROB WELDON

I'd like us to work on a meditation that leads to shapeshifting—to seeing the world through the eyes of other forms of life. It's called therianthropy. – Thalia

But magic existed before science, because it did. It did. And when people figured out how things worked, they called it science and the magic seemed to go away. People love to explain the mystery out of things. – Kevin O'Culled

And your Emporium cat, the feline Consumerian, he shall remain. He raises the average IQ of the room. – Yksian Tapiola

And while we're alive, we're fighting entropy. Our body is constantly dying and renewing itself, trying to keep its shape in the face of destruction of form, before we finally succumb and return to sand. – Yksian Tapiola

Animals understand us better than we give them credit for, but we also anthropomorphize them, which causes us to further misunderstand them. It's a delicate balance. – Jasmine Waters

CHAPTER
ONE

HARPER

H arper Rose stopped by Consumia's Spiritual Emporium to buy a few things: some herbs and mushroom powders, an essential oil, some ground saber tusk. CSE didn't specialize in rare herbs, but they carried what little extra she needed for today's particular concoction. They also carried several herbs she'd grown herself, some of which may have been illegal, but they never asked. Probably didn't care. She used to joke that if she swept the floor of their Dark Arts room, she could cast a random spell from the residue.

To be fair, Harper made the scrape-the-floor joke about several places she regularly visited, like spice shops in alleys, Russian and Asian markets, outdoor farmers markets, and small secretive distributors in downtown Los Angeles who operated from behind an aluminum door and may or may not open it for you based on your appearance.

Besides the herbs here, she loved the aroma of dusty air, fresh wood, essential oils, and incense. Although the various fetuses and animal parts on the shelves were hermetically sealed in jars, she still sensed the alcohol and formaldehyde. All manner of life was present here. Alive, alive and dying, dead in a suspended decomposition, decomposing, and organic ingredients of pre- and post-life, plus pre-cast spells to push things along in any of these directions. Dead or alive, life here was continually shifting to another state.

She found the last vial of imported cat saber tusk, both delicate and sturdy, with a ring on the cap to easily make it into a pendant if she so desired. The portion was just enough and would save her another trip downtown.

She went to the front of the Emporium and picked out a couple of Organica candles from an arrangement near the counter.

Kat was working the register today. For as conventional as Harper appeared, Kat looked the part of working in the realm of mysticism. She didn't know Kat well, but assumed she didn't worship Satan or have a demon fetish, regardless of what her black clothes, black hair with recently bleached white bangs, and snarky demeanor suggested. Maybe it was Harper's extra twelve or thirteen years of maturity, or maybe she just had more to hide, but she'd learned to present herself as more unassuming. Overall, she liked Kat and thought she'd be an interesting project, someone to groom with wisdom and advice. And it wasn't just Kat's feline-sounding name, either, although that didn't hurt.

"Hello, dear," Harper said when she approached the counter. "Would you hand me a vial of agarwood?" Or oud, as those who peddled knockoffs often called it. The Emporium carried the real thing and it wasn't cheap, which was why even a ten-milliliter vial was kept under the glass of the front counter.

"I love this," Kat said, her tone conveying no additional excitement as she placed one of the nearly black vials on the counter.

Harper picked it up and unscrewed the tiny cap, taking in the bouquet. She held it over for Kat, who leaned in to inhale, her eyes apparently massaged by the scent.

Connie—*the* Consumia of Consumia's Spiritual Emporium—wouldn't approve of Harper's plans tonight, and Harper had no intentions of telling her, nor anybody else. Harper wasn't interested in the other things the Emporium sold: the T-shirts, the costume jewelry, the optimism. Even though they were known to sell the macabre: the preserved, crushed, or ground animal parts (and rumor was, even human), much of it was relegated to the Dark Arts room, so maybe Connie had an out-of-sight-out-of-mind mentality.

"Just what do you think people plan to do with this stuff, sweetie?" Harper imagined asking her. But as a shop owner, Connie was always so nice, smiling, greeting Consumerians, and handing out complimentary tea, that she likely had no clue what some of her customers really believed in, and Harper wasn't going to raise the issue. She hadn't seen her here today, anyway.

Harper's next stop was a bakery in Burbank called Poncho's, where she picked up a decorated anniversary cake. She hated cake. Didn't think Giovanni particularly cared for it, either. But she needed this distraction for everything to run smoothly. The cake was the...err, icing on the cake.

~

AT HOME, she placed the powders and spices on the counter and the cake in the refrigerator. She retrieved an antique green bottle of pre-prepared fermented red grape elixir infused with homegrown herbs. This had taken time to mature and had been sitting in a cool, dry place in a vintage cabinet in the dining room. She set the bottle on the counter with the other items.

At some point, all five of her cats made an appearance in the kitchen, curious as to what she was up to:

Spike, the biggest and oldest cat, a brown and gray tabby, paced the floor, the house, checking doors and perimeters. He was piqued, ready for action. He rarely showed affection, but came up behind her and head-butted the back of her calf to get her attention. Without looking, she reflexively shook her foot at him in frustration. He uselessly swiped a paw at her ankle and continued vetting the area.

Chico, heavier and white, rubbed against Harper's leg as she worked. She did her best to ignore him.

Jagger, with long gray hair, lay on a mat inside the back door, facing Harper, rarely lifting his head to look.

Steve was a lighter gray, distinguished by his patch of white fur on his chest, and sat in the kitchen doorway observing the scene.

Cherry, a bright red, strawberry, and white calico sat watching three feet away on the counter. Since Cherry was her newest cat, she hadn't seen Harper make this potion yet, and it was no surprise she was the most curious.

Harper worked under a framed picture that said, "Caelum super me, Terra infra me, Ignis in me." This meant "Sky above me, Earth below me, Fire within me." She knew enough Latin to read old texts of spells and always tried to think in Latin as she worked, rather than translating.

She ground some herbs with an old Petoskey and

Charlevoix stone pestle and mortar, the ground cat saber tusk helping to pulverize the other ingredients. She added a powdered fur and whisker donation from her own cats, more herbs, as well as catnip. She mashed and crushed and twisted and ground, putting her shoulder into it, forcing the organic into the stone as much as freeing microscopic bits of stone into the powder itself. People didn't realize how difficult it was turning most things into powder. It took strength and patience.

A dash of dried cat feces was added last. This didn't take long to mix in.

Once the concoction had reached the consistency of a silty salt-and-pepper gray powder, she rubbed it between two fingers. It was chalky to the touch, with softer organic bits sticking to her fingers, the fine dust coating the inside of her fingerprints.

She washed her hands. As disgusting as the ingredients were, this was more to protect herself from accidental poisoning.

Even though she had cross-referenced the recipe from an ancient book, potions for her was an inexact science, performed by feel, eyeballing the measurements as she went along. She based the quantities on how much saber she had in her possession, since it was the most limited in supply. There would be no extras, just like last time. And she'd sworn that time would be the last.

Which reminded her, Giovanni believed her pestle and mortar set was made of limestone. She had corrected him several times, but had to admit that Petoskey, being a rare fossilized coral found in Michigan, looked similar to limestone. It was Michigan's state stone, and rare enough that a person was restricted to removing only twenty-five pounds from the ground at once by state law. If someone found a rock larger than that, which was extremely uncommon, the state would confiscate it and it'd become a museum piece. So, Petoskey made a great mortar.

The pestle was made of Charlevoix stone, which was a different species of fossilized coral also found in Michigan, darker, with smaller exoskeletons. To her, the set looked like a snakeskin pestle with a bowl made of fossilized eyeballs.

The set had a substantial financial value from the stone alone, but carved into the set, who knew what it was worth. It was living stone. The microscopic Petoskey and Charlevoix dust her P and M created was important to many of her creations. She was attached to the set the way chefs were attached to a particular cutting board or knife. It was broken in, grooved, and polished by use. It had long grown past financial considerations. It was invaluable.

She opened a bottle of wine, a good Bordeaux, as Giovanni would expect this evening, and poured herself a glass to drink while she worked. Gio could have the rest of it for all she cared. But she predicted he wouldn't have the opportunity to finish it.

She slid over a pour-over coffee contraption, a freestanding copper wire base with a removable glass basin at the top, and placed a Pyrex measuring cup underneath it. She put a brown filter in the basin and spooned the powdered mixture in as if making coffee. She then uncapped the jug of years-old fermented elixir, scrunching her nose at the smell (one never got used to the odor), and slowly poured it over the powder, wetting every bit, in effect "brewing" the concoction at room temperature.

After all the elixir had dripped through the filter, she removed the cup and placed a second measuring cup underneath and poured the potion through the powder (now a pebbly mud), a second, then a third time from cup to cup, harnessing all the essences of the concoction.

The final substance was consistent in hue and, except for an oily black rainbow glistening on the surface, looked like a German mulled red wine or digestif.

Then, with a funnel, she slowly poured the cup of potion down the neck of the bottle of Bordeaux, replacing what she had poured for herself. She always half-expected a dramatic sizzling sound, but it never happened. She recorked the bottle and swirled the contents gently for a marriage of flavors, powers, and intentions, the energy charging right there in her hands. She knew when she poured a glass, it would look virtually indistinguishable from the unmolested wine she was drinking.

She set the bottle on the windowsill in sight of the half moon. It wasn't a requirement of the recipe, but as with so many other potions for her, exploiting the power of moonlight felt like an essential step.

Seventeen years ago, after the first time she'd made this concoction, she'd immediately thrown out the leftovers and cleaned the dishes, fearing any remaining evidence. A couple years later, she wished she'd saved the leftovers, or at least the fermented grape elixir base. So when she did end up needing to make the potion again, she set some of the elixir base aside for future use, hoping all the while she'd never need it.

CHAPTER
TWO

GIOVANNI

As Giovanni Susurrus drove to Consumia's Spiritual Emporium, he was mildly disappointed Harper had insisted on having dinner delivered tonight. A one-year anniversary called for a nice restaurant. He'd been worried she would break up with him recently, but she never did seem to want to go out much, even if it was a celebration.

His phone lit up with a Mote, which was a notification from the Omnist, the app for Consumia's Spiritual Emporium.

MOTE:

Speaking in tongues: an old language, or a new one, or a jumbled mess.

. . .

SPEAKING *WOMENISH*, he thought. No, he needed a better working relationship with *Harperese*, specifically. He felt like whenever he spoke up with his preferences in food, movies, volume of music or voices, whatever it was, he wasn't heard, and when he was heard, he was shut down. Thusly, they ended up doing what she wanted to most of the time.

And he liked eating out. He often worked from home with a three-monitor setup so he could be nearly as efficient as at his Warbler Brothers' office. He was a post-production effects editor, so he spent untold hours staring at screens. It affected his circadian rhythm, so sometimes he needed to get away from the desk to recalibrate, see the sun and other people, and not cook or order in. And he did a pretty good job of not taking these frustrations out on Harper. *Slippery slope*, as they say. Once you realize you're the problem, it's probably too late.

Plus, he was allergic to cats, and they and their dander would be everywhere at Harper's house. Gio wondered how much Harper even liked her pets. She didn't baby or play with them the way others did with theirs. In some ways she fit the stereotype of the crazy cat lady, and in other ways she didn't. The only display of affection was at feeding time, when they'd rub against her legs. She would yell at Spike or Jagger to get off the table, and for the most part, they listened. They seemed to go right up to the line, but never cross it.

He suspected she was going to ask him to move in with her.

Because Gio's condo had a "no pets" rule, Harper would never move there, but he didn't want to move in with her, either. She had a creepy old Craftsman-style house set in the foothills of the Verdugo Mountains in Burbank. Not the most accurate in recognizing architecture styles, he had made the mistake once of calling it a Victorian, which she'd immediately corrected with a thick layer of condescension.

Still, it was probably a hundred years old. Her family had been the only owners; Harper's grandfather died in a bedroom. When Gio spent the night, he would hear noises and voices below the level of language comprehension. Possibly original plumbing suffering through old age with achy, popping joints. Multiple times he heard a door creaking its way open down the hallway. Probably the wind, but the effect was profound.

His place would be easier to sell and she could keep her cats, she would say. It was a big house, big enough for a family to grow. She had been explicit about never getting married, but having turned forty this year, her clock was ticking. She'd dropped hints about being more than just a mom to five cats. Marriage or no, she probably wanted a baby.

HE PARKED down the block from CSE. Like many other businesses along this strip of Lankershim Boulevard in North Hollywood, they didn't have their own parking lot. Consumerians were beginning to gather in front of the store and in CSE's Basil Alcove for a Lodge tonight. An easel announced that the Omniscian named Organica was speaking, and her merchandise was specially priced on racks near the front door and register. Organica was a proponent of living close to the land, growing your own food, veganism, that sort of thing.

The Organica merchandise display was serendipitous; Gio didn't have to think too hard about choosing an anniversary gift for Harper: a marble pestle and mortar set curated and blessed by Organica. He passed on the idea of buying Harper more candles.

The Emporium's resident goth Kat rang him up. "I would totally eat my yogurt out of this," she said.

"Expensive bowl," Gio said, people-watching.

He saw CSE employees Paula and Derby greeting Organicans in the Basil Alcove, the audience area in front of the stage. He was mildly surprised Harper hadn't suggested attending Organica's Lodge tonight. Maybe she didn't know about it. He had a soft spot for Organica, as it was in front of that very stage, listening to her speak, that Gio and Harper had first held hands.

So yes, buying Harper a gift blessed by Organica showed he was thoughtful and sentimental. Besides, this was in her wheelhouse. Harper loved growing herbs, spices, and rare plants. Examples included rosemary, sage, thyme, oregano, chives, basil, peppercorns, parsley, dill, cilantro, and mint, plus many more that were foreign to Gio. She harvested her own sea salt from the mountains. He wasn't exactly sure how she acquired it. Maybe it was from the desert. Still.

Her regular limestone pestle and mortar set was ready to spend retirement displayed on a shelf in her front room, next to an ancient soapstone bowl used for pulverizing maize. Even if the P and M was a family heirloom or something, she could set it out as a collector's piece. He wasn't implying she should get rid of it, by any means. She could now spare it from further damage. He was thoughtful this way, too.

Driving home, an advertisement for Consumia's Spiritual Emporium came on the radio and he caught himself laughing out loud. He had just left there. Connie voiced the ad like a used car dealer.

"Your life, your afterlife!" she said. "You have natural power, come tap it!"

~

Gio saw a CSE event postcard on Harper's kitchen counter, next to their logoed, biodegradable black bag. He'd waved off all this when Kat was ringing him up, instead buying a gift bag that he now left in the car to surprise Harper with when the time was right.

"You went to the Emporium?" he said to Harper. Although they both frequented CSE, there were unspoken rules: Organica was hers. The Omnist app was his.

"Oh, I picked up a couple candles," Harper said. "For tonight."

There were more than a hundred candles in various stages of use throughout the house. Every room, nearly every flat surface: kitchen, dining, bathrooms, bedrooms. Back patio. But she'd felt the need to get two more, which were apparently the ones already on the dining table.

"The only house heated by candle," he said. She didn't respond.

One of the five cats jumped onto the dining table and Harper stomped in its general direction. "Chico! Down!" she said.

He immediately jumped down.

"Will you light some candles?" she said. "But not the new ones. We'll light those when the food arrives."

Gio did this without question, picking ones that had been previously lit, but wondered how it was that the cats hadn't burned down the house with all their running and jumping around. It was an accident waiting to happen. An old curtain, *poof!*

He could swear Chico had jumped on the table to watch him more closely. This was why he hated cats. They were always staring at him, jealous of competition for Mommy's attention.

And they didn't seem to like him much, either. It's not like he swatted at them or yelled or anything. He avoided contact, trying not to aggravate his allergies. So naturally they rubbed against him or jumped on his lap when he sat on the couch. At least Harper always swooshed them out of her bedroom before they went to bed. He appreciated that.

But the dander remained, evidenced by his waking up with swollen, itchy eyes. He had nightmares several times that he woke up to a cat sitting on his chest, staring him in the face, and sucking the air out of him. He'd once left his jacket on the living room couch, and when he went to pick it up, one of the cats was sleeping in it. It was perfectly curled into the collar and shoulders, so after Harper removed Jagger, Gio couldn't wear it until he washed it.

"Isn't that cute?" Harper had said.

It wasn't cute. It was evil.

He suspected if he were to move into the house, one of the males would piss in his shoes or something. They would ramp up their covert attacks. Rubbing Gio's legs had already progressed to rubbing under his chin when he was lying down. That spot would break out in hives, itching like a cluster of baby mosquito bites. He knew the shoes were next; he could feel it. Then the cats would only be limited by their imagination.

In Harper's defense, she often reminded him to take his over-the-counter allergy medicine before coming over, but she also seemed to enjoy watching him suffer when he forgot. And now that he thought about it, this was as good a time as any to take his pill. He popped one into his mouth, grabbed her glass of wine, and took a drink to wash it down.

"Hey, easy!" she said, swiping the glass away from his lips. "I'm only having one, so don't drink mine."

It had only been a sip; it wasn't a big deal. She could pour more for herself. It was very good wine. She had chosen well.

MOTE:
Instead, try thinking in tongues.

THREE

HARPER

When Gio said he needed to run out to the car, she knew it couldn't be good. If he'd said he forgot his allergy medicine, that would've been understandable, but he'd already taken it. She had a special potion tea she'd authored herself that scrambled the drinker's thinking. Not a ton. They wouldn't black out or hurt themselves, but maybe lose a little memory or train of thought. It'd rearrange their thoughts in a more positive direction. *It has a beneficial effect on the world!* For an instant she figured Gio may have accidentally drunk some, but he hadn't. She'd mixed her herbal potion with some looseleaf tea this morning and put it in a mason jar on the counter where it remained undisturbed until she brewed it. She'd need it in a few days, maybe a week or two, whenever authorities were bound to call on her. She'd be a responsible, concerned girlfriend, offering them a tea. They'd refuse, but she'd pour one anyway. Officers liked their caffeine. She hadn't met one yet who didn't.

Maybe Gio was bringing in sparkling water, since she never had that at her house. She preferred natural spring water and preparing her own beverages and tonics to anything prepackaged.

She heard the car door slam and Gio's footsteps as he bounced back up to the house. She heard jolliness in his feet. Something about the way the shoes contacted the pavement. The happy scuff and slide.

She'd warned him once early in the relationship to not let the cats slip out the door, and to his credit, he always carefully opened the door to make sure no one was ready to launch. There never were, but it was a test of how well he would obey the rules of her house, how conscientious he would be.

He had a peculiar look on his face when he handed her what was obviously a CSE gift bag. She had one just like it in a closet. He was clearly pleased with himself.

"Not a big deal," he said. "I know how much you love curating your own seasonings."

She removed the tissue and took out a heavy box that said "Organica" on it. The pestle was the size of a piece of string cheese, the mortar the size of half a grapefruit. Along the rim was etched a quote:

Soul feeds the food and food feeds the soul.

A fine item for somebody else, anybody else. God help him.

He hadn't been paying attention when she explained why she loved the pestle and mortar set she already had. Of course, she'd left out details about witchcraft and such, but he'd seen her frequently using the P and M for herbs and spices, especially her own harvest. She was clearly attached to it.

If it'd been the thought that counted, he'd failed again. His logic seemed to be that if her set was merely an aging tool, he'd buy her an updated one. Newest model. The man had power tools he never used, but would never sell, either. For him, taking them out of the box and storing them on shelves or display hooks in his walk-in closet or office was better than not having them at all. But she knew better than to buy them for him as gifts. Unlike his tools, her ancient P and M wasn't for show. It served a purpose greater than he could know.

And they'd promised each other no anniversary gifts. Both were in their early forties, so a year together wasn't as big a deal as when they'd been, say, in their twenties. He'd broken the no-gift promise. Although this wasn't a big deal, considering the overall situation, she felt more vindicated than ever. This was a clear example of an overarching issue that she'd been dealing with for a while: he didn't pay attention, and when he did, he didn't listen.

"Thank you, sweetie," she said, giving him a peck on the cheek. He was so pleased with himself she wanted to smack him.

"We should've cooked for ourselves tonight," he said, "and broke this sucker in."

The statement called for no response. She put the P and M back in the box and set it at the far end of the counter.

"But ordering in's fine." He rocked himself from heel to toe. She could tell he didn't know what to say. "That works."

At least he didn't put up any resistance about ordering food. They generally took turns paying for meals, as she felt it was only fair, but he didn't hesitate to take charge tonight. Maybe he'd gotten used to not eating in restaurants all the time. He claimed to not mind cooking, but never offered to help if she'd already begun a meal. And he never offered to cook at his place, either. To her, eggs and toast and Wide-Eyed Wyatt coffee in the morning didn't count.

"Regular or spicy garlic?" he said, reading from a menu on his food delivery app.

"Definitely spicy garlic." For the edamame. She wanted him to eat intense flavors to mask any potential off-notes in the wine.

"I kind of want salmon in my poke bowl instead of tuna. I'll be different."

"Give me salmon, too," she said. *Why not.* "And extra sides of ginger and wasabi." *The cats will eat well tonight.*

Well, not the wasabi.

FOUR

KAT

The rungs of a witch's ladder could be made of hair, feathers, twine, or beads. Each knot could be a separate charm, and a ladder was a series of them. The bestsellers at Consumia's Spiritual Emporium were collections of spells that enhanced one other. Like humor, charm, and gregariousness for an introvert who wanted to make friends. Or strength, courage, and perseverance for someone who needed to tackle a big life challenge. One of the most popular was for beauty, attraction, and love.

A Consumerian named Stacy was browsing the witch's ladders in the Dark Arts room. Her hair and dress were similar to Connie's, as product made her head-scaped and highlighted hair nearly a helmet, and her expensive (possibly knockoff) brand-named fashion was designed to impress. But whereas Connie's face was warm and lit up easily, Stacy's face was stern, and her mouth, with radials of cigarette-lines around her lips, was ready to share her constant dissatisfaction with the world. "You know pre-casting spells is ridiculous," she said. "One should cast their own ladder charms."

"Well, most Consumerians aren't witches, and this way they can bring a spell home," Kat said. She was using a chalk pen on a chalkboard to announce the arrival of new O'Cult potions, drawing a flange with a cork in it in a far corner, a beaker bubbling over with foam in another.

"Or you should at least be in the presence of the person casting it." Stacy flicked at a witch's ladder for enhancing wisdom, knowledge, and curiosity.

"Think of it like a check that's already been signed and filled out for the dollar amount. The Consumerian just has to write in their own name."

"It's cultural appropriation," Stacy said. "This is Connie's prayer to her God of Money, stealing from the Wiccans. How do you know some of these ladders weren't cast by vengeful witches who disagree with all this commercialization? There could be dark spells mixed in to bring bad luck or illness or even death."

"Because they're made by people like Thalia and Kevin O'Culled. They would never do that. We support them."

"At best, these are watered-down ideas. Generic kitsch."

"I take it you see nothing you like, huh?" Kat was known to relax and swim in sarcasm, but she also didn't want to end up like Stacy one day, inventing problems to distract from her own insecurities.

"I'm here for Organica. This section's useless. It's just a way for Connie to make money off depressed people."

"Are you implying it's better to make money off happy people?"

Kat put the black board back on the wall and returned to

the front counter to help Paula at the register. She saw that the Basil Alcove had completely filled with Organicans. There was often a rush of customers to the registers before a Lodge, either guests purchasing snacks or items related to the Omniscian, or other customers hurrying to make purchases before the event began. She hurriedly rang up three customers in a row.

People started clapping as Organica made her way through the front door. There was a woman on either side of her. One was glowing, soft, supple, and traditionally feminine, made up in such a way as to not look made up. The other had a crew cut, a strong jawline, and sinewy arms. Almost military, but in a jean jacket and white T-shirt. Both were striking in their own way; both had brown, innocent, saucer eyes; and Organica was somehow like both, and neither.

A thirty-something woman approached the register holding one of the new witch's ladders. She set it down to pay for it. "What's this here?" she said, tapping a black velvet box on the counter with a small touchscreen on top. It was something Connie had recently added to the point of purchase to draw people to the register. It seemed to be working.

"It's called an 'L.A. Obscura.' It takes a picture of the aura around your fingertips."

"How much does it cost?"

"The picture's free. Here, I'll show you." Kat turned the box to face herself and put her hand in a hole in the front. "You have to tuck the velvet all around your hand to keep out the light...and go like this on the glass."

Kat made a spider shape with the fingers of her other hand, showing what her boxed hand was doing. Then she hit the touchscreen on top to wake it up, and pressed a red button like that of the camera on a smartphone. "Voilà!"

"Does it print?"

"No, but look. I just type in my info and it sends it to me."

Kat typed in her number and a second later, she got a text. It was an image of five dime-sized coronas, the heat from her fingertips. There were blue and red with flares of white shooting off them. L.A. Obscura was written across the top and their logo and address were at the bottom. Meme-ready. She showed the image to the woman.

"Whoa!" The customer began to turn the box toward her.

"Let me wipe it first," Kat said. There was a small dispenser of alcohol wipes on the counter and it took three seconds for Kat to clean the glass inside, then she turned it to face the customer.

The woman repeated Kat's steps and soon was looking at the photo on her phone. "That's so cool."

"So you want to buy this?" Kat picked up the witch's ladder on the counter.

"Do you think it'll help me find someone I lost contact with?" the woman said. Her eyes asked as much as her words.

"What's the story card say, again?" Kat said, opening the card.

"It says it's for help looking for something."

"That could work. There's another one back there, too." Kat walked around the counter and headed for the Dark Arts room. "I'm Kat, by the way."

"Jessica."

"Are you looking for a family member…a friend?"

"A friend. He used to live in my building. We'd go up on the roof and get stoned and stay up late and listen to music and talk. He used to come up with the best and craziest ideas. We'd think of all the impossible things that may actually be true. Like how people are collectively the mind of the universe. Through us is how the universe conceives of itself."

"That's intense."

"Then one day he just disappeared. I must've missed his

moving day. Just never saw him again. I've been thinking about him lately and tried to find him on social media, just to reconnect and say hi, but it's such a political hellhole now. I kind've figured he wouldn't be there. Then I thought maybe a spell would help. Of all people, he'd appreciate it if it turns out this is how I found him."

Kat pulled another witch's ladder from the display and handed it to Jessica. "This one could work, too. It's a communication spell. I used one like this to talk to my husband."

"Your husband?"

"It worked." Kat had never worn a wedding ring. They were supposed to get tattoos on their ring fingers, but they'd never had the chance. "Do you have a photo of your friend? Just hang each of these next to each other on a wall and recite the incantations. There are three in the card: one to listen better, one to express yourself better, and one to reconnect with somebody from your past."

CHAPTER
FIVE

GIOVANNI

W hile Harper was in the kitchen unwrapping and plating the food, Gio turned off the wall lamps in the dining room so that the candles were the only light source. A bulky, brown tabby was sitting on the chair he planned to occupy. The biggest one in the house. Not wanting to touch it with his hands, which would have meant washing them again, Gio lifted one socked foot and gently nudged it.

It lifted its head and looked at him as if to say, "What the hell?"

Still standing on one leg, Gio nearly lost his balance and held on to the back of another chair to steady himself, then pushed his foot under the cat a little harder, enough to lift him an inch or so, majorly pissing him off. The cat squawked and hissed and gave his foot two faster-than-the-eye-could-see swipes with his razor-sharp claws and jumped off the chair.

"Spike! Are you okay?" Harper called from the kitchen.

"What?" Gio said. *He* was the one injured in the incident.

"Where'd he go? Is he all right?" She entered the room with a couple plates and set them on the table. The smell of garlic was overpowering and delicious.

"You could tell which cat that was?" Sometimes he thought she had extrasensory powers. Spike was the oldest and most aggressive of her kitties. She claimed he was seventeen. Gio only remembered what they were called because she'd made collars with their names on them.

"Of course, they're all my little men."

"And girl."

"And girl. Now don't touch anything. We're making a toast first." Harper disappeared into the kitchen and returned with a bottle of wine, an empty glass for him, and her own half-full glass. She sat down, removed the cork, and poured the wine for him.

"And what's up with calling one of them Steve?" Gio said, sitting down. "Why not a cat name like Fluffy or Tiger? I don't think you've ever answered that."

"Well, I think calling a cat 'Fluffy' is disrespectful." She held up her glass. "With your beer gut, how would you like me to call you 'Mr. Wiggles' when you move in with me?"

"Touché." They almost toasted, but Gio stopped cold. Wait a minute. She'd snuck that right in. His prediction had been correct, tonight was more about convincing him to move in.

His foot was burning. The scratch. It felt simultaneously dry and wet, itching and bleeding and sticking to his sock. He set the glass down and rubbed his foot. First things first.

"You know it's bad luck to not drink after a toast," she said. "You nullified it."

"*That* was the toast?" Sneaking in a "moving in" comment? He knew he was smiling. This was the way she acted when she was being sweet. She wasn't snuggly physically, or even verbally, like other girls he'd dated. Occasionally holding hands in public was maximum PDA for her, if she ever went in public. Basically, she told it like it was. You knew when she was mad. You knew where you stood. She had no veneer. "But that Spike. It was so fast. Little needles for claws."

"He doesn't mean it. Not the way you think, anyway."

"Real toast this time?" Gio picked up his glass. "You get a do-over."

"Okay, then. To my darling Giovanni, thank you for being you. Thank you for the marble pestle and mortar. And thank you for doing laundry yesterday. You've opened my eyes to what living with you will be like. And so, tonight is my gift to you. Happy anniversary."

She wasn't even asking. She was telling it like it was. He liked this. There was something sexy about the way she toasted with a glass from a hundred-dollar bottle of wine.

"A red with salmon. Bold move," he said, clinking their glasses. "And so, cheers and thank you, Minxy. I love you."

She often responded negatively to nicknames, but if she was going to tease him with a name like Mr. Wiggles, at least her nickname was a compliment.

They both sipped. The wine tasted off. He'd had a sip from her glass earlier when washing down his antihistamine and the pill may have affected the flavor. He made a face that Harper picked up on immediately.

"Eat an edamame," she said. "I should've paid more attention and made you eat something with your pills."

She was nearly psychic. Gio reached over and took a pod, popping and sucking out the bean. Bits of fresh garlic and red pepper drifted off the husk. Delicious. He took another sip of wine. A little better this time.

"The cats are all staring at me," he said.

"It's the salmon bowls."

"Seriously, it's all of them at once. I've never seen them do this before."

"Drink. You need to relax. I should've given you a glass of wine to take the edge off when you first got here."

He took another sip, bigger this time, a drink. "Is this from the same bottle as yours?" He ate another bean. His heart was racing. "How old is it?"

"You're just having another panic attack. I just corked it and poured my glass before you got here. Swear. It's the same bottle."

The cats started making noises. Not meowing in the traditional sense, but more staccato and rhythmic. Their teeth were showing. The noises were equal parts growl, chirrup, and chatter.

"No, I mean the vintage. It's turned, I think." He took another big drink so he could swish it around in his mouth, searching for what was off about it. "Like it's gamey. And too much sediment."

"'Gamey'?"

"I don't know the right words. Gamey up front, chalky sediment, then like an ammonia aftertaste."

"You know what urine tastes like?"

"It tastes like—you know what, I think a cat pissed in it! And why aren't you drinking yours?"

"Listen to yourself. I *am* drinking mine; we just toasted. I'm just pacing myself and have another bottle ready to open. I want to get dinner in me first."

"Here, taste mine..." He held out the glass for her. His hand was shaking so badly that, even though half the glass had been drunk, some of the sloshing wine splashed out. She took the glass, likely as much to keep it from falling out of his hand as anything else.

"What's happening?" He punched his legs and whipped his head back and forth. "I can't open my hands."

"Calm down. Breathe. You'll be okay. It's just a panic attack."

"Aauugghh!" Gio's stomach clenched and he buckled forward in pain. "Did you poison me?"

The cat chanting continued, evolving closer and closer to something like language. His field of vision was expanding, and in his periphery, he saw Spike, Jagger, Chico, and Steve surrounding him. Their eyes were expectant. Knowledgeable. Evil.

He was glad he'd turned off the lights, as everything was brighter now. He no longer even needed the candlelight to see.

"Why yes, I think it's safe to tell you now. I did poison you." Harper's tone had become pedantic and pleased. "I did, I did, I did. And I meant it when I thanked you for doing the laundry. Like I said, you opened my eyes as to what living with you would be like."

Harper got up and went to the hall closet. She took out a fistful of something and came back. "You see these panties you washed and folded so nicely for me, Giovanni?" That wasn't normally where she stored panties. "They're not mine! They're not mine, Gio!"

They were Hazel's. She was a co-worker of his at Warbler Brothers.

Gio was shrinking in the chair. His socks had fallen down and his legs were pulling up out of his pants toward him, his point of view sinking. "Whose are they?"

His voice had morphed into something unrecognizable, but Harper seemed to understand him just fine.

"You slept with somebody in my own house! How could you?" she said.

The cat vocalizations were becoming understandable. Like banshees or harpies. Sirens? He didn't know his myths and legends well enough. The cats crept closer to the table, low to the ground, hunting their prey. He had always thought her cats had brilliant eyes, but now that they were trained on him, they were more soulful and pained, almost human.

"Gio, Gio, Gio?" said a cat.

"Can you hear us yet?" said another.

"Giii-ooo!"

"Aauugghh!" he screamed. "The cats are talking. The fuck? Aauugghh!"

"That's why I'm christening you—" Harper lifted her arm and dropped it in his direction, anointing him with an imaginary sword— "*Mr. Wiggles.*"

"Mr. Wiggles!" said a cat.

"Fat cat, fat cat!" said another.

The cats were moving closer.

"Wiggly Wiggleman!"

"What nice ears you have, Mr. Wiggles."

"And of course you can hear them, precious. You're learning their language. And I have to say, your teeth are coming in nicely."

His clothes were blankets now, large and heavy. He pushed backward, escaping claustrophobia just as his pants fell to the floor. And the salmon bowls smelled more delicious than ever.

He screamed again, convulsing in misery, baring his incisors as he tried to lick them and felt a startling absence of lips. His arms and legs were itching, and when he scratched at them, he found he had claws instead of fingernails and they cleaved through fur to find skin. His arms had become another set of legs. He was sitting within his hoodie's collar, not unlike Jagger had done several months back.

The cats were enjoying the show.

"Mr. Wiggles!"

"Perfect name for a little scaredy cat."

"Not so tough, huh, Mr. Wiggles?"

He was thinking much faster than before. Maybe from a different sense of time or the quickness inherently needed for feline survival. Harper seemed to be moving at half speed, although he could hear her speaking just fine. Motion and sound otherwise weren't syncing properly.

The cats were threatening him. Maybe they were laughing at him the way they always had, but now he could hear what they were saying. The room, although relatively bigger since he had become smaller, felt congested with too many creatures located in one place. He needed to flee.

He shook himself free and reconfigured himself on top of his clothes. He arched his back and stretched and stretched and his range of motion seemed limitless. He could seriously increase his length by mere extension.

His phone Moted and he jumped on the table. Checking his phone was a human habit, so he still had that, but jumping on the table was not. His vision had been perfect when looking at Harper from a few feet away, better than his human 20/20 had been, but up close the notification was blurry. He jumped backward from Harper's incoming arm, and managed a glance of his phone from a couple feet away.

MOTE:

Turning water into wine, thoughts into beliefs, beliefs into delusion.

. . .

HE DIDN'T KNOW if he was more creeped out by the meaning of the Mote or the blurriness of his vision up close. If the Omnist was aware of his predicament, it should tell him how to escape. Or reverse the potion. Harper snatched the phone away.

"You're not going to need this anymore. A text from your girlfriend? Too late! Maybe if she comes over, I can change her into a kitty, too. Wouldn't that be nice of me? You guys can spend the rest of your lives as cats. My cats. My rules. And you can hear me have sex with my new partner."

The culprit had been the wine and, impulsively, he dove for the bottle. He nearly missed, glancing it with a paw. He wasn't graceful as a cat, yet, learning how to move in this new body. As the bottle toppled, Harper caught it.

He liked flicking his tail. It was like a joystick for balance.

Harper swiped at him and he jumped straight up, feeling as if he were in the air for several seconds, and swung his tail to change direction. He toppled a wine glass.

Again, Harper caught it as if used to this sort of thing.

She collected the bottle and both glasses and headed out of the room.

Gio jumped off the table and slid through the doorway ahead of her into the kitchen. Although still uncoordinated, he felt more svelte and angular than anticipated. He was much faster than Harper, thinking on a different plane.

He could smell what was wrong with the wine. How could he have missed it before? It was nearly overpowering, but there was something else in it, a couple somethings, that were attractive to him. And not the grape or yeast esters or ethanol that humans craved. But catnip, pheromones, and something ancient. Thousands-of-generations ancient. He also smelled cat waste.

Seeing Harper headed for the sink, Gio attempted to jump

on the counter and fell short, his legs cycling as he slammed back into the floor.

Harper set the bottle and glasses on the counter and turned her attention toward him. She seemed pleased he hadn't been able to jump that high.

"You need to calm down, Mr. Wiggles."

He needed to know what the bottle was all about. He'd learn more by smelling it up close. It was right there. He backed his ass up the way he had seen cats do countless times, winding up, ready to spring. Just as he jumped, succeeding this time, another cat came flying out of nowhere. Swooshes of white and blood-red fur. It was Cherry. He didn't need a collar to remember her name. Despite his heightened sense of time, Cherry's motions were still almost too fast for him to comprehend.

While Harper was trying to swipe him off the counter, Cherry tried to get at one of the glasses, knocking it sideways. Harper managed to catch the glass before it broke, and with that same arm motion, took a huge gulp. The rest of the glass. A triumphant, celebratory mouthful of the remainder of her glass of expensive Bordeaux.

She looked pleased. She had won. Nothing had broken. She set the empty glass in the basin, turned on the water, and poured the remainder of poisoned wine down the drain, holding Cherry back as she did so.

"No, Cherry, love," Harper said. "No, no. This is the last we're going to see of this."

CHAPTER
SIX

HARPER

Harper didn't feel well at all. She buckled over and held her stomach. She knew immediately she'd made a mistake, and she tried to force herself to vomit the potion, but the cramping of her muscles felt like it was doing the opposite and holding everything down. She had drunk from the wrong glass trying to save a ten-dollar gulp of wine.

Her teeth felt like they were being bashed in by a brick and a rusty shovel, back and forth. Grinding them into shape. Her hearing and vision, including the ability to see colors, were changing. Most painful was the bone-crushing shrinking.

She hated Gio more and more as the fur grew in, itching. In a few minutes, after she was done cooking, she planned to rally the troops and sic all the cats on Gio. This was her house, and with her little accomplices, they would force him out. Even if it were only she and Spike acting as enforcers, Gio was a goner. But help from the others would make his forced exile overwhelming and final.

She could already understand some cat communication, as she had cast herself a spell for it years ago, but now realized it had been woefully inadequate. On the verge of being a sham. The language she heard spoken between Cherry and Gio as cats was crystal clear.

"My name isn't Cherry, it's Jehri. J-E-H-R-I," Cherry was saying to Gio. "Harpy calls me Cherry for some reason."

Maybe because cats weren't supposed to be cherry red. She was red, strawberry, and white calico with the softest fur ever.

"I like that, calling her Harpy, like a devil from hell. Similar to a banshee, right?"

"I thought she was breaking up with me the night she changed me. But you have to really care about somebody to hate them this much."

Harper tried to say something, but "Aauugghh!" was all that came out.

"I did it! I did it!" Cherry said.

"She's still here," Gio said.

"Now Harpy has no choice! She's a cat forever!"

Maybe Cherry had done this on purpose, and now the cats were relishing in her misery. Harper could hear other cats tearing apart the sushi salmon bowls on the dining room table. One of the bowls hit the floor. The older cats, like Spike and Chico, had seen the human-to-cat metamorphosis before, and didn't need to again if it meant risking missing out on a gourmet dinner.

On her knees, she hid her changing face in her hybrid-human paws, closed her eyes, and tried to block out the bright lights of the kitchen and the razor-sharp migraine slicing her cranium in half. She'd never felt pain like this before. She tried to focus on their conversation to distract from her agony.

"What did you look like as a human?" Gio said.

"I was a redhead," Cherry said.

She was selling herself short. Jehri had been striking, with delicate skin that burned at the mere mention of sunlight.

"What do I look like?" Gio said.

"Black and white," Cherry said. "Big patches of white with little patches of black inside and big patches of black with little patches of white. Like a yin-yang."

Gio started twitching and moving rapidly in small circles. "Aauugghh! My skin is tearing," he said. He flailed on the floor as if on fire.

While Harper was still shrinking, nearly cat-sized now, Gio was growing again. His fur was disappearing into his skin, the claws and teeth retracting. Still growing. Still screaming. "Aauugghh!"

If Gio was becoming human again, Harper thought maybe he could save her. He still loved her, right? "Please, please, change me back!" Harper said, hoping he could still understand her. "Help me!"

Spike and Steve trotted into the kitchen. Harper could smell salmon on their breaths.

"Mr. Wiggles!" Spike said. "You can't change back! You're one of us now!"

"I don't think so. Look at him," Steve said.

In a final throe, Gio flung himself onto his back, and completed shapeshifting into a human. He was nude, of course, with his clothes still in the dining room. He acted as if he were suddenly aware of this, cowering and patting invisible pockets on his thighs.

"But we get Harpy now!" Spike was frolicking, clearly worked up from all of the excitement. "This'll be so much fun!"

They were surely going to kill her, or at minimum, torture her. This was a travesty.

Gio rolled to his knees and pushed himself to his feet. He stumbled to the dining room.

Harper fought herself free of her clothes and sprinted across the kitchen floor past Spike and Steve, uncoordinated as a baby giraffe. Legs splayed, she slid into the wall and bounced. She redirected and ran full speed into the dining room, where she slammed into Gio's bare legs as he shook his pants. Rice was everywhere.

Convinced the other cats were on her tail, Harper ran down the hall, claws click-clacking the climb of a rollercoaster across the hardwood floor. She bounced off a door jamb into her bedroom, and ran under the bed.

CHAPTER
SEVEN

KAT

After Organica's Lodge had died down, Kat sent Paula and Derby home, and soon enough, the Emporium was down to its last customer.

"It's time, Alex. I have to close up," Kat said to the woman, who was looking at the premade salads in the refrigerator.

"Lunch for tomorrow," Alex said, picking out a kale and artichoke salad and an oat-based beverage and setting them on the counter. Alex was a Consumerian first, as her Executive Saint pin showed, and an Organican second, rarely missing one of Organica's Lodges. "You look sad."

"I'm just tired," Kat said. It had been a long shift. They'd been busy tonight and she'd been social for hours.

"Don't worry, a girl as beautiful as you won't have to wait long for a man to come knocking."

Kat liked Organicans well enough, but they pretended to care more than they did (as much as she pretended to care less than she did). Both parties were probably wrong to an extent. Alex meant well, but Kat certainly didn't want anyone to come knocking.

Organica was a fine Omniscian, but Kat preferred listening to Yksian, who wielded scientific facts as proof everyone was doomed to die alone. It was comforting.

Shockingly, even traditionally beautiful women like Alex who came through the store would tell Kat how pretty she was. That hadn't happened so much in high school or college, but maybe other women had been intimidated by her when she was younger. Or maybe her energy was different in Los Angeles than it had been in Phoenix.

She closed and locked up the Emporium.

KAT DROVE BACK to the house that belonged to her husband's family, a wedding present, or a grievance present, as she called it. It was where Jesse had lived the first years of his life. Then his family moved to Arizona before Jesse began high school, renting this house out for a few years in the meantime.

Kat met Jesse Maris at Arizona State University and they dated for a couple years before the accident that had taken away his ability to walk, possibly permanently. They slugged out his therapy together, then got engaged and moved to the house in L.A.

As he continued to regain his strength and mobility, he insisted running was his way of showing fate who was in charge. Maybe, in retrospect, he'd been a bit stubborn. He didn't need to run a marathon. He had never run one before.

The wedding ceremony took place seven months ago at the halfway point of the L.A. Marathon, and then mere moments after their vows, Jesse collapsed after re-entering the race stream. He'd been a husband for a duration measured in minutes.

The Maris house was too big for a single woman, a widow in her twenties, living alone. Her boss, Connie, had been sweet, offering to let her stay at her place for a while if she needed company, but the idea had made Kat uncomfortable, like she'd be imposing. Besides, Kat *had* a place to stay. But she wanted a dog, someone to greet her when she walked in the door.

She threw her bag on the couch. She spent a little while decompressing, removing makeup, and changing into comfy clothes. It was November and she hadn't really slept well in the last seven months, since Jesse died in the spring. Fall was her favorite season, but not this year. Seasons were now inconsequential. She had a new routine for evenings like this when she was too burned out to do anything, but too awake to sleep.

She went to the back of the house into the den addition and turned on a set of three small lights with red shades, creating a moody martini-lounge glow. Then she sat at a small bar with three stools.

The bar top had been Kat's idea. It was made with Jesse's ashes sprinkled in it, swirled like supernovae. Galaxy bursts of blue, red, and orange, the colors of his aura. Some mica for a touch of glitter against a black backdrop. The dust explosions scattered his elements throughout the universe. Shining a phone's flashlight into the surface revealed endless depths, much deeper than one would expect from half an inch.

Kat had sent the ashes away to a woman named Ekko in New Mexico who made epoxy resin jewelry from cremains, using small amounts, like a quarter teaspoon for a keychain.

But for this project Ekko had needed a lot more, so Kat sent all she had. A couple weeks later she received a delivery of three eighteen-inch square tiles that she laid down as the new bar surface. She had then poured another layer of epoxy resin over the top to join all the edges and create more visual depth.

And she liked this better than keeping an urn. Jesse's ashes had been split between his parents and Kat, and they were doing the traditional urn thing. Ekko had sent back the extra ashes she didn't use for the tiles and Kat sprinkled them in the garden. Jesse had enjoyed growing peppers for his own hot sauces, and would now continue to do so. This bar was a way for Kat to interact with him every day rather than hiding him in a vase or wooden box on a shelf.

If she ever moved, she would have to take this bar with her. Jesse would approve.

Ekko had also thrown in a free matching pendant, with a card relaying her condolences and hope that a necklace would be easier to wear than a tile. Mixing humor with condolences was a delicate skill, and Kat had appreciated it.

Otherwise, Kat had taken over Jesse's man cave. Here she would lie on the couch with a giant iced tea on a CSE-branded coaster and a movie streaming on the smart screen on the wall.

The largest room in the house, it had a fireplace with a sandstone mantel with two couches in front positioned at a right angle. Despite its cathedral ceiling, it was also the coziest room. Whereas her friends would sit at a breakfast nook or a kitchen table in the morning, she'd sit at the bar with a yogurt, orange juice, and her tablet.

Tonight, she stirred a cup of hot bedtime tea and took a sip.

Hanging on the wall behind the bar was a picture of Jesse laughing at something while mixing a martini, shaking the tumbler over a shoulder. The angle suggested it was shot from bar level. Kat remembered saying something funny to elicit this candid expression.

She stood up and walked around the bar to stand in front of Jesse's photo. Next to it hung a witch's ladder just like the one she'd recommended to the customer Jessica. "Just give me a sign you can hear me. That my prayers aren't being wasted."

Nothing. As usual.

She had wedged the story card for the witch's ladder behind the photograph. She lifted the frame to remove it. She knew what it said, but read it anyway. It told her to speak to his eyes in the photo so he could see her thoughts. To impress her thoughts onto the photograph itself, invisible, but permanent. But each photograph could only hold so many prayers, and after that, she would need to use a new photograph.

She'd previously wished for Jesse to speak to her in her dreams, to let her know he was well and still with her in spirit, and he had. Several times. She'd then wished for his mother, Priya, to stop insinuating Kat had contributed to his death. She'd implied Kat had forced Jesse to run beyond his body's capabilities, when, in fact, it'd been the opposite. He'd become obsessed with proving life was mind over matter, courage over body. But she'd seen no sign of her mother-in-law "forgiving" her.

Staring at Jesse's photograph, Kat wished for company in the big house. "If I can't have you here, then maybe a dog. But don't worry, Jesse. I'm not lonely for people, if that's what you're thinking. I don't need friends. Only you."

This picture may have been full. Maybe she'd have to find a new one to hang here.

Her phone, next to her cup of tea, buzzed with a call. The display said was Priya Maris. "Hi, Kat, did I wake you?"

It was late, but Kat didn't sleep much. Besides, her

schedule at the Emporium required a mixture of day and evening shifts. "I just got home from work."

They caught up on small talk for a few minutes. A late November heat wave had wildfires burning in Arizona. Elderly people without air-conditioning were dying. Jesse used to talk to his mom a couple times a week, but Kat only did when she saw Priya in person. Now though, Priya checked in with Kat a couple times a month.

"You know the property tax is due," Priya said. "The value of the house went up a lot this year, so that means the taxes did, too."

"I really appreciate you letting me live here." Kat couldn't help the skyrocketing housing costs, which meant rents were rising, too. The deal Priya had made with her was that Kat would pay a small rent that covered the cost of property taxes. It'd be a fraction of what a rental family would pay, but the Marises also wouldn't be losing money outright.

"It was thirteen percent," Priya said.

That meant Kat's rent was going to increase by that amount. "I understand."

They exchanged their goodbyes and hung up. For a moment, she'd hoped Priya had called to apologize for making her feel guilty, but instead had called to notify her of a rent increase.

Kat felt tugged at and turned to her right. There was an unbelievable painting that pleasantly sucked at her soul every time she entered the room. After seeing Priya's negative reaction to it the first time she'd seen it, Kat had put the painting on the same wall as the door so you'd have to be inside the room to see it.

Connie had given it to her. It depicted a widow with a hole where her heart should be staring into an open grave. Her long shawl disappeared into the hole in her chest, then magically fluttered back up at her from the grave. Those two holes, painted with Black Vertigo, appeared as if they went straight through the painting itself, into the wall behind it, into another universe. It was otherworldly and slightly nauseating, an illusion you wanted to touch to reassure yourself of your balance, your place in the universe.

Without metaphor, Kat saw herself as that woman.

She was she.

CHAPTER

EIGHT

GIOVANNI

After putting on his clothes, Gio could barely stand, falling into the dining table and holding himself up with two hands. This was as dizzy and nauseated as he'd ever felt. He dropped himself into a chair covered with rice and edamame and tried to equalize his heart rate and breathing. He felt like he was going to pass out. His muscles were tingling and sore to the bone, and he didn't want to move. The hard wooden chair had never felt so comfortable, and he checked to make sure his tail wasn't twisted.

But he had no tail.

MOTE:

Do you feel you're a Gift? Or a Gift in the returns line?

• • •

HARPER HAD RUN OFF. The other cats had moved back into the room and were staring at him from five equidistant points. Like a pentacle. He'd been correct in thinking the cats didn't like him. They were exes. But he couldn't hear them talking anymore.

He needed to think. He couldn't think. Human-cat-human transfigurations weren't normal. He'd somehow survived this. These cats had been cursed by a spurned, malicious woman, and who knew for what reasons. They didn't deserve this fate. And Cherry...Jehri...had caused Harpy....Harper...to drink the potion. At least that's what it seemed like. Cherry had sounded understandably happy Harper had turned into a cat. Justice.

Going home to sleep was out of the question. Driving would be too dangerous in his condition. He wasn't hungry; his stomach was uneasy. He wondered why he hadn't peed as a cat with his bladder shrinking out all the liquid, unless the water somehow shrunk, too. As if that mattered now.

Sleeping here may be difficult. The other cats may not be an issue. They may have disliked him, but their behavior could've been merely a display of dominance. But who knew what a spurned Harper would do? She really was a witch. When he'd first met her, he was attracted to her infatuation with natural forces and the earth. He thought it was cute. The magic wasn't real, but the reasoning behind it was interesting. Harper living a sort of fantasy lifestyle had made her more real to him in a way. More than merely harmless, it was a healthy headspace. Or so he'd thought. It hadn't been just organic food and moon cycles. Sage smudges. She had real power, and she'd, in effect, killed five of her exes and tried to do the same with him.

Cherry, who was watching from the point where the dining room led to the hallway, turned and started walking away. She was good. She hadn't tried to intimidate him when he was briefly a cat.

Gio got up, shuffled past Jagger, watching from a shelf on a hutch, and walked down to Harper's bedroom. Cherry entered before him, but when he turned on the light, it startled her and she quickly ran out. Gio closed the door so Harper couldn't escape. He got on his hands and knees and looked under the bed. Harper kept a few boxes and a suitcase under there.

He heard a shuffle as he moved a box and first saw the reflection of light from her eyes. That was spooky in its own right, the way cat eyes looked in the dark, but he recognized hers, specifically. Her fur had become dark as a moonless night, so eyes were all he saw. "Harper, I can see you," he said, short of breath. Even getting on his hands and knees had wiped him out. "Come on out so we can talk."

Harper shuffled farther back, which meant she was now closer to the other side. He wasn't going to play that game, chasing her back and forth. It dawned on him she may have been hiding from the other cats as well. She needed to feel safe.

"Okay, then. We'll talk later."

Gio stood up and looked around the room he had slept in many times. The windows weren't climate-efficient. Old single-paned glass, possibly lead, with paint smeared a touch over the frame's edges. There was a tree outside the window and this side of the house was well shaded from the sunrise. The drapes were thin and layered and seemed to absorb the smells of the house, but sometimes moved in a draft.

He found a plastic bowl in the kitchen that he filled with water and placed in Harper's bedroom. He closed the door behind him as he left. The cats were still staring at him as he slowly walked through the kitchen and out the back door. Maybe fresh air would help. The backyard was quiet, but his hearing was more acute now. He heard more life shuffling throughout the ravine beyond her property. He imagined he could differentiate between the smell of an unseen opossum and rat, and between a raccoon and coyote that were farther away.

"The back door's open you guys," he announced into the house. "You're free to go, if you want."

The cats no longer had their usual caregiver. If they still possessed the equivalent of human souls, which he suspected they did, they may prefer their freedom. He wasn't into the idea of caging animals against their will. Years ago, he'd had a black dog named Goodnight and he always felt she'd picked him more than vice versa, and he'd loved her to death. That feeling of being chosen was important for them to be together.

He walked throughout the house to make sure the cats all heard him. "Here, kitty, kitty. You can go out the back door if you want. You're free to go, kitties."

He was still woozy and had a headache. He rifled through Harper's medicine cabinet looking for painkillers. Harper was the type who chewed on a piece of rare bark or something when she had pain. Surprisingly, he found some expired ibuprofen and took three. He drank a full glass of water and returned to the hallway, the geographical center of the house.

"I realize now you're all Harper's exes. You didn't ask to become cats nor to be imprisoned here. I have no beef with you, so please go in peace if you so desire."

Gio knew how Hazel's underwear had made their way over here. He'd found them at his condo, assumed they were Harper's, and brought them over with a handful of her clothes yesterday. Then, to be nice, he did her laundry. He'd had a change of dirty clothes of his own here to throw in. When he'd found the underwear, he should've thrown them away, and maybe none of this would've happened. *Seriously, Hazel, who leaves underwear behind?*

He'd had a work meeting last week. Harper had been distant, rude even, triggering his anxiety about her breaking up with him, so when the meeting ended, he needed to blow off steam. He and a few coworkers on the project went for drinks at Tony's Darts Away, a craft beer and vegan establishment in Burbank.

And Hazel, a production assistant on his team, she'd laughed at his jokes. Made him feel funnier than he was, something Harper never did. It boosted his ego. After a few drinks, he'd forgotten about his relationship stress, work stress, and limited access to a social life.

Hazel went home with him and spent the night. It was a mistake, and he regretted it immediately in the morning. She'd kissed his forehead when she headed off for the office, stirring him out of bed, and that was the last sign anything intimate had happened. Her emails remained exactly as professional as they'd been before, and they'd talked twice on the phone without an ounce of acknowledgment on either side. It had been a one-time thing for both of them.

But the indiscretion hadn't occurred at Harper's house like she'd assumed, but at his condo. She'd been so angry she didn't think how he would've been able to pull off a stunt like that (and why). She almost never left the house. Maybe when she was delivering herbs to a store or distributor, but even then, what would he have done? Have Hazel over for a quickie when Harper was gone? As if any of this helped his argument.

~

He heard a cat wailing like it was being tortured in Harper's bedroom. He opened the door to find two cats on Harper's bed. One of the tomcats had mounted his girlfriend, so he slammed his hand on the bed. The cat ignored him, continuing his mission. Gio was more forceful the second time, actually pushing the cat off her. It was Spike, the dominant one, who hissed and swiped a paw at him, then jumped off the bed and ran out of the room.

Harper had already begun hooking up with an ex-boyfriend so he could hear her, just like she'd promised. Then again, if she hated that guy enough to turn him into a cat, maybe it wasn't consensual. He shifted from anger toward her to anger toward Spike. Harper was lying on the bed licking herself. He simultaneously hated her and felt sorry for her.

He hesitantly reached over to pet her, half expecting her to swipe at him. She was the blackest cat he'd ever seen. Her wide, green Eurasian eyes illuminated her face. It was only a little while ago he'd told her he loved her during their anniversary toast. He gently stroked the top of her head. She didn't purr, but accepted the gesture.

"Poor Harper," he said sarcastically. *Sar-CATS-tically.*

Petting a cat. Who would've thought? He hadn't done that since he was a teenager, back when he believed he could control his allergies by sheer force of will. She rubbed her whiskered cheek against his hand. Cats had glands there. She was marking him. Maybe it was a vindictive gesture to provoke his allergies. Even as a cat, she was trying to torture or punish him for his sins against her. He did take an antihistamine before he changed into a cat. Who knew what his immunity was like now. That would suck if he'd become allergic to himself.

It was even harder to stand up than last time. He paused at the door, an arm on the doorframe. "I'm sorry, I have to close this again. I don't know how Spike got in. Maybe he followed me when I brought the water. But I'm keeping it closed for your own safety."

He saw Jagger in the hallway and Chico in the kitchen.

They walked slowly and craned their heads to keep an eye on him. It was eerie. He hadn't taken attendance yet, so he wasn't sure who'd stayed. It was possible Spike had left after the fracas in the bedroom.

Gio closed the back door and barely made it to the couch before collapsing. By definition, his shapeshifting had been twice as exhausting than for any of the other cats. He'd had two changes back-to-back.

Cherry jumped up next to him and climbed onto his lap. He petted her.

"What are you doing? You know I'm allergic. I've told you that before." Her eyes were an incredible olive green, but now he saw them as more human than before. They were catlike human eyes, not the other way around. His mind had been opened to the concept.

"What do I look like now?" He lay his head on the armrest and throw pillow. "Just kidding. I know you can't answer."

She blinked sleepy-slow. He pivoted so he could lift his legs onto the couch. Cherry moved closer to his head, and lay next to his chest. He turned sideways.

"How're you able to keep Spike off you?" he mumbled. "He's the dominant one, right?"

Of course, Cherry didn't answer, but he knew she understood him. One moment he saw an innocent house cat, the next he saw all the human knowledge and experience that little body contained. He would be okay with Cherry sleeping behind his knees. That was what allergy medication was for. He picked her up and placed her there. The exhaustion was overtaking him, and he struggled to keep his eyes open.

"I'm going to keep calling you Cherry, if that's okay. It's your cat name, and how I know you...Cherry."

She purred. He didn't think he'd ever heard any of Harper's cats purr before.

CHAPTER
NINE

HARPER

One of the things she hadn't thought about before was the sense of touch created by whiskers. She could close her eyes and be perfectly aware of her immediate surroundings. This made slinking under the bed, between boxes and a suitcase, not just easier, but fun. She enjoyed the smell of dust bunnies as long as the whiskers kept enough distance between them and her nostrils. This space was cozy in a way she'd never experienced before.

But she'd also never felt so alone and vulnerable. As a cat, the house felt bigger and colder. She assumed fur would help more than it did. She wished Gio was here so she could sit on his lap. The bastard. Still negatively affecting her life.

She'd never expected a spell to bite its conjurer. It was mutiny. No, she'd been stupid and got the potion wrong. Her eyeballing, gut feeling method had failed her. It was Cherry's fault for knocking over the glass. In retrospect, the reason she'd changed was easy to discern: She drank from the wrong glass. She took Gio's place. The universe remained balanced, but with her on the wrong side. She'd learned through the years that thoughts affected potions greatly, as they were part of the spells. Incantations could exist merely in the mind. Whatever Gio had been thinking when she accidentally drank the remainder of potion could've also affected the spell. In effect, because they'd both ingested it, he was a co-conjurer. It was Gio's fault. Again.

As she heard Gio move about the house, talking to the others, she wondered how obvious and serious her alternative lifestyle was to him now. The garden in back. Wolfsbane. Mandrake tinctures. Motherwort. Herb Passiflorae. Fortune Eupatorium. It wasn't just basil and oregano.

The plants on windowsills, trapped between curtains and glass, creating a makeshift greenhouse.

The candles, oils, incense, and smudges. A miniature Emporium.

The books with no titles on the spines, or in Old English or Latin. He wouldn't be able to read these.

The special boline she used for harvesting and chopping herbs was hanging just inside the back door. Shaped like a crescent moon, it was next to a mirror with a wooden star frame. Her neighbor Linden had made that frame for her. He was perennially in a good mood. It was annoying. At first, she'd wanted to throw the mirror away on principle, but found it useful to see the movements of her cats behind her when she was near the back door.

Her cauldrons were hidden in plain sight. Smaller ones were holders for squat candles, larger ones for plants on the patio. Like the P and M set, she had a favorite, one that housed a rubber tree. She could remove the tree and its smaller pot, and with a quick rinse from a hose, the cauldron was ready to go.

That one was used in the fire pit at the far end of the backyard where the ground was rockier. The stones were charred from performing repeated rituals. She had no immediate neighbor behind her. Well, technically she did across the ravine, but the terrain wasn't really hike-able, and they'd never met.

One of the first potions she'd made in her teens was a disorientation spell, where she added a couple pinches of mixed herbs to loose-leaf tea. It was a relatively harmless spell that made people forget details, but remember a general positive feeling about the experience. She'd used it on her grandpa once when she'd come in hours late from frolicking alone in the San Gabriel Mountains and knew she be in trouble. An impending argument. She made the tea while being chewed out, and they sat at the kitchen table. Soon, he was talking about her dead grandma and dead mom, his wife and daughter. His memory of the conversation the next day was just them bonding over tea at four in the morning. He didn't remember her coming home late or him being angry, nor the topics of conversation. Just that a conversation happened and was positive.

As much as that potion had the power to make people bond with her, she didn't need, nor want, people to like her. There was power in friendship, but also in mystery and fear, as well. She only used that spell when she'd be in trouble otherwise.

～

As for safety, Harper knew catfights were usually between males for either territory or a mate, and once one of the participants slinked away with nothing more than a couple scratches, it was over. But where was the research on cats who were former humans?

The one she needed to keep an eye on was Spike. He'd attacked her once, and may do it again. He was the oldest one of the bunch, her first metamorphosis. He didn't creep around, lowering himself as he stalked like the other cats did. He stood tall, tail down, as much bulldog as cat. He was Harper's first success on a couple levels.

As a human, Spike's surname was Spychowski, which lent itself to an easy nickname. He hadn't been the typical man she was attracted to. He was bulky and hard-headed. She was usually drawn toward the more sensitive, thoughtful, intelligent, and artistic.

When they'd met, her grandpa had recently died and her house felt large and lonely. She was twenty-two and he was a thirty-year-old lighting technician for one of the major studios, drove a heavy-duty pickup truck that he waxed monthly, and, although he hadn't gone to college, he watched college football with his buddies. A USC Trojan fan. At first, she liked that he made her feel safe. He was simple and frustrating and largely fairly consistent. Not a lot of drama.

Then the relationship became basic. He liked this and she liked that. He believed men were one way and women were another, and that was the way it was. Preconceived roles. He was loud; she was quiet. He was wrong a lot, but if he said it louder, it made it truer. He had nothing interesting to say. Ever.

Then it became a chore. She couldn't stand him. She hated his taste in music, movies, clothes, everything. They had virtually nothing in common. She decided she'd like him so much better as a pet, somebody to be with her in the house. As a dog he would've been all up in her space, though, communicating too much. Too needy. But as a cat, they could keep their distance and she could be the sole provider. It was her house.

So that was settled.

She had to convince him to drink the wine, as his usual vice was domestic beer. She wasn't sure if the potion had been concocted correctly, as it was her first time, and didn't know how noticeable it would be in the wine.

Her first instinct was to get multiple beers in him first, then dare him to eat the hottest peppers she grew in the backyard. He couldn't refuse a perceived threat to his masculinity. No pepper could beat him.

Standing in her kitchen, she pretended to drink from a glass of the polluted wine. She fed him fresh peppers of increasing strength, daring him not to cool his mouth. When he finally needed something, she handed him the wine knowing he wouldn't wait. While she poured him a small glass of water, he chugged half a glass of wine.

"Slam it," she said. "I have more."

He pounded the rest of the glass, as no wine could defeat him, either. She assumed he couldn't taste any off notes through his scalding mouth.

"That's horrible!" he said, gasping.

"Yeah, but can you do another pepper?" she teased.

He wouldn't, not because the pepper had beat him, he said, but because he claimed he suddenly had an atomic headache and had to sit down.

The transfiguration was fascinating. His arms cramped awkwardly. He kept rubbing his feet against his calves. He pounded his head into the coffee table. It was refreshing to hear Spike begging for help, and for someone to explain what the fuck was happening to him. His voice slowly shifted from that of a tortured, whiny man to an angry, confused feline. He became a brown and gray tabby, hefty and solid. No nonsense. Like his truck.

Which, in turn, she'd left in a parking lot near the USC campus downtown, and tossed his wallet over the gate of a sports bar's outdoor patio so it would be found by staff when they opened, giving the impression it was the last place he'd been. She'd taken the bus back to Burbank.

She'd made sure to keep texting Spike daily. Texts like "Where are you?" and "Why aren't you answering?" would make great bits of evidence to prove that she'd not known his whereabouts.

He escaped on the fourth evening. She was taking out the trash when he darted out. She regretted not locking him in the bedroom while she did chores, but let it go quickly. He couldn't exactly *tell* anyone. And if he changed back in some alley, naked and rambling, no one would believe him. She just hoped the spell would stick.

Spike had now "disappeared" both literally and figuratively, and an officer finally came around to ask questions. Harper invited him in. She offered him tea, but he declined. She poured two anyway, only hers was sans potion. The officer explained Michael's studio and union had reported he stopped showing up for work.

"I don't know where he is," she'd said, sitting down at the dining room table. It was easy to lie when you were telling the truth. Maybe Spike was in a rescue, neutered. She showed the officer the texts, all unanswered.

The officer sat down, too, and eventually sipped his tea. He'd said men like Michael often returned a few weeks later after a bender in Las Vegas or a trip to a secret family in Montana.

Harper was formal, cold, and polite, but also not dismissive, defensive, or flippant.

He sipped, look about the room. Sipped again. There was no apparent evidence Spike had ever been in this house, and Harper was honest about rarely leaving.

"Not really sure why I'm here," the officer said. The potion in the tea had worked as quickly as caffeine. "Just touching all bases after striking out, I guess. Just dotting the 'teas' and crossing the 'eyes'."

At least that's how she heard it.

By the officer saying something nonsensical like that, but in the ballpark of his intended meaning, it told her the spell was working. He'd soon fill out his report where he'd staunchly defend her presumed innocence. He'd swear there was nothing suspicious about Spike's disappearance in relation to her.

About a week later, she discovered Spike sitting on her front steps, dirty, hungry, thirsty. He didn't strut with pride, sulk, or run away. Rather, he scratched at the door and walked in like he'd only been away a few hours. She had no idea where he'd been. She gave him some turkey lunch meat and a bowl of water. He was ravenous.

Once he returned, Harper almost felt bad for forcing the change on him without his consent—but only to a point. If only he'd been a better, different person. A different, better person would've needed no spell. If only he had taste in anything. Even if she disagreed with somebody, if they had *decent* reasons for liking something, she could respect that. Spike's answer why he liked something was, "Because it's good." Or if she asked what he wanted for dinner, he'd answer, "Anything good." If only she hadn't dated him.

So, to make up for it somewhat, rather than only feeding him conventional cat food, she decided she'd cook for the both of them. Not every night, but several times a week. If she made chicken, turkey, beef, or fish, she'd withhold the seasoning until after she'd separated a portion for him. He was grateful, tearing into the meat much like he had before, when he was human. As much as she made a better "cat mother" than girl-friend, he made a better cat than boyfriend.

After each transformation, Harper would sit with the new cat and tell them if they escaped and were caught by animal control, she wouldn't search for them. And if they weren't euthanized, they would certainly be neutered. So escape at your own risk.

Harper then presented each cat with a personalized collar with their new name. These didn't include phone or registra-tion numbers, in case they escaped. She didn't need people trying to contact her. And she didn't abuse the cats. Gave them space. Fed them well. There were worse ways to live.

HARPER HEARD Spike outside the bedroom door. He was calling for her, not tauntingly or angrily or apologetically, but just to come and talk. His "English" wasn't as fluent as Cherry's and Gio's. Maybe being a cat longer makes you lose your sense for language. Less vocabulary and syntax. After they "spoke," she couldn't remember anything he said as a direct quote. More like a distilled essence of what he meant.

Basically, Spike said, now that Harper was a cat, the house-hold consensus was that there was no longer hope for any of them ever changing back. Spike, as it was, had given up hope years ago. They were all cats now and the sooner Harper accepted it, the better.

It was difficult to determine how much of his human personality remained. He didn't seem as bitter as she expected.

More resigned with age, and he never acknowledged the fact he'd mounted her earlier. He didn't think it was a thing. There would be no justice in the cat world.

She decided she'd be safer in the bedroom for the time being.

CHAPTER
TEN

KAT

Consumia's Spiritual Emporium was often slow in the middle hours of a weekday afternoon. A few customers may wander in on late lunch breaks looking for organic snacks or bottled beverages, or perhaps a few restless students looking for entertainment after class.

An event was taking place tonight in the Dark Arts room, CSE's location for edgier content like skeletons, potions and spells, dead critters in formaldehyde. Séances. By sequestering these items in the back room, sales of these items didn't go down, they actually went up.

Coffin Club was a bi-weekly event hosted by Linden Vowel, where Consumerians would decorate and sometimes build their own caskets or coffins from scratch for future personal use. Terminal diseases encouraged limitless humor in a part social club, part arts-and-crafts setting. Guests were often older or widowed, or cursed with a life expectancy measured in months, but advanced ages or morbid prognoses weren't prerequisites nor ubiquitous.

In practice, Linden's gatherings were more about self-help than practical woodworking. The group consisted of some of the happiest and friendliest Consumerians, a tone set by Linden himself.

Linden entered through the front of the Emporium. He smiled and waved at Kat. "Just going to grab a box before it gets busy," he said.

"You need any help?"

"I'll call if I do."

Three girls entered the Emporium, somehow all talking at once, and Kat recognized the voices of two of the three before she even looked up from her phone.

"Hi, Kat," Chelsea said.

"Hi, Chelsea. Hi, Lizette." Kat knew they appreciated her flat tone. Teenagers tended to be more respectful when she used it.

Lizette was a shy brunette who granted a tight little inconspicuous wave Kat's way. Chelsea and Lizette had interesting piercings and makeup, mimicking musicians they liked, which reminded Kat of herself in her school days.

A third girl, frumpier, with un-plucked eyebrows and no apparent makeup, trailed them.

Lizette paused in front of the easel that announced that the Omniscian Jasmine Waters's Lodge was tonight. "We should totally go to this," she said to the others. "She's a pet psychic."

"I need to take that down," Kat said. "Jasmine had to cancel."

Linden waved high over his head from the entrance of the Dark Arts room. "Ladies!"

"Hi, Mr. Vowel," Chelsea said, bored now with Lizette's

failed suggestion, and confidently led the others to a necklace display.

The girls consulted with each other about which items were better and what they meant, the plain girl reading a story card to them. "'A brush to brush, a friend to befriend, a charm to charm, a dead end to end.' It's a brush for fixing a bad relationship."

"Ewww," Chelsea said, filming her own reaction with her phone. She was a popular PikPoketer, which meant CSE would get a plug to her thousands of followers. Apparently, the plain girl had chosen an uncool item. "I have no problem telling someone to go away. I don't need magic for that."

The eagerness on the plain girl's face faded. "I think it's for fixing, not ending."

Chelsea looked at what Lizette was holding. "What's that?"

"It says it's a spell to make you more successful at casting spells," Lizette said.

"But if you're not good at casting spells, how do you know you did this one right?"

"I don't know," Lizette said, tilting her head curiously at Chelsea's camera phone. "Stuff starts working?"

Eventually, the girls approached the checkout. Only Lizette had an item to purchase.

"So how do you ladies know Linden, um, Mr. Vowel?" Kat said. "From here? I can't imagine you taking shop class."

"I do," the frumpier girl said.

"Oh, Kat, you don't know Delwen," Lizette said.

"Maybe it's better that way," Chelsea said. She and Lizette giggled.

"Mr. Vowel spoke at our school after Mateo died," Delwen said. "He built a bench for the basketball court, and we had an assembly to dedicate it to Mateo's memory."

"In case you didn't catch that," Chelsea said, snorting, "Delwen takes woodworking."

"I think that's cool," Kat said.

"It's almost all boys." Delwen was neither embarrassed nor proud. "I'm only one of two girls in the class."

"Yeah, if those are the kind of guys you want," Chelsea said.

"My husband took metals class and learned how to make jewelry." Kat lifted a silver pendant of a phoenix off her chest. "He made this."

The girls all leaned in to take a closer look. Delwen *oohed*.

"Oh, I have a pentagram, too," Lizette said, sliding over the necklace she was purchasing. Kat guessed she may've been buying it to piss off her parents, thinking it was satanic.

"This is a pentacle," Kat said. "That means it has five points. Since there's no Jasmine Lodge, I just found out we're about to have one painted in the Basil Alcove. I can't wait to see it. A pentagram is when it has five sides."

"I've only heard them called pentagrams," Chelsea said.

No bag was needed for Lizette's purchase, but Chelsea filmed herself picking up a postcard event calendar and walking with it. "Bye, Kat!" the girls said at the door.

Linden parted the skull-beaded curtain for the Dark Arts room.

"Miss Katty-Kat, Katmandu," he said. "Now that I think of it, do you prefer being called a cat-woman or cat-person?"

"I'm more of a dog person," she said, walking around the counter. He must've used a half-dozen nicknames for her by now. A name like Katherine Lyons had led to many throughout her life.

Linden had propped open the fire exit. There were a couple shelving racks flanking the sides of the door where some works-in-progress were stored. He usually kept the one he was working on here as a sample for others to follow.

"It's not so much the heat but the humidity," he said.

"What?"

"It's not so much the weight but the bulk."

Linden's humor. When Kat didn't laugh, he said, "I can usually finagle one of these myself, but I just realized I left my hand truck at home. If you could help me carry it out the door?"

The wooden box was well crafted and unadorned. It reminded her of the bar top at home, which, prior to the addition of Jesse Supernovae, had been stained pinewood. Functional, plain, not ugly. Utilitarian. She and Jesse had then made it their own. Personalized it. Soon, now, someone would make this coffin their own.

She could see why Linden needed to move it out, as there was no free space on the shelves. Unloading the boxes was often bittersweet, like when one was completed and the decorator said they'd come back for the next meeting, but sometimes didn't. An unfulfilled promise for another visit was a preferred outcome to a sudden stop without explanation.

Kat grabbed the handles on the side, and they slid the box off the shelf. He was correct. It was lighter than it looked. They walked it out to the alley, where his truck was backed up close to the door with its gate open. They slid the box into the back.

Linden clapped his hands once.

"Ope! Gotta run, now. Thanks, Kat." Linden climbed in his truck and started the engine. "I'll see you in a few hours."

When Kat turned around, she startled a gray cat walking in front of the dumpster. He then ran through the back door into the Dark Arts room.

"Kitty, no!" she said, uselessly. She hesitated, wondering if she should keep the door open to chase him back out. He was standing in front of the display counter, and as she walked toward him, he continued on through the aisles of the Emporium. He wasn't running from her, nor slowing for her sake. He was a Consumerian, browsing as he went. Or maybe he was looking for something in particular.

"Come here, kitty."

He wasn't wearing a collar, but he looked clean and healthy. His fur was nice. He wasn't starving. But he was definitely wary around people. Or strangers. She was a stranger.

"I'm not going to hurt you."

She imagined all people said this to strays, regardless of their intentions. "Do you want to be a member of the Emporium? Are you a *Cat-sumerian?*"

Pets rarely understood what a person was saying. It was her tone of voice. He could tell she was asking a question, the voice curling up at the end like italics. Pets appreciated italicized voices.

The back door slammed shut, as the doorstop must've come loose. This happened a lot due to its loose jamb and broken hydraulics.

"I'm going to pretend you made the door close. So that seals it, you can stay until Connie gets here." Kat walked back to the Dark Arts room to double-check everything was copacetic there, half expecting another cat or Linden, and found nothing. She returned to the front counter to text Connie.

CHAPTER
ELEVEN

GIOVANNI

Gio woke up on Harper's couch feeling sick. Getting worse. He'd been too tired to go to a bed or retrieve a blanket, covering himself only with his jacket. His bare feet were cold. Cherry was gone. It felt like the flu, so he emailed his project manager to say he'd likely spend a day or two in bed. Even working from home, he couldn't work under the weather. State of mind, state of body. Managers and coworkers sometimes argued that if he could sit up and check email, he could edit. This was experientially untrue.

His project manager responded with her wishes to get well, cc'ing Hazel, who emailed him right away, separately. "Are you okay?"

This was the first time Hazel had asked a personal question since she'd spent the night. He responded that yes, he was under the weather but otherwise fine.

"Is this something I should be worried about, too?" Of course she'd be concerned. They'd been intimate.

"No, this is probably just a flu," he wrote. And a hell of a flu. "Just came on last night."

In his defense, he could send a few emails, scroll a few newsfeeds, and generally do light stuff on his phone when he was sick in bed, but not the heavier lifting of sitting at a desk dealing with post-production editing programs for a movie. That took more energy, and he couldn't focus that long and hard. His head hurt epistemologically just thinking about *thinking* about it.

He took a couple ibuprofen.

HE MUST HAVE FALLEN BACK ASLEEP, because it was now late afternoon. His face and neck were hot. The ice in his glass of water had melted. He took a sip, wishing it were sparkling, scratching on its way down. He got up to put more ice in and opened the back door.

"To all cats that can hear me," he announced, "I will continue to clean the litter boxes and fill your bowls with food and water while I figure out what to do. Unlike before, I will occasionally leave a door open. Nobody is keeping you here against your will."

In case they changed their minds after sleeping on it. He felt like he was practically daring them to leave. But they were human. Maybe they wanted to leave. Maybe they wanted to stay. But at least they'd have a choice.

Why did he cheat on Harper? He was to blame. Had all her exes cheated? How did he not see that all this time they were little people, that this wasn't just a metaphor? *They're all my little men.* What would've happened if he hadn't become human again? There would've been seven cats locked in a house until they either killed each other or starved to death. This open-door policy was as much a message of peace to the exes as it was an exit.

"And nobody is allowed to mess with any other cat or I will lock you in a room by yourself. Kitty jail. Otherwise, if you stay, consider yourself under my protection until I figure out how to change everyone back." *If* he could change anyone back.

He walked around the house taking attendance. He counted Spike, Chico, Jagger, Cherry, plus Harper. There should've been six. He forgot the name of the missing cat.

Without putting on socks or shoes, he plodded out to his car to get a can of sparkling water he knew was there. Harper's neighbor, Linden Vowel, was trucking a coffin up his driveway between the houses.

Not something you see every day.

"Hey, Gio," Linden said. "Hop in!"

THE FIRST TIME they'd met, Linden was out in his front yard edging the walkway when Gio parked his car. He was doing a job a lot of homeowners paid somebody else to do, but Gio would later learn Linden was the type who took pride in doing his own yardwork, making furniture, and fixing up his house.

"Howdy, Harper-friend," Linden said. He was old enough to be Gio's dad, and shaped like an egg with legs.

"Howdy, um, Harper-neighbor."

"Name's Linden," he said, shaking with a hand that was sweatier on the back than the palm.

"Giovanni," Gio said. "But Gio's fine. What you're doing right there, that's why I live in a condo."

Linden took off his hat to wipe his forehead with the short

sleeve of his T-shirt. His comb over looked like a hat. It really did. Lift one hat to reveal another one made of hair.

"I want to finish this up cuz I got a full day tomorrow. I teach high school wood shop, and then I'm hosting Coffin Club."

"What the hell's a Coffin Club?" Gio imagined somebody making blunt weapons with pieces of a casket. "Is that a school thing?"

"'What the hell's Coffin Club'?" Linden parroted. "We're a group at Consumia's Spiritual Emporium that encourages people to approach death in a positive way. Not that you're dying, mind. Maybe it's not right for you. Maybe you don't need it yet. But if you're going that way anyway, you should pop your head in and say ouch."

"Ouch?"

Linden leaned the rake against his shoulder and pressed his hands against his ears, popping his head like a blackhead. "Ouch!"

It was Gio's first taste of Linden's oddness.

"Coffin Club's a way of dealing with the devil, and the devil's truly in the details," Linden continued. "People decorate their boxes with their favorite sports teams, murals of childhood landscapes, houses, pets. Nothing's off limits, except the unimaginable."

"Huh."

"Imagine that, huh?"

Was this guy fucking with him?

"That means I go to a lot of funerals, more than the average bear," Linden said. "As Yogi Berra said, 'Always go to other people's funerals, otherwise they won't come to yours.'"

"I guess that's true, isn't it?"

"Truer words never been said."

Harper came outside looking for Gio. The way the neighbors greeted each other; he knew something was up between them. His first instinct was that Linden seemed like a nice guy, but maybe that was his schtick as a teacher. Shop class wasn't odd in itself, but teaching people to build and decorate their own coffins was definitely left of center. Maybe he was a bit of a home-and-yard freak, acting as the self-appointed head of an unofficial neighborhood HOA. Since Harper had a lot of cats and did nothing with the front of her house, maybe they'd clashed.

It seemed to him Harper didn't want Gio talking to Linden. She put an arm behind Gio as if he didn't know which direction to walk. "Linden," she said.

"Harper," Linden said. "Nice to meet you, Gio pet."

Gio pet? Like a terracotta figurine?

Once inside the house, Gio asked Harper what she thought about Coffin Club.

"Not much," she said.

He looked up Consumia's Spiritual Emporium and saw they had an app, too, called The Omnist. He signed up, spending an hour or two answering the initial wave of questions.

Almost immediately he received his first notification.

MOTE:

Why Motes? Because they are the tiniest flakes of spiritual knowledge floating in the ether.

~

"SERIOUSLY THOUGH, COME WITH ME," Linden said now, wheeling the coffin into his garage.

Gio was barefoot, felt like ass, but went with him anyway.

He was too sick to be straying this far from a place he could lie down.

"Harper got your shoes?" Linden said.

"Something like that." He'd never even put socks back on after being turned into a cat last night. Couldn't exactly say that.

Gio was immediately envious of the abundant power tools and saws. No car had been stored here for years. Maybe ever. Harper's house didn't have a garage, just a shed in the back. For all he knew, Linden built them both.

Linden laid the hand truck flat and nodded toward one end. They picked up the coffin and set it along a wall. Linden grabbed a rake and used it to point at Gio's feet. "I'd give you one, too, but you look hobbled."

"I'm surprised you're home," Gio said. "I thought Coffin Club was tonight. I saw a sign yesterday."

"I got a couple hours before I get ready. And by get ready, I mean, put on some deodorant. That's how you know I like you."

Linden's eccentricity was on full display. Without something to concentrate on, one arm moved energetically into a pocket, out of it, fixing his collar, shifting his shirt. Shifting the rake from hand to hand. To the uninitiated, it looked like he was dispersing nervous energy. "So, where's Harper today?"

Locked in her bedroom.

"In bed, not feeling well," Gio answered. "I'm not either. Then heading out of town."

"Oh, where're you guys going?"

He hadn't planned to see anyone when he stepped outside, much less have a prepared alibi for Harper's whereabouts. He just ran with it. "She's going to visit family in Michigan. I'm staying here. Work deadline. Plus, I can take care of the cats."

"And the yard?" Linden's eyes were laughing. He was teasing. "I sometimes mow that little patch of grass in front and trim some of the jungle when I'm out here already."

Except for the actual garden in back, Harper's yard was unkempt. Both overgrown and half-dead. "Maybe wait until she's gone though. Don't want to rub her fur the wrong the way." That was a joke only Harper would get.

They walked down the driveway to the front yard. Gio gingerly stayed on the pavement rather than step on the dry, poky scrub grass.

"I'm sure those are good cats," Linden said. "She promised to keep them inside, and I'm sure that's true for the most part, but something's tearing up my backyard, destroying birds' nests, and eating the eggs. I mean, domestic cats kill four billion birds a year. That's their number-one predator."

"Sounds like a crow."

"I can hear the cats howling in heat if the windows are open. It brings other strays into the neighborhood."

"Raccoons?" Until last night, the only female of the bunch had been Cherry, and he'd never heard her in heat. "Squirrels?"

"I'm broken, you're broken, we're all broken." Despite the content of the conversation, Linden was playful. "But she needs to get those cats fixed."

Linden poked at a cluster of dried leaves with his rake. Then he said, softer, almost regretfully, "I've been asking her about it for years."

Odd that Linden would be concerned with whether someone's indoor cats were fixed. *Then again, they do escape. Or someone could leave the back door open.*

"Anyway, you should count the cats," Linden said. "I saw one before school today roaming our yards, so maybe it didn't get too far. Maybe it was hunting birds, I don't know. I love animals, but if you have cats, they need to be fixed. Who knows what trouble it's getting into?"

That may have been that one cat, What's-his-name; the one that left. "I told you I'm allergic to cats, didn't I?"

"Then you're a perfect cat-sitter. I'd help you look right now, but I've got to finish out here." Linden scratched the hair hat under the baseball cap. "I'll tell you what: I'll give you that box in there if you take those cats to be fixed while she's gone. When she finds out, tell her they'll live longer now. It's true. They live a lot longer when they're fixed."

Even though Linden's tone sounded like he was joking, the fact he brought up the pets again made Gio think he really was concerned. If he only knew the truth. And after what Harper had done last night, Gio knew whose side he should've been on this entire time. He just couldn't say anything about it.

His phone buzzed with a Mote.

"Still got the Omnist, huh?" Linden said as Gio took his phone out of his pocket.

"I should probably delete it. Maybe it's telling me to go back to bed," Gio said. He hoped it did. He felt like shit. "It says, 'The secret of the universe is a reflection of mortal phenomena.' Whatever, right?" He shoved the phone back in his pocket.

"Makes sense, don't make sense." Linden pointed the end of the rake at Gio. "Now, make *dollars* and I'll perk up."

"By box you mean that coffin, right?"

"Caskets are rectangles, coffins have six sides, but they're all boxes until they're filled. And we all got to go sometime."

"Speaking of which..." Gio looked down at his bare feet. Linden's gaze followed.

"Go," Linden said, pretending to shoo him away with the rake. "You look like hell. Get out of here. You're slowing me down."

He didn't have the heart to tell Linden he preferred to be cremated.

Which reminded him. At some point he would need to file

a missing person report for Harper. She wasn't dead, of course, but as the boyfriend he'd be the main person of interest in her disappearance. He was innocent, yet needed an alibi. She'd be legally dead, eventually, but he figured he had some time, first. A little.

Enough to spend the rest of the day asleep and recuperating in the spare bedroom. He closed the back door and took attendance again to see anybody else had left.

Just the initial one.

He put on socks, a second shirt, and sequestered himself in a spare bedroom. He closed the door to keep the little allergy makers at bay.

TWELVE

HARPER

H arper sat on the sill, wedged between the curtains and windowpane in her bedroom. Her house was draftier as a cat. Even though she enjoyed the smells that wafted in, she needed to feel warmer. Not only was it like a greenhouse inside the curtains, but she could see all the critters she wanted to play with. And to her, "play with" now meant "scout and pounce and bat around." She wasn't even hungry. The goal wouldn't be to kill but to sharpen her hunting skills, and if the critter died trying to escape the game, so be it.

She kept replaying the anniversary dinner over in her head. Gio had drunk the potion and she watched him morph into a cat. She'd put the wine bottle and glasses on the kitchen counter, and out of nowhere Cherry had launched herself at them. Harper had been positive the "safe" wine had been on the left. That was the one Cherry had knocked over, and Harper caught it and drank it. She'd obviously been wrong.

And what had the Omnist been trying to tell Gio? It annoyed her that he constantly checked it. She'd made that crack about a girlfriend texting him, but she hadn't actually seen the message. Harper didn't use the Omnist, didn't need it. She was a lone cat. A lone witch. No coven. And even if she belonged to one, it wouldn't have been through CSE or its watered-down mass-marketed app. Love of the Emporium aside, Harper was her own witch.

But Giovanni loved the Omnist. She wasn't sure how much he believed in it or followed its advice; he didn't believe in magic. At best, the Omnist encouraged self-improvement. At worst, it interrupted their conversations, their dinners, their movies. Most of the time when he was messing with his phone, it was with the Omnist. It was constantly pinging him, giving advice, asking questions. She supposed it made him feel deep.

She smelled Chico nearby. Jumping from the sill, to the nightstand, to the bed, to the floor was quick and easy. Her agility had already improved. Chico was in the hallway outside the door. Since he was more traditionally religious and a natural-born animal lover, maybe he didn't hold a grudge against her and enjoyed being a cat.

She smelled him drifting away. She called for him to no avail.

~

As a child, Chico Medina had wanted to be a veterinarian. Had too many pets. Mended hurt animals. Nursed baby birds. He acquired student loans for four years of college with a biology major and an ecology minor, but hadn't graduated yet. Since he'd also been working thirty hours a week, he was on a six-year plan to graduate with middle-of-the-pack grades. The work-school double life eventually became too much for him and he dropped out. When Harper met him, he still worked with animals, but didn't have a degree.

She was initially attracted to his positive attitude and closeness with animals. But he never seemed to get angry, and that infuriated her. He was religious almost to the point of caricature, and although he seemed careful never to be condescending, she always felt he harbored negative thoughts about her. Like he believed she was going to hell anyway, which allowed him to have more patience and understanding with her. It was spiritual arrogance. So his unspoken reasoning for not being condescending seemed condescending to her.

When it was time to break up, she needed him gone, but didn't want him to leave. He didn't consume alcohol, so getting him to drink a wine potion would be an accomplishment. But she could use religion as her entry point.

"We should do our own communion," she said to him one day.

"Come to my church," Chico said. He was clearly happy at the proposition. "It'll be something we can do together. I always knew your soul longed for everlasting peace and the grace of God."

"But I don't want to be part of a social group. The glad-handing and pretend smiles. People who don't care how I'm doing asking me how I'm doing."

"Do you think *I'm* fake?" Chico wasn't argumentative. Just curious. She hated it. Where was he hiding his anger?

"No, no, not you," she said. "I'm just saying I crave a personal relationship between me and God. I mean, you and me and God."

"Okay. Let's start there. I'm not sure us doing it ourselves will count as a first communion, but we'll give it a shot. Maybe you'll come along for the ride after you see how nice the car is."

"Maybe. Let's just call this a proof of concept. If all goes well, we may end up being together a lot more."

He seemed to like this idea.

At Consumia's Spiritual Emporium, she bought a shiny brass pill box, which appeared to her like a container for sacrament wafers. It had a hinged lid with a deeply engraved cross filled with blood-red resin. It wasn't a religious cross, necessarily. It looked Swiss. She preferred the nationalistic inference. She then bought unleavened communion wafers online to put in it.

On the night of her "first" communion, she dressed nice. She'd done this with her grandpa many years ago, going to his church and ignoring everyone there until she was fifteen, then never went again. But this was different. She wanted Chico to feel he was in charge. Paternal. A shepherd. She knew she should wear white, but wanted to wear black. A much better color for performing rituals. She chose a flowing gray cotton dress with white lace as a compromise. Comfortable. Plus, she shaved her arms and legs and oiled herself in a scent that reminded her of the Fertile Crescent. She felt exotic for such a domestic, personal ritual.

She and Chico moved the coffee table back against the couch, and put pillows to sit on in the middle of her old Persian rug. Harper placed a five-arm candelabra of tall white candles on a silver tray on the coffee table next to them.

Spike the cat had been restless the night prior, apparently aware of what was going to happen. Rather than swipe at her ankles like he normally did when she passed, he rubbed against her shins while she concocted the final preparations.

Tonight, he lay on the couch with his front paws close together, ready to spring into action at the first sign of danger.

Harper came in from the kitchen with two shot glasses and placed the laced wine near Chico, and the normal one near her. The house was dark but for the candles.

They readied themselves by kneeling on their respective pillows. Harper's dress billowed out around her. She felt like a schoolgirl in ninth grade. She didn't like it.

Chico smiled.

He read a passage, angling the book in the candlelight to see better. She hadn't bothered to research or prepare better for this because these words didn't matter, and Chico should be changed over before the end of the ritual, anyway. They wouldn't have time to argue about it. And she didn't care.

He placed the sacrament on her tongue. The wafer was dry and stuck to it immediately, and she pulled her tongue in like a conveyor belt. She'd never been one who enjoyed having others hand-feed her, but she found this turning her on. Too late. Maybe it was built-up excitement for witnessing another transfiguration.

Chico lifted his shot glass to hand to her, but she grabbed hers instead.

"I'm supposed to offer it to you," he said.

"Already have it."

He nodded at her to drink.

"Cheers," she said, unconcerned with coming across as sacrilegious. It was delicious.

In turn, Harper read the same passage to him, placed a wafer in his mouth, and picked up his shot glass. Unlike a traditional communion, where the shot may be smaller and the wine may be unfermented juice, she needed to make sure he got enough potion into him. A sipper could lead to disaster.

"I know you don't drink," she said, handing the glass to him, "but this is special. It's from a hundred-dollar bottle."

"It *is* special," Chico said. "It's the blood of our savior." He looked at the glass with skepticism. "It's a lot more than I'm used to. You don't mind if I just have a sip, do you? I drink a special imported non-alcoholic..."

"Just knock it back. All in one go. Trust me, it's worth it. For me."

He drank his shot and coughed. "That's awful." But he'd drunk the whole thing.

"Oh, come on," she said. "You're a lightweight."

"You paid a hundred dollars for that? Next time give me the hundred and I'll have Spike there provide some of his finest."

"You'd willingly drink cat urine?"

"I mean, for a hundred dollars..." He probably wasn't kidding. But this way she got to enjoy some nice Bordeaux.

"I don't feel right," he said. He scratched at his arms. Then his cheeks. "Maybe I'm allergic?" As he changed, he started screaming and clawing harder at himself. "What's going on?"

"Just calm down, dear," Harper said. "This should be easier for you than it was for Spike. You're so much more the animal lover, and sympathetic to the plight of cats."

He dug at the sides of his face so hard she expected blood. But instead, she saw little whiskers creating new shadows in the candlelight.

"Are these whiskers? I'm turning into a cat?" He knocked into the coffee table and the candles fell over, extinguishing their light. She saw him fall over in the dark, the impact rattling the bones of the old house. "You mean...Spike's an ex? You're evil!"

"Come now, that's all relative, dear. Religion is such a bore."

"Evil!"

Finally, the anger she'd been waiting for. She knew he had it in him. "Let's not call each other names, now, dear," she said. "We have to learn to get along."

"Oh! My! God! Why?"

That was completely garbled now, and Harper could barely make out those words. "Name in vain, sweetie." She must research a spell for communication with cats. "Be a good kitty."

"Aauugghh!"

Between the yellow-white floaters still in her eyes from the deceased candles, she could just make out Spike jumping off the couch, his hunched form sneaking up on Chico as Chico shrunk to his size. She reached over and pushed Spike away.

"Easy, Spike. No jealous boyfriend stuff."

Chico made a fine white cat and nearly glowed in the dark. But of course he did. His fur represented the white robe of the devout. Since he was known to hike a lot and be one with nature, she left his hatchback wagon at a trailhead in the San Gabriel Mountains.

Making the forgetful, scattered, trusting tea potion was much easier than the transfiguration potion had been, but it was far less satisfying.

Harper presently found herself by the bedroom door making semi-guttural noises, hoping Chico would come back. It was a reflexive bodily activity, like hiccups or hyperventilating, neither of which she'd been prone to do as a human. She didn't realize she was doing this at first, but when she noticed, it felt natural. Soft and deep and quiet. Like the opposite but companion noise to purring. She hadn't made these noises since she was a kitten.

She'd never been a kitten.

She was in psychological pain. It was the feline equivalent to crying herself to sleep. But she was lying on her side by the door, not hiding under the bed. Everything felt heavy.

She snapped to awareness again when she sensed a cat sniffing the crack under the door. It was tomorrow. No, it was still yesterday.

"Harper, are you there?" Chico said, softly but firm. He had a good bedside manner. "You're sobbing. Are you in pain?"

His communication skill was better than Spike's, but the words still pressed into her brain as more emotive than vocabularic. Whereas Spike was pretty much all cat now, Chico was mostly cat. She pictured him with his paws together, head down, checking under the door like he was sublimating to his God. His fur was fluffy white, like a soft robe. Maybe it was the power of suggestion, but his collar always seemed part of his image. A white robe and a choke collar.

"My sense of time has shifted," she said.

"Definitely. So you're okay?"

"Is one day really a week now? Who would've thought that one human year really does equal seven for a cat?"

"Kind of. Not really, though. It's more elastic. But I'm getting old and it doesn't shift that much anymore. It flexed a lot at first. How long have I been a cat now? Fifty years?"

That was insane. But this elastic thing made sense. She could feel time stretching as her brain got used to her new senses. It dawned on her that the sense of time was itself a sense. The most obvious thing that she'd never thought about. And cats were already fertile within their first year. Comparatively, humans weren't reproductive at seven. So, from their perspective, cats aged quicker early on and slowed down later. Humans were opposite. Time passed quicker as they aged.

"Chico, honey," she said. "It's only been like twelve or thirteen years for you."

"That's not possible. I...can't... Don't lie."

"When we change back to human, you won't be an old man yet. Still in your forties."

"I'm an old cat. I don't have a lot of human memories. I've forgotten most of them. I have more way more as a cat. Most of my life I've been a cat. I'd be an old human with almost nothing but cat memories."

This wasn't worth arguing about. Maybe the feline mind reworked memories. Made him a different person.

"You'll help me, right?" Harper said. "We'll get out of here. Change back. We can do this."

"I don't know if I can, Harpy. You stole my life from me. I could've helped so, so many animals by now. Saved so many souls from suffering. That's what I was put on this earth to do, and you stopped my purpose cold."

"Then help me, Chico. You need to forgive me. I'm a cat, just like you. We're all cats. You were put here to help all of us. You can finally help all the cats now."

Chico wouldn't really be an old man when they changed back, would he? What was the lifespan for a cat that used to be a human? Would they live as long as a cat or as long as a human? Or something in between? There would be no ASPCA charts or graphs to reference. She couldn't spend the rest of her life like this. Her oldest, Spike, had already been a cat for seventeen years. Old for a cat, but not all that rare.

She needed to go back. Spike had been a cat so long he'd accepted his fate as such, and here was Chico, a better communicator, and using it to transmit his resentment. He'd rather stay a cat and see her punished for her sins than see all of them become human again.

"I'm sorry, Harpy," Chico said. "I cannot help you. It's for God to lay his judgment upon you."

THIRTEEN

KAT

Wet paw prints led across the top of the front counter to where the cat was sitting, stoic and regal. Instead of dashing for the door, he watched customers as if observing a royal procession moving past. Kat had set out a four-footed marble water bowl at the other end of the counter, the splashing from which had made a small circumferential mess. Odd, since Kat had never seen a cat behave like this before. He'd splashed and rubbed his front paws in the water like a raccoon. Like a doctor rubbing wet forearms together.

The water was dirty, so Kat changed it out and put the bowl down on a fresh paper towel.

"You're doing this on the counter?" Connie said as she walked in.

"It's where he wants to be. Look at him. He already knows more about the store than we do."

The cat glanced at them, then returned to surveying. Even though they were talking about him, they weren't worth the trouble. He had dignity.

"And is that Organica merch you're using as a cat dish?"

Connie needn't have asked, as the answer was written along the rim:

Soul feeds the food and food feeds the soul.

It was the mortar half of a P and M set.

"Well, it's a bowl," Kat said. "It's heavy and won't move too much. And it's the perfect size for a kitty."

"We have Jasmine's animal dishes over there." Jasmine, the pet psychic Omniscian, sold her own brand of animal-related merchandise and treats.

"I know. I don't know why, but the mortar felt right."

"We can't sell it now," Connie said.

"Why not? It's a floor item without packaging anyway. People know it's dirty when they buy it."

"Do I really have to explain this to you?"

"So don't sell it. I named him Mortar because of the bowl. He's really smart. He's a Consumerian, and he can't wear an Executive Saint pin, so we should make him a CSE collar instead. Have Lucador make one. Or modify one of Ornatu's wrap-around bracelets. We can let Mortar pick one out for himself."

"I see you've been thinking about this," Connie said. "Well, regardless, he belongs to someone. I'm going to make a flyer."

"You like it here, right Mortar?" The cat didn't respond to the name, just continued observing. Kat wanted him to direct that inquisitive look in her direction, for him to be more curious about what made *her* tick.

Gawd, she was envious of the attention of a stray cat.

Connie took several pictures with her phone but Mortar kept turning his head away, eventually jumping down from the counter to avoid her. He was well-behaved, but Kat was learning he was stubborn about certain things. Like he didn't want his photo taken.

"I guess this is good enough," Connie said, scrolling through the shots as she walked to her office.

Mortar jumped back up on the counter and stared at Kat. She occasionally scratched under his jaw as curious, smiling Consumerians approached to inquire about him and kiss the ring. She continued to speak for him. The Ol' Chap. He wasn't a stray they were adopting; he was a new Consumerian adopting them.

Connie returned and handed a flyer to Kat. "Could you tape this where customers can see it?"

Kat watched Connie walk away to put one up on the bulletin board by the door and then on a couple of poles outside. She crumpled hers and tossed it into a waste-paper basket.

"You look like you want to say something, sweetie," Kat said to Mortar. "Go ahead." But asking him to communicate felt like a form of teasing, creating psychological discomfort. He was more mature, beyond teasing, so she swore not to torture the poor creature. She had always baby-talked to animals, but it was different with him. He deserved a conversational tone.

"Where's Connie?" Consumerian Stacy said, suddenly standing near the register as if she'd elevated from the floor. Kat wondered what the contrarian's next issue would be.

"She's putting up posters for this little gentleman," Kat said. "This is Mortar. He's a stray who wandered in today."

"You know I'm allergic to cats."

"Now, how would I know that?" Of course Stacy was allergic. And if she wasn't, she'd say she was, anyway. Kat cupped her hand to pet the top of Mortar's head, while he both leaned into it and averted his gaze.

"Allergies aren't fun," Stacy said.

Kat didn't want to engage with her, and instead focused her attention on the cat. Connie was soon there to provide reinforcement. "Hi, Stacy. Lert me guess; you're allergic to cats?"

"It's not just me, you know. It's something like ten percent of all people."

"Me, too," Connie said. "And if I can suck it up, so can you." She lowered herself to Mortar's level, "Isn't that right?" It was that baby voice again. Poor kitty. Connie probably wouldn't admit it, but Kat could tell she was falling for Mortar. It was easy when he was such a debonair little man. "Poor thing just appeared today. We're trying to find his owner but he has no collar."

Stacy reached out two fingers in front of Mortar's nose. Mortar sniffed, then quickly lost interest.

Even though Connie had basically explained the same thing as Kat, it rolled off her tongue better. Connie had charm. She lit up. "He's not yours, is he?" she asked Stacy.

"Oh, hell no. Cats would eat you if they could," Stacy said.

"You don't think this lil' guy would do that, do you?" Kat said.

"I'm already here to look death in the face. That doesn't mean I want it to happen tonight!" Stacy laughed coldly; the situation was apparently not as severe as Stacy wanted it to sound.

"I'll be sure to keep him out of Coffin Club," Connie said.

Coffin Club would be less fun tonight with Stacy's presence, but Kat had to give her credit: Even though Stacy complained about nearly every Omniscian, Lodge, and other event at CSE, she managed to try them all at least once. Maybe she just needed fresh material for her complaints.

Otherwise, Mortar received lots of attention serving sentry on the counter. Lots of petting and cooing customers. Mortar seemed to know exactly when to dip his head or lift his chin and puff out the starburst of white fur on his chest, and seemed to enjoy listening to people talk.

SPECIAL BLACK CAUTION tape with yellow lettering blocked access to much of the floor of the Basil Alcove. Instead of displaying "Caution," however, the tape read "Consumia's Spiritual Emporium." There was a freshly painted pentacle and an Old Norse style compass in the middle of the floor.

But enough room remained between the main floor and windows for access to the tea kiosk and tables. Dani the tarot reader set herself up at a table near the front door, rather than at her usual spot deeper in the Basil Alcove. She performed free readings at CSE to attract customers to her own store, L.A. Obscura. There wasn't much preparation needed: a black tablecloth, a candle, and an antique cookie-tin receptacle with a twenty-dollar bill in it as a starter. She went to the front counter.

"I see a beautiful, wonderful box here," Dani said, patting the L.A. Obscura on the counter. She also sold them at her own store of the same name. "How much are you charging?"

"They're free."

"Huh. I charge five dollars."

Kat shrugged. "At least it's an advertisement for your store." Kat moved the box over and tapped on a business card taped to the glass. "Cross-promotion. See?"

"More importantly," Dani said, mollified but clearly still annoyed, "you have a new kitty. Him or her?"

"Well, not neutered yet, so..."

"Oh, a little man, I see."

"This is Mortar," Kat said.

Dani petted the cat with thick, gentle hands that looked made to hold an axe.

"Sorry Jasmine cancelled tonight," Kat said. She could swear the cat understood her by the way he shot a look at her. "Will you hand me the sign off the easel? I keep forgetting to take it down."

Dani went to retrieve it. Mortar seemed to tire and put his head down.

"As you can see," Kat said as she received the dry-erase board, "Thalia and Kevin used the opportunity to do some handiwork on the floor."

"I see that. It's beautiful."

"Hopefully, you'll still get lots of clients."

"There's a Coffin Club. I can lean the readings more positive, play to the crowd. Cheer them up."

Which meant no Mortoscopes. A Mortoscope was a fortune Dani devised which combined astrology, tarot, and numerology to determine a death sign and produce a more complete fortune. Providing a date of death may be unwise tonight.

"How would you do that?" Kat said. "Just lie about what the cards mean?"

"I know people who do that, but no. You never know what your customer knows. I rely more on, you know..." Dani lowered her voice. "I can tell you of course...card tricks."

"Tarot card tricks." Of course. If one could learn tricks with a normal deck, they could certainly do it with tarot. "Sleight of hand?"

"While you're distracted talking about your finances and health issues. Maybe a dead husband."

Kat froze. It had only been seven months.

"Oh, dear," Dani said, reaching across the counter to lightly touch Kat's forearm. "Bad example."

"It's fine." It wasn't fine. But whatever. It was a mistake.

More customers wandered in.

"Time for some sleight of feet," Dani said, and went back to her table to look official or mysterious or something.

An Executive Saint named Patrick approached the counter. He was a retired security chief for Warbler Brothers studios, solidly built like a forty-year-old body builder, and had the best/worst comb over ever. He was holding a frayed, broken pet collar. "I heard you telling someone a cat showed up here," Patrick said, handing it over. "And I saw this out back. Think it's his?"

It said "Steve." No phone number or address or tags.

"It was by the dumpster," he continued. "Clasp broken. Looks like it either got caught on something and he yanked it off, or he found a sharp edge somewhere to break the clasp himself."

She could feel it through her skin. Something about it. She set it behind the register.

"Steve's a weird name for a cat," Patrick said.

He was right, but she didn't want to talk about it. Patrick was also holding a box of cricket snacks.

"Horror D'Oeuvres," Kat said. That was the brand name for Yksian's insect treats, which also included mealy worms and ants. They tasted like chocolate-covered, overcooked crispy rice. "My favorite."

"Oh, hell no," Stacy said, walking past. Fortunately, she disappeared as quickly as she'd appeared. In case Kat needed a dissenting opinion.

"I don't know. I like them," Patrick said.

"Me, too," Kat said. She rang him up. No bag needed. Patrick left.

"Your name's not really Steve, is it?" Kat said in the cat's direction. Steve lifted his head. "Should we add your name to the posters, maybe?"

Steve lowered his head.

"Nah, your owner would know your name," Kat said. "And no more Mortar. I guess you're Steve again."

The collar joined the crumpled flyer in the wastebasket.

WHEN KAT WAS ON BREAK, she went to a pet store to buy some cat food, a litter box and fill, and a black pet carrier that looked like a cross between a gym bag and a miniature screen tent. Waiting in line at the register, she thought about how last night she wanted a dog, and then today, a cat presented himself. Even if it was only until they found his owner, it felt like, for once, the universe was looking out for her.

She brought a bag of cat food into the Emporium with her, leaving the rest in the car. Steve was in his new usual spot on the counter, seeming to recognize her as she walked past him.

"Steve, are you hungry?" Kat said. She hoped nobody had tried to feed him Lucador's beef jerky or any chocolate crickets while she was gone. Jasmine's treats were fine, but would get expensive fast. She petted him and looked at the waste basket behind the counter. No new food packaging. "I bought you some dinner."

She went down an aisle and found a tiny O'Cult-branded twelve-ounce iron cauldron. Like an iron teacup, really. This was heavier than the mortar. She unboxed it, poured in some kibble, and set it on the counter next to the water.

Steve looked at it, uninterested.

"Dinner," she said in a baby voice. She cleared her throat and said it again, correcting herself. She was talking to an adult. "Dinner."

Maybe he hadn't been hungry.

COFFIN CLUB WASN'T a late-night event, over by nine p.m., and Linden, Connie, and the guests were gone within thirty minutes. Without a Lodge—which sometimes kept them open until midnight—Kat closed up as soon as there was a moment with no customers in the Emporium. She went out to her car to retrieve the carrier and brought it in. She set it on the counter and unzipped it.

"Come on, Steve, we can do this." He stared. "You've been in a car before, haven't you?"

Steve jumped down and trotted around the freshly painted pentacle, and hopped onto the short stage. He sat down and faced her. It seemed like this was where he'd reunite with his owner. Like maybe they were a Consumerian.

"Are you saying you'd rather stay here?" Kat said.

Still, Steve acted as if he understood her, but also didn't care. Maybe he was someone with whom she could attempt to reason.

"You can stay here if you think that's better for you. But if you'd rather come visit my house, you need to get in the bag."

He kept looking at her.

"I'm not going to take you to a shelter. And we'll come back here tomorrow. I have to bring you back, anyway. Connie's going to expect you to be here."

She moved the carrier to about six feet from him and backed away. He continued to look at her. This was hopeless.

She sat on the stage between Steve and the carrier. Steve walked onto her lap, asking for attention. She petted him. She could just put him in the bag. But she couldn't. She really couldn't. He was a cat with a human name who'd come to CSE of his own volition, and she believed he should leave the same way.

"Well, I guess I should bring in your litter box from the car."

At that, Steve entered the carrier. He turned around, sat, and waited for Kat to zip it up.

"Or maybe not."

CHAPTER

FOURTEEN

GIOVANNI

H e still felt ill, worse than yesterday. It was like a bad flu, the worst he'd ever had. His head hurt. His muscles hurt. His eyes hurt. He was running a temperature. He certainly couldn't edit video footage like this, so he reported sick to work again. He would probably be kicked off his current movie work project. They had a deadline coming up and this would be his second missed day.

MOTE:

Your body experiences essential fulfillment.

. . .

HE WASN'T ABOUT to go to the hospital and try to explain how he'd completed a round trip transfiguration of human to cat to human. Maybe he'd picked up some sort of cat flu. There was a bird flu, a swine flu, a mad cow disease, so why not?

He had to figure out what was going on. He Giggled "cat flu." What he found wasn't influenza, per se, but toxoplasmosis, a parasitic disease spread through cat feces that apparently infected an estimated ten percent of people in the U.S. Although most infected adults never developed any overt symptoms, some people experienced fever, fatigue, muscle aches, and tender lymph nodes or blurred vision. Like the flu.

He fit this description. Regardless of whether the victim felt ill or not, the disease messed with their immunity, turning them into a lifelong host. Although it could infect most mammals, the disease could only reproduce within the cat family. So humans could get infected, but couldn't transmit it. He may have had toxoplasmosis.

He searched for information about humans morphing into animals. What he found mostly fell into the realm of cryptozoology, the study of mythical creatures. He was piqued by an American legend about a "bipedal feline." Like Bigfoot, but with a cat's head, tail, and paws. Of course, they were rarely sighted. Maybe they were blurry, too. This didn't fit the situation, but maybe he was on the right track.

He read about werecats, people who were like werewolves but changed into cats under the full moon. Harper's exes weren't werecats. They didn't kill or attack humans, or change back and forth. Some people believed werecats were illusions created by demons to trick humans. But the situation he was in was *real*, not a myth or a legend or a fairy tale. The proof was right here in the house.

He got an email from Hazel. "Should I go get checked out?"

It sounded like a trap. He would never recommend

someone *not* get checked out, but if he said that, he'd be implying his condition could be a sexually transmitted disease. He'd answer this later. He was too sick to be on the computer this long.

He rubbed his eyes after looking at the screen for too long. Sore, blurry, itchy. This wasn't surprising, since they'd been comparatively widened to provide a broader feline field of vision when he was briefly a cat. Everything was still sore. He went to the bathroom mirror to inspect his eyes. He could swear he still had catlike qualities, but after blinking and refocusing, maybe that was psychosomatic. This condition probably wouldn't affect his work, when and if he went back to it.

He'd done virtually nothing the last day and a half, including eating. He wandered into the kitchen to take stock of the food situation. He saw the cats had barely touched the cat food he'd put in the dishes. Jagger chirruped at his foot, asking to be fed, which brought Spike and Chico in as well. Harper would cook most of the cats' meals. The cat food was merely backup.

Giovanni hadn't thought of himself as a cook before, but also hadn't considered cats to be literal people in feline bodies before, either. "Hold on a sec," he said. "Let me see what I should do for you guys."

He went back to his laptop to research cat diets. Besides the obvious meats, which would make up the majority of their diet, they ate eggs, spinach, rice, oatmeal, cooked carrots, peas, and pureed pumpkin. The key was to serve the food warm, as if from a fresh kill, and unseasoned. Sparingly, due to sugar content, they could also eat bananas, blueberries, and strawberries.

He was still too sick to attempt to drive or go shopping. He found some chicken breasts to grill and sweet potatoes to boil and mash with a fork. He separated the food into two dishes for those in the main house to share, and brought a third dish to Harper in her bedroom. She was curled on a pillow and lifted her head when he entered.

"I can't believe you would do this for everybody," he said, setting the food on the floor. "I heated it up. I read how cats prefer food the temperature of fresh murder, so eat it before it stops moving."

Rather than acknowledge him, she stared out the window as if there were a bird or squirrel nearby. The drapes were closed. Maybe she heard or smelled something.

"Are you listening to me?"

Harper remained still as a bust. She no longer hid from him, but didn't seek affection, either. It was difficult to tell when speaking to a cat if they had the presence of mind to intentionally ignore you or not.

"If you had it your way, I'd still be a cat, just an addition to your collection of exes. That was the plan; that's what you do. Seriously, who is that evil?"

He smelled fresh feces and urine. He hadn't put a litter box in the room.

"Whatever," he said, closing the door behind him. He looked in a utility closet and found a cracked litter box that he filled and returned to the bedroom.

"It's your wood floor so I don't care if you decide to ruin it, but in case you want to be lady, you can use this." He squatted to clean the floor. She would probably use the box. She'd had the presence of mind to go on the floor, not on her rug.

HE'D MADE a cup of fresh loose-leaf tea Harper had apparently blended before their anniversary dinner. He poured a mug and went out back to get some fresh air, but didn't know how long he'd have energy to be out of bed. He'd already burned all his mental energy for the day.

Cherry joined him.

There was a solemn old fountain back there that added the bucolic sound of running water to the relatively peaceful Verdugo Mountains ravine behind the house. He had no idea how old it was. In the center was a four-headed, weather-worn stone dragon, each head facing a cardinal direction. It was easily hundreds of pounds. It was majestic and probably impossible to move without a forklift. Harper had allowed weeds to wrap around much of its base. The bowl was waist-high and acted as a bird bath. He couldn't fathom how she could attract birds to her garden without them ravaging her plants and flowers and seeds. Maybe the garden was protected by spells. Three days ago, he would've considered her rituals performative, with no real outcome. Now, he wondered if anybody had ever seen this fountain without later being turned into a cat.

Cherry hopped up onto the rim of the fountain. The most beautiful cat with the healthiest fur and most despondent eyes. Feline malaise. He petted her. He decided he would never spurn a cat's desire for human affection ever again, allergies be damned.

"You're sad because your best chance to become human again is stuck as a cat, too, aren't you?" No cat had ever looked him in the eyes for so long, their gaze saying so much. "I'll figure this out."

He forgot what he was thinking about. The only thing he knew for sure was that he needed rest. He again forgot where he was. He laughed at himself. He looked around and realized he was at Harper's. He and Cherry went back inside. The tea seemed to be making him happier, but more tired.

He was surprised to see a dining room in his condo. It had

grown since he'd been outside. Right, he was at Harper's. He climbed into the bed in the spare bedroom. He forgot he was trying to sleep, then forgot he was sleeping, then forgot he'd been awake. He forgot he was sick. Forgot he was at Harper's. Forgot he was alive.

He woke up in the middle of the night feeling the house was eerily possessed. He'd slept eighteen hours yesterday, and would be close to that total again when it was all said and done, if the loud silence and quiet noises of patrolling cats didn't keep him awake.

No wonder this place used to freak him out so much. His mind had sensed the cats telepathically chittering below the threshold of physical hearing. The house was indeed haunted, just not in a way he could've predicted.

Mote:
   The heart explores the mechanics of silence.

Okay. He was just thinking about silence.

CHAPTER
FIFTEEN

HARPER

When Harper had first met Jagger, she was attracted to him sexually, but as she'd learned with previous boyfriends, that desire weakened the more she got to know him. But if either were to break up with the other, she needed to be the one in the cat seat. Catbird seat. Whatever. She'd never been broken up with, not since Jeremy in ninth grade.

On Easter Sunday afternoon, she and Jeremy had made plans for him to come over and share their baskets, watch a movie, and play with the family cat. She'd gone to church with Grandpa, then remained in her pretty dress and fancy hair so Jeremy would be impressed. She waited. And waited. No call, no show.

She'd sat there for two extra hours in her flower-patterned

church dress, feeling like an itchy kitchen drape. Jeremy. That little shit. And then he dodged her at school in the halls, at lunch, everywhere, for another week.

She finally cornered him coming out of the boys' room.

"And just where were you on Easter? You were supposed to come over."

"Playing football with the guys." He acted like anyone would know that.

"I waited for you, and I know you know you fucked up because you're avoiding me."

"Avoiding? I thought we were already broken up. We haven't talked in like a week, isn't it obvious?"

She didn't hit him, but she wanted to. And she swore she'd never be broken up with again. And she hadn't been. And like the stealthy hunter she was, they never saw it coming, all thinking they had the relationship under their control. Until they didn't. It'd been fairly easy to trick them into drinking the potion.

But Jagger's breakup and changeover had been a little different.

His human name was Mick and he was a tall, skinny, long-haired artist. His surname wasn't Jagger; that was something Harper called him after the change. Jagger sounded more like a pet's name.

Although his career was in animation, which meant long hours in front of a computer, he was an artist to the bone in the more traditional, "granola" sense. He attended events like Burning Man in the Nevada desert for the lifestyle, Comic Con in San Diego for the animated arts, and Bonnaroo on a farm in Tennessee for the bands. But he attended all of them for the community. His ultimate goal was to create an "adult animated movie"—not XXX adult, but animation that wasn't aimed at children. He wanted to blow minds.

Mick was the only boyfriend who'd caught on that Harper practiced a darker side of witchcraft, not just worshiping the moon and casting enchantments for good luck, health, or vitality.

One day she had been in the backyard at the edge of the ravine, burning a potion in a cauldron, casting a spell.

"That smell...what are you doing?" came a voice from behind her. Mick was an hour early and making the yucky face at her. He had no poker face; he was prone to telegraphing emotions.

What the hell, she thought, just tell him the truth. "I do this once a year," she said. "Otherwise, the animals come and eat everything in the garden."

"But we're the ones encroaching on their territory, building farther and farther back into their feeding grounds. It's not their fault. What else are they going to eat?"

"They don't have to eat what's mine. I'll throw the scraps in the ravine."

"But you compost."

"They can eat someone else's garden."

She expected more anger out of him, but he seemed fascinated. "I do love the idea that you're using nature to affect nature, though," he said.

"I thought you'd be mad."

"I don't like what you're doing, but I'd love to know why an animal would avoid this area for a year now."

"The answer's written on your face."

He was still making his yucky face. The spell was affecting him. The wind had shifted, blowing the thin, black smoke at him. "Ow," he said, rubbing his eyes, now red and watery. "No, I mean the smoke and smell will go away. Why won't the animals come back next week or next month? What will they sense has changed about the backyard?"

"I can show you if you want to learn more," she said.

Harper was marginally entertained by Mick's willingness to trust her and try new things, which injected new energy into the relationship for a few weeks.

Twice he said, "Let's not do this one again," stating they'd made the world a worse place for others for their own benefit. But he never said no to a first-time charm, even when they gave the neighbor across the street a cold for parking three straight days in front of Harper's house.

But he still whistled while he slept. And he never cleaned the surface of his phone; she nearly gagged thinking about his greasy finger streaks reflected in the sunlight. And he would bring it into the bathroom with him. And he could listen to The Grateful Dead or Phish all day, every day. She was okay with that genre of music in general, but in smaller doses.

She, too, was an earthy, nature-bound soul, which was why she'd been attracted to Mick in the first place. They'd met at the Organica booth at a vegan beer festival, although she was neither vegan nor a beer nerd.

She learned Mick was the type of person who got free tickets to a Phish or Goose concert by offering to pick up the tailgaters' trash in the parking lot before and after the show. Carrying around other people's stinking, sticky, sickening garbage in wet, biodegradable bags. *No, thank you.* She wanted to arrive on time and leave on time, not be a janitor paid in barter. Or preferably, stay home altogether.

No, she was still going to break up with him in her own unique and increasingly skilled manner. Transfiguration was an art, and as far as she knew, she was the only artist who currently worked in the medium.

Mick always had a thing for cats and was good to both of Harper's, even if Spike had never really taken to him. One day Mick was playing with Chico, dangling a hacky sack bindle dusted in catnip for Chico to chase. As Chico dove through the air and swiped a paw, Mick would lift the bindle just out of reach and the cat would fall backward, twisting awkwardly, just barely landing on his feet. It was almost as if Mick's goal was to get him to actually land on his back.

"Ever thought about seeing the world through the eyes of a cat?" Harper said. "You know, for your art?"

"I've thought about it. Dogs, cats, birds. A ketchup bottle. Bathwater."

"I don't mean as a mental exercise, but from their actual perspective. Seeing the world as they actually see it. I don't know how to put you in the mind of one of those other animals, but a cat, that I can do."

"What do you mean?"

"I mean I can make a potion that will temporarily give you the vision of a cat."

"Like becoming colorblind?"

"I think they can see blue. Maybe yellow."

Chico stopped jumping and looked at Harper. She reached out and clapped her hands on the dangling hacky sack, creating a fine cloud of catnip. Chico jumped and chomped at the air.

"But see," she said, "doesn't matter what color the catnip is."

"He can smell it."

"He can smell it." She rubbed her palms on her thighs. She shouldn't have done that. Now the cats would be all over her that night. "Let's do vision first. We'll do smell second."

"You're yanking my paw. You're just going to dose me and tell me I'm a cat and I might believe you."

"No, I promise this is real. How about Sunday?"

She liked the idea of giving him a taste of what it was like to be a cat, because she herself was curious. He could give feedback. She could tweak and perfect her recipe.

That weekend she brewed a small potion that would augment his vision. Each cat sense was a chapter of the main spell, but unless they were all combined in the proper order with the other key ingredients, the effects would be minimal and temporary. She hoped the doses were low enough that he wouldn't develop any sort of telepathic communication. She didn't need a message from Spike or Chico getting to him.

THAT WEEKEND, to keep things relatively consistent, she added the potion to red wine.

"This is going to be so cool," he said, drinking.

After a minute, Mick lifted his eyebrows as if they'd grown heavy. Then he rubbed them. "I have a headache. My eyes are burning."

He tried to get up from the couch.

"Sit still," Harper said, easing him back with one hand.

"I want to see my face." But he didn't push forward. His eyes had widened and enlarged like he was wearing a pair of novelty glasses. He looked at his hand up close. "I can't see my fingerprints, it's too blurry. But when I do this..." He held his palm as far as he could from his face. "I see them just fine."

She dangled the bindle in front of him and he swiped at it.

"Motion is cool. I can predict movement a lot quicker. Or I've sped up so much, everything else is slower now."

Chico was on the floor, crouching like he was going to jump at the bindle, but never did.

Harper held a book open across the room, and even in low light, he was able to read it.

"We should make single-serving vials of this to sell at desert parties," he said. "We'd blow so many minds."

Spike walked to the edge of the room to watch for a moment before continuing on into the kitchen.

"The cats keep looking at me," Mick said.

"I'm sure they sense something's different about you." She hadn't expected paranoia to be a potential side effect, but the cats had indeed been watching him.

The spell lasted about an hour. It was almost over.

"I'm so tired," Mick said.

"Cats do need more sleep than we do."

"Now I know why." He yawned, stretching by extending his arms and arching his back.

"Did Spike or Chico say anything to you?" Harper said.

"No...what? What do you mean?"

"I was hoping understanding them would be an interesting side effect. Just checking."

She'd heard each of them say something, but Mick hadn't.

Good to go.

THEY TRIED out the feline olfactory spell the following weekend, and afterward Mick told Harper about journaling both experiences.

"It's like taking psychotropic drugs, but with laser-focus," he said. "No mind wandering, it's all free-floating consciousness. They're visits into an entirely new world, one sense at a time. I'm able to write about it from the inside out."

"Hearing is next," Harper said.

"No, that's just more of a tease. Let's skip hearing and go full feline."

It seemed he may have wanted the transfiguration for himself more than she did. She was impressed.

"Let's do Sunday again, but in the morning," Harper said. "It's a powerful spell so it may last longer, but we'll get you back in time to have dinner with me. We'll have sushi."

She'd seen him with a set of isolated cat eyes, then a cat nose with wet nostrils. She wondered what his face would look like framed by whiskers, fur, and pointed ears.

"Maybe we'll give you some finger paint for your paws," she said.

"Nice," he said. "I'm on the verge of creating a completely new movement in art with you as my guide and muse. This is like going from the combustion engine of humanity to the nuclear reactor of all life."

So Mick was the only boyfriend who knowingly and willingly drank the potion. Her only lie had been about changing him back. His ashen hair had transferred with him to cathood, and he had the longest, dirtiest looking hair of all the cats. She left Mick's car parked at a pickup lot for busses bringing people out to a five-day vegan food and music desert festival.

"Despite you changing us into cats," Jagger was currently saying through the door, "we never doubted you loved us. Our issue is that, for you, love means controlling our environment, our diets, our entire lives. And until you changed yourself into a cat, you had control over all five of us."

"Almost six." Almost Giovanni.

"Listen to you—you're proud of it!" Jagger said. "And I could argue you already controlled Gio. You didn't need to turn him into a cat."

"He cheated on me."

"And now that you're a cat that still bothers you? What about Cherry? She never cheated. Never would. Out of all your exes, I probably get along with her best. She's a good person."

Harper had forgotten about Mick's emotional intelligence. She'd learned Spike had lost much of his language skills over the years, and Chico lacked a little around the edges. But Jagger seemed as sharp as ever. Like Jagger was somehow keeping his kitty Alzheimer's at bay.

"I take it you're still angry then," she said.

"Anger's the wrong word. It's more like I think we've all matured, but you haven't. Your success at witchcraft has stunted your evolution."

"I don't need to hear this shit."

"You turned us into cats so you could keep us around and break up without losing us." Jagger was on a roll. "It's greedy and egocentric and uniquely human." Jagger paused. "Wait, Gio is coming."

Shuffling footsteps, then they stopped.

"Pet me, scratch, yes, pet," Jagger said. "Right there, yes."

"You're pretty okay, too," Gio said.

Gio opened the door holding a green pet waste bag over one hand to clean Harper's litter box. His eyes were red, puffy, and swollen, and he was still caring for her. Jagger was right, now that she was a cat, the concept of infidelity concerned her less. It was nice being a part of a colony with Gio in it. She was still angry, but he was steady. Safe. Even if it meant she was kept locked in a room.

"Harpy," Gio said flatly, like acknowledging an uptight coworker while passing by their desk. He had just started calling her that, since Cherry had told him when he was briefly a cat. He didn't mean it affectionately. He picked up her waste.

The thrust of her feelings for Gio a year ago had been: "I

want you so fucking bad I could squeeze you until you stopped breathing, literally love you to death."

Now it was: "I want to fucking kill you so bad, cheater, but feed me first and drag your hand along my spine to the end of my tail, yes please, that feels so good."

But he didn't touch her. And she wasn't going to ask for it, either.

His stability, boring only forty-eight hours ago, was now attractive. He was mostly ignoring her. She liked that. Cats were wild and people were safe. That's the way it was supposed to be.

"But I hate you and would eat you if I had to," she said, then remembered he couldn't hear cat thoughts. "And it's not Harpy, it's Harper!" came out as a traditional meow.

"Bye, Harpy," he said as he closed the door.

"Asshole!"

CHAPTER
SIXTEEN

GIOVANNI

Gio went to the backyard the following morning. He wasn't normally outside this early, and the birdsong reminded him he was on the edge of nature here, the border of sonically active canyon country. In a year of dating Harper, he had seen deer, raccoons, coyotes, bobcats, opossum, skunks, rabbits, and snakes near her property. Things he didn't see as much or ever near his condo. He only lived about four miles away, near his office at Warbler Brothers, but it may as well have been a different state.

He was feeling better. Marginally. Her house was physically forcing him outside. His newly broken fever needed respite from the house's cold, dark, damp, depressing air that smelled like musky cats. Even as a cat locked away in the bedroom, Harper's negative energy was permeating everything.

Mostly shaded this early in the morning, the backyard was

cleaved with angled shards of sun. It was nice. The contrast of warm light and cool shade made him feel healthier. Made his body pay attention to the awakening sounds and scents. He'd wrapped himself in one of Harper's robes which, being too small for him, felt more like a long smoking jacket. It was cozy. He hadn't bothered tying his shoes, nor pulling them over his heels, his feet squashing the backs into makeshift slippers.

Few of the front yards on that block had fences, but apparently the backyards did. Harper's fence was old and wooden and had once been painted white, the remainder of which was sun-damaged, peeling, and split. The fence separated the yard, not only from neighbors, but from ravine wildlife. Two six-foot-wide sections had collapsed in back and the overgrown weeds were patted down from animal traffic. It was an open door to the canyon, a path straight into her garden.

Harper had complained once that Linden called the fence separating their yards a termite haven. But of course he did. Because it was. Linden had offered to build a new fence if she paid for half the materials, and when she resisted, he came back later and offered to pay for all of it. She complained about that, too, claiming the posts were technically on her side of the property line and she wasn't planning on changing anything.

He patted an armpit that was moistening his T-shirt under the flannel robe and saw Linden walking to the side of his garage to dump sawdust into a green bin.

"Hey, Giovanni. Mood gorning," Linden said, hyucking.

"Moanin'." Gio played along. He shuffled toward him, to where a slat was missing in the fence. His head hurt, but it wasn't due to time of day. Nor Linden. "Shouldn't you be at school?"

"Chores first." Linden dumped the sawdust, shaking the trash bag clear.

Gio never really understood morning people. He would

rather stay up late editing, or even all night, than get up early and do chores. Maybe he was changing. "Ahhhhh..." he said.

"Nice robe. Present from Harper?"

"That obvious, huh?" At least she didn't wear pink or have little bunnies or hearts all over it. It was thin flannel that was wearing thinner, in a shade of brown popular in the seventies. But still, it was too small for him.

"I've decided to give you a present, too," Linden said. "This should fit better, though. You're, what, five ten, two twenty?"

Gio looked down at himself. The robe barely covered his belly, and parts of his boxer shorts were exposed.

"Don't look so disappointed," Linden said, patting his own midsection. "At least you got a couple inches of height on me to distribute that weight."

"You could take that show on the road."

"Beer bellies? Belly flops?"

"Guessing heights and weights."

"Maybe when I retire. But listen, I was trying to bribe you too much when I offered you the new box. You can have it, the one we talked about. I was just joking about you needing to cure the cats of their reproductive abilities. But since I give them away anyway, I may as well give one to you. In case you want to stop by a meeting, you'll have something to decorate. And hopefully you won't need it right away." Then sing-song, as in a nursery rhyme, "Dirt, dirt, dirge...we all end up as dirt."

Giovanni didn't really want a coffin, but he needed to be neighborly and not raise suspicion about Harper's disappearance. Linden was being generous.

"Help me carry it over." Linden did that windmill arm sweep. It was a gesture that Gio assumed worked well for teachers corralling students on a field trip, but this time he was directing Gio down along the old fence to where the front yards began. "Come on back!"

He hoped he wasn't about to become the target of a hard sell, whatever it was Linden was selling. Religion, insurance, a maintenance plan, post-mortem makeovers.

"What's so funny? You laughing at my waddle?" Linden said, exaggerating his left-right tilting for effect.

Gio hadn't been laughing. It'd take too much energy. But Linden did sort of waddle on skinny legs that held up a Humpty Dumpty body. "*Waddle* you talking about?" Gio said.

"Hey, that's my joke!" It probably was.

Even with swollen sinuses, Linden's garage smelled welcoming in the morning. Gio had always enjoyed the scent of freshly cut wood or grass. It was still "overnight cold" in there, and the floor was relatively clean. A general sweeping had been done recently.

"You caught me recycling sawdust. Sometimes I add a little to my mulch, and I've given some to Harper in the past for the garden. But I make more than we can reasonably use. I've probably filled half the ravine. You want some? I can have a full bag for you by next week."

"No need. Condo." Gio looked up and around the space. "Did you build this garage?"

"Sure did. I had help though. And I was a bit younger. Before my back filed for divorce." Linden snapped his elbows as if stretching. "Quite a bit younger."

The box still lay along the wall where they had deposited it, and they each picked up an end. With Linden in the lead, shuffling backward, he steered them down the driveway.

"I don't think it'll fit in the car," Gio said, realizing where they were headed. "Let's bring it in the house. I have a buddy with a truck who can help me take it home."

Gio didn't think there would be room at his condo, either. Maybe he could keep it here and store collectibles in it. Put it against a wall with some shelves in it. He imagined a previous version of Harper filling it with soil to serve as an elevated garden box. Not a bad idea, either.

It must have been quite a scene for people driving by on their way to work, a couple guys carrying a coffin to the front door. They set the box down long enough for Gio to take his keys out of the robe, since he had exited out the back. Maybe the neighbors were accustomed to Linden's odd behavior. What a rumor mill he and Harper must've fueled on that block.

They set the box in the middle of the room.

"This is fine. I'll figure it out," Gio said.

"I should head to work." Linden brushed the palms of his hands on the front of his pants. "I should learn to shower *after* I do chores, not before. Then again, I'm going in to work with more dust anyway."

"Thanks for the coffin." Gio resisted an urge to poke it with his foot the way potential buyers did with a used car.

"Don't forget, it's just a box until it's populated. Have fun with it."

CHAPTER
SEVENTEEN

KAT

Kat had taken Steve home the first couple nights, hoping he would fall into a routine of sorts so when Connie finally admitted his owner would never show, he'd already be hers. Steve trusted her. He didn't hesitate to get in the carrier to go to her house or back to CSE.

He refused to eat the vitamin-enriched dry cat food she'd purchased for him, so yesterday she bought him soft canned food, of which he only nibbled the edges. It was meat pudding, really. After not really eating for the first thirty-two hours, she ended up cooking him fish late last night.

He tore into that feast.

"Look at you," Kat said. "It's like you were waiting for me to be a chef. I can't do this every day. At least Jesse used to cook half the time."

Steve stopped eating his salmon filet and looked at her. Sad eyes.

"Oh my God," she said. Maybe his name wasn't Steve. "Jesse?"

Soul jumping was a thing. She bent down to pet him as he went back to eating. "The witch's ladder worked, Jesse. You came to me."

He stopped eating again and looked at her. No, she was being stupid.

"I'm sorry, Steve. Not your fault."

A therapist would say acquiring a pet is good for a widow's mental health, but they probably drew the line at believing he was her dead husband incarnate.

STEVE JUMPED to his usual spot on the counter at the Emporium. He seemed as interested in tonight's Yksian Lodge as everyone else.

Consumerians pressed backward from the Basil Alcove into the aisles of the Emporium like it was a sold-out night club. There was a spook of goths, a whimsy of Doctor Who fans, and a potter of science-fiction and fantasy enthusiasts who used social media to brag about something as archaic as reading. Displays near the front counter featured Yksian's new book and his Horror D'Oeuvres snacks.

The lights dimmed and the intro music began, ominous swirls of soft orchestral strings that started quietly, but would build soon enough.

A Consumerian couple, Mitzy and Ted, were at the back edge of the audience. They had pulled a chair from a table in the Basil Alcove and Mitzy was sitting on it, Ted standing behind her. Trapeze artists, they would normally be on tour, but she was very pregnant, due any day really, so they were taking a year off and would be in L.A. until at least spring. They were facing the stage, backed up to almost where Kat stood at the counter, avoiding the press of the crowd.

Steve jumped off the counter and trotted past them into the audience.

"They say don't let a cat near a pregnant woman," Ted said to his wife upon spotting Steve.

"I think it's supposed to be babies," Mitzy said. "No cats around babies. The cat will suck out the baby's breath."

"Because the soul can jump to a cat instead."

"You've got it all wrong. If it's a soul jumping, that's from a dying human to a pregnant cat."

Kat didn't feel like inserting herself into this conversation. Jesse had gone to the stage and hopped on a cabinet to view the crowd from there, facing the Consumerians. He was certainly stealing no souls, and Kat's own soul planned to stay where it was.

Steve. His name is Steve.

Connie stood beside Kat behind the counter, at the only section with a view of the stage.

The music bottomed out just as Yksian's assistant Mackenzie hit a spotlight to reveal him sitting on a maroon and purple velvet throne. His long, straight, jet-black hair fell mostly behind his shoulders, but thin strands hung over each cheekbone, exactly wide enough to avoid obstructing his ice-blue Scandinavian eyes. Steve was sitting on his lap, head cocked, listening attentively.

With no introduction, Mackenzie, grad school-aged with librarian glasses and straight platinum hair, left the sound and light controls and took her place in front of a microphone to Yksian's side. Even standing up straight, as if balancing a smartphone on her head, she was the same height as the six-

and-a-half-foot-tall Yksian was while seated. She began reading from Yksian's new book:

"The common scientific theory on the origin of life is that it evolved from a primordial soup. These chemicals churned and swirled in the elements, changing electric charges, coagulating and bifurcating until these elements began reproducing on their own. Then life begat life and slowly grew more complex as, over billions of years, the environment filtered out what didn't work. I find no fault in this."

"Then explain..." said a guest. The crowd laughed, but Kat couldn't make out the rest of what they'd said.

Mackenzie wasn't rattled, and continued. "And the opposing view is that we didn't evolve but were placed here by a god, creating companions for himself in his own image out of sheer boredom. This also is a common belief. Having been bored myself, I appreciate this, too."

Mackenzie cleared her throat while some people laughed. Despite the content, she sounded less like a TED Talk speaker and more like a student reading an essay. Some statements ended in a strong down note for punctuation.

"But I propose a third idea, and that is, 'What if we live in a simulation?'

"This creator would be technologically incomprehensible to us. Unbelievably so. Imagine if they created us on an enormous biological computer, larger than our known universe, with numbers tweaked by hand."

Yksian lifted his goblet, toasting someone in the crowd without expression, and slowly took a sip.

"As an aside, I say 'they' because the creator here is not binary. They are gender chill, yet encompass all genders.

"The multiverse theory, of which I am a proponent, still holds here, since the basic equations that make up our universe are only one possible iteration of the program. Infinite variations of numbers can be inputted into the equations. Nearly all universes immediately collapse after their respective Big Bangs, the products of their equations incompatible. New universes are constantly appearing and disintegrating, bubbling and popping like a cosmological primordial soup. But the tiniest of fractions of them, like our own, survive.

"This particular iteration of the program, the universe we see all around us, means we are living within an experiment that initially booted up in an event we call the Big Bang, and who knows if the program has a defined end. To us, it could run indefinitely. Or until we destroy ourselves. In short, since we evolved within a program, we are nothing, do not and cannot exist outside of it, and cannot enter our creator's universe.

"Just as we have pets within our households, we are pets to our creators. Our decisions may feel important to us, but they are inconsequential to them. Billions of people with trillions of inane questions and issues. All this from just one of their billions of planets that contain life. They proverbially pat us on the head, bored with us."

Mackenzie turned her head toward Yksian. Both he and Steve were listening intently. Yksian micro-nodded, which was a massive shot of encouragement coming from him. She turned back to the book.

"Our lives are linear; we see ourselves moving forward in a straight line. But to a creator in a higher dimension, they see the curvature of our space. How the line we draw is not straight at all. With a telescope, we see how light bends from the gravity of a star, but if you were traveling with that beam of light, you would believe you were moving in a straight line.

"To our creator, we appear to move in a path no straighter than that of a butterfly, a bumblebee, a gnat, or my favorite, of course, a bat. From that view, they see our potential lives blossoming out in front of us, unbeknownst to us, like a four-dimensional decision tree. They see the nearly infinite branches. They don't see our exact futures, but the collection of our potential futures. Potential decisions, potential life choices, all accessible to us. Almost all of them which are not taken. To cross metaphors, our pathetic, squiggly flight of a bat is just one infinitesimal line moving through a tree with billions of branches."

Mackenzie closed the book. "That is our life."

There was a moment of silence, no one moving or speaking in the near-dark.

A few people slowly began to clap but it petered out.

Silence again.

"T-t-tell us how to avoid d-d-death!" said a man in the crowd.

Kat knew that voice. It was Balbutio, an older gentleman who claimed to be the God of Stuttering, and figuratively shook his cane at the blasphemous approach to religion Connie employed at the Emporium. Kat had heard about Balbutio crashing a Coffin Club where he'd accused Yksian of being a vampire. Ridiculous.

Mackenzie stepped away from the microphone.

Yksian stood up with Steve tucked into the crook of his elbow, his snakehead goblet of wine in his other hand, and leaned down to the microphone adjusted for Mackenzie's height. He said in his slow, wet, bass, "Let it be so."

A couple people laughed, which then spread throughout the room. People cheered.

"Why do you think they're laughing?" Kat said to Connie. "Is it like how emergency workers laugh while dealing with dead bodies? I swear, if I had seen one of them laughing when Jesse..."

Kat stopped herself.

120

"He's just Yksian," Connie said. "A crusty, brooding...giant nerd. You can't help but laugh."

"Steve seems to like him."

Yksian posed in a gentlemanly stance, sipping wine, staring into a middle distance while a low, droning note played through the sound system. He apparently wasn't going to talk anymore, and the presentation wasn't over until he finished his wine. The crowd was obedient and mostly silent. This was the performance, being in his presence in artificial twilight.

Steve looked like he was napping in his arms, but then Yksian squatted and placed him gently on the stage. Yksian handed the goblet to Mackenzie, who refilled it and set it on a table along the wall.

"That's our cue," Connie said. She weaved through the crowd and when Yksian saw her, he nodded once and stepped off the stage. His head was still above everyone else's. Mackenzie raised the brightness of the lights a quarter of the way, where they would remain for the rest of the signing.

"Greetings everyone," Connie said into the microphone. "And thank you for coming to the release of Yksian's new book, *What's Not Real in a Simulated Universe*. Yksian will be signing at this table right over here. If you'd like something signed, please form a line going that way, and if you need to buy a book, we have stacks of them with Kat at the front counter. There is a two-item limit for signing, so please be respectful of that."

Just like that, two lines formed, all attendees maintaining a murmuring reverence. Usually crowds this large bustled with conversation, but Yksian had set a quiet tone that persisted.

Balbutio was first in line for the book signing, pressing his barreled chest through an old suit. He already had his book opened to a page. Kat hadn't sold him one. Even in the low light from where she stood, Kat could see his suit was wrinkly, dusty, moth-ridden, and whatever other clichés you could apply to poorly stored dry goods. He looked excited. Excitable.

"Say, etern-eternal-eternally yours! To the Great Balbutio!" He announced his own name like an emcee would from stage. It was easily the loudest sound in the Emporium.

Yksian signed and handed the book back to him without comment, then reached for the next guest's book. "Greetings," he said, deeply and not unpleasantly, to the next fan.

"Eternal life!" Balbutio was waving his book. "Do y-y-you deal with that? You know it. I know it. W-w-we—" He was rushing out words faster than his mouth could say them.

"Excuse me," the fan said, forcing himself against the table and edging Balbutio to the side. "I'm Xavier, but you can sign it to X-Y-Z."

"Yksian is a v-v-v-undead!"

"Those are my initials," Xavier said. "We'd sit next to each other in class. Xavier...Yksian."

"Unclean! V-v-vampire!"

Even though there was a line of people in front of Kat waiting to buy their books, all focus was on the spectacle of Balbutio. When Connie put a hand on Balbutio's shoulder and spoke to him, a murmuring chittered through the crowd. Yksian continued signing books and Mackenzie stood shotgun against the wall, playing with her phone, waiting for something to do.

"Ahh," Kat said to the first person as she rang him up. "Two books, huh?"

"One's for my son at school."

Quite a few Consumerians also bought Horror D'Oeuvres. A few people bought items from other Omniscians—a monogrammed Lucador cape, a silver unicorn Ornatu ring, an Organica hemp produce bag. They were selling more kombucha than any other beverage.

Yksian was like kombucha. The first taste could be fairly repellent. But oddly, you craved more, and soon enough, you loved it. Now you would stand in line for it. Twice.

Connie opened another box of books and stacked them on the counter, bagging purchases large enough to call for it. CSE postcards made good bookmarks.

"You think people understood what Yksian was talking about up there?" Kat said when a customer was stalling, inspecting a branded tin of mints.

"You mean what Mackenzie was saying?" Connie said.

"You know what I mean."

"I don't know. I'm sure a lot do. But he's a star. I think people like him no matter what he says or does. He can just stand there drinking wine and they'll cheer."

"So this book's shit, is what you're saying."

"Not at all. I'm just saying they'll love him no matter what he does. If the book's good, that's a plus."

"What you're saying is you have no idea what she said up there and you'll never read the book."

"That obvious, huh?"

AFTERWARD, Kat was speaking with Yksian.

"You think there's any evidence for the simulated universe theory?" she said.

"It can't be proved one way or the other," he said. "But consider this, and I say this in the book: If I can create a model universe on my computer, and within that universe it creates its own model universe, and so on, I think I've made a point. Just imagine the regression going in the other direction now, too. Bigger and more complex."

Steve was on the counter perched near Yksian, watching

the dissipating customers. Kat feared he'd want to leave with Yksian. Steve turned to face her and blinked slowly. He was content. It's like he knew what she was thinking. This soothed her. She slow-blinked in return.

"And your Emporium cat, the feline Consumerian," Yksian said. "He shall remain. He raises the average IQ of the room."

CHAPTER
EIGHTEEN

HARPER

Harper had learned from Jagger that Steve left. He hadn't been obligated to come say goodbye, but he should have, since she felt closer to all of her exes after they'd become cats. He certainly could've escaped many times over the last several years, so why leave now? She hadn't been sure a change from cat back to human could be done, but they'd all witnessed Gio do it.

It was possible.

But how does one un-ferment a grape, un-crush a cat saber tusk, or un-brew a potion? If any of them could find a way, it would be Steve.

～

"Actually, it's Steven," he'd said the day they met.

She hadn't even bothered to come up with a better nickname for him as a cat. He would've ignored her or found a way to logic-trap her into calling him Steven again. "Steve" was as wayward as he'd allow. He was a brilliant human, and probably a brilliant feline.

After dating a teetotaler like Chico and a drug enthusiast like Mick, she found Steve refreshing. Maybe this was a common theme with her. Each boyfriend was an overcorrection to the disliked traits in the previous one. Steve partook but wasn't a partier, was logical to a fault, and had a PhD. He worked at the Jet Propulsion Laboratory in Pasadena.

"Actually, JPL is in the city of La Cañada Flintridge," he told her that first evening. "Pasadena is just the mailing address."

They'd met at a bookstore in Pasadena. Browsing new releases.

"Ah, it says this book's a 'tour de force,'" he said in a baritone made for radio. His hair was salt-and-pepper gray and either inexpensively cut, so little did he want to pay attention to it, or expensively cut in order to give that impression. White button-up shirt and dress slacks.

Harper looked around and realized he was talking to her. Or to no one in general, but she was nearest.

"That's a good thing, right?" she said.

"I make it a point to never buy a book that's described as a 'tour de force.' It's overused to the point of meaning nothing. The X-15 rocket, now *that's* a tour de force."

"Tell me more," she said, not wanting to hear more about rockets. But frankly, it didn't matter what he said. She just wanted to hear his voice up close, vibrating and tickling her ear.

"We can talk over some wine next door, if you'd like to accompany me."

Turned out he'd been killing time in the bookstore before a wine tasting class. She joined him, they hit it off, and they signed up for repeated tastings together. Their next two dates were planned meetups there.

After that first class, she feared if they ever got close enough to need to break up, she may have to do it in a more traditional manner. He would recognize spiked wine long before bringing it to his lips.

The first time he came to the house, Steve saw the sign in her kitchen, the one that said, "Caelum super me, Terra infra me, Ignis in me."

"Ah, I see we have a Pagan in our midst," he said.

"The earth is my cathedral," Harper said. "You know Latin, I take it?"

"Scio parum," he said. That meant "I know a little." He was faking modesty. He explained it was a hobby of his and he'd taken a class in college.

She showed him ancient books on herbology, alchemy, and astrology so he could translate parts she'd been unsure about. She was pleased to know she'd been correct more often than not, even when a particular word or passage may have been a straight-up guess. She didn't show him one particular book, of course.

As a boyfriend, Steve Sanders never admitted to being wrong. To be fair, she couldn't think of many instances when he *was* wrong about something, but that wasn't the point. He didn't make an effort to allow her to feel right sometimes. Or justified. Or that they were equals. She couldn't tell him about a problem without him giving advice or telling her how she'd been wrong or had gone about it the wrong way.

She would listen to him talk to peers or coworkers and notice how he was so much more patient with them, allowing them space to think things through out loud, not cutting them off. And he allowed them to be partly right, granting them points in an argument even when he disagreed. She was never granted points.

She was miserable. He was intelligent with a great voice. That was it. And frankly, she never saw what he saw in her, either. They were nothing alike.

What she ended up doing, though, was impressive even to herself. She put time into her solution, planning for months.

She began by fermenting wine at home, mashing the grapes by hand. She earnestly attempted to make good wine, and although it wasn't horrible, it wasn't very good, either. Passable at best. She'd had a little practice fermenting grapes and other fruit for potions, but those directions were more like minimum requirements. Real wine required precision with temperature and duration. Here, she was trying to impress Steve with complexity, body, legs, bouquet, and notes.

He tasted her first batch, clearly forcing himself to finish a glass to show support.

"Keep at it," he said. "You'll get better."

Anchoring his expectations there, she made more, heeding Steve's copious advice.

"Actually, order this yeast... Add it when..."

When it was ready, she poured the equivalent of several glasses into two saucepans on very low heat and added whole cinnamon bark, lemon peels, allspice, and clove. A shot of orange juice. Peach slices to top it off. And one of them was spiked with her special potion. It'd still taste terrible, but would appear a valiant attempt at homemade mulled wine.

She poured two mugs, one from each saucepan, and brought them to Steve out on the couch. "I hope you find this batch an improvement," she said. "I followed your tips to a T."

"I'm sure it is," Steve said.

"But the mulling is my own recipe with some herbs I grew

myself," she said. "In case it catches you off guard." It surely would. "Then afterward we'll open the good bottle, the one you brought."

The beverage was warm, not hot, so he could drink it quickly. They snacked on a spicy nut mix.

"You know the guys at work consider peanuts to be good luck," he said while chewing with his mouth open, like he was with the guys. At least he didn't lick his fingers.

They toasted and drank.

He made that expression where his lips stayed closed but his neck muscles tightened as he forced it down. He coughed lightly. "Normally, I'd never eat spicy food with a red. It ruins the wine. But this is nice."

That meant he found it terrible, but was blaming the nuts. And what the hell, a little good luck from the peanuts wouldn't hurt, either.

"Actually," he said, showing support for her burgeoning hobby by forcing down the entire mug. He then edged a slice of peach up the rim with his finger, "luck is an illusion of logic..."

As a cat, he was plain but handsome, with short, salt-and-pepper-gray fur and a starburst of white on his chest. Harper left his car in a parking lot near Union Station as if he'd left town on a bus or a train.

CHAPTER
NINETEEN

GIOVANNI

Gio was standing in the Basil Alcove, his first visit to Consumia's Spiritual Emporium since buying the gift for his ill-fated anniversary. The easel set up between the two halves of the store said, "Welcome Thalia!"

He scuffed the bottom of his shoe on the edge of a black-, white-, and red-painted design he could swear wasn't on the floor before. It was large and there were too many people standing on it to see it in its entirety. There was one perfect cat paw print placed neatly in the paint where he stood. It added a touch of friendliness.

He was feeling better after three days spent mostly in bed. Earlier, he drove for the first time when he went grocery shopping, and for once avoided the prepackaged frozen and microwavable dinners. Harper didn't even own a microwave. Today, he'd figured out he could cook two or three meals' worth of food ahead of time for him and the cats, saving the rest to reheat later. This would save time.

He sipped complimentary tea from a paper cup and the heat hit a bad tooth, causing him to flinch. He was positive his health plan from work covered dental, and he could afford the copay, but there was always a work project or some other pressing excuse. The events this week provided ample reason to procrastinate.

But the second sip bothered his tooth less, and he found the experience almost enjoyable. Like toying with a hangnail. Then, on subsequent sips, he felt nothing odd at all.

Gio tried to think like Harper. She'd gone to Thalia's first Lodge a month ago. What would she have done here? Would she mingle and suss out future victims? Bond with Thalia? Stand back and take mental notes?

MOTE:
Are you waiting for something to wait for?

MAYBE. There was subtext in that Mote, so there needed to be subtext in his answer. Something to think about, anyway.

Gio saw his retired neighbor who owned the condo across the hall from him, Henry Vellichor, pouring himself a tea. As usual, he was wearing a Detroit Tigers hat. He was staring. Gio realized he'd been poking his now not-so-painful tooth with a finger, so he stopped. Manners.

"Tooth still bothering you?" Henry said when he walked over.

"I'm getting it looked at soon," Gio said. He couldn't recall telling Henry about it, but he must have. Gio didn't usually talk about that sort of private stuff. Odd the details neighbors remember you said in passing.

"Good to see you," Henry said, raising his paper cup and moving on to greet another acquaintance.

~

THALIA WALKED ONSTAGE and mimicked blocking the sun to see out to the far end of the Basil Alcove. It was maybe half full.

"I'd say this is double the amount of people as last time. So, thank you, thank you everyone for showing up." She spoke in a surprising monotone for such positive words. It was hypnotic. She didn't sound depressed, but...something.

"Thalians!" someone in the crowd said.

"Hi, Jessica. Nice to meet you, by the way. This is only my second Lodge, so I'd say calling the audience members 'Thalians' might be a bit premature. But I can see there is serious curiosity in the Valley for knowledge about the divinity of all life."

Applause.

"And you may have noticed the new design on the floor. It's a nine-foot pentacle, with an old-timey compass. Now you know that north is that way, if you didn't already. And there be dragons." She pointed at an aisle on the Emporium side that had figurines of animals, both real animals from nature, and fictional.

There were certainly dragons there.

Gio had browsed there earlier and wondered if some of the overpriced figurines were pre-owned and some were repurposed from a dollar store. All had little story cards attached, telling tales of animation, spirits, and other forms of magic.

Thalia continued: "Another Omniscian, Kevin O'Culled, and I painted this ourselves, so don't criticize our artistic skills too much. And don't worry, we'll be standing in a circle and using that thing for its intended purpose in a little while."

Gio was already in place, then. Paw marked the spot.

"But before that, I'd like us to work on a meditation method that leads to shapeshifting—to seeing the world through the eyes of other forms of life. It's called theri-anthropy. Basically, this means focusing your mind on becoming another animal. The easiest for us to visualize morphing into are dogs and cats, followed by horses, birds, and farm animals; basically, ones that humans are most familiar with.

"There have been instances where a person has achieved the highest level of concentration and literally become the animal they were imagining. Becoming a common pet is also the safest, since you're less likely to cause much alarm. If you morphed into, say, a mountain lion, you'd risk being shot, or drugged and released far from home, lost and unable to return. Of course, literal shapeshifting is extremely rare, but it's learning how to concentrate deeply that's important. We want an out-of-body experience that allows us escape the limita-tions of daily life. We can discover new modes of thought and altered states of consciousness. Wouldn't that be great?"

"Are you a witch?" someone said.

"I've been called a witch, and I practice what some people used to call 'white magic,' but that's more like slang for the uninitiated. I believe we all play a role in each other's lives, with everything affecting everything else. And we're born with most of the tools we need for survival in this and other planes. Our quality of life is based on what we do with those tools."

"Do you believe in God?"

"I don't *not* believe in God. I'm more of a pantheist, which means I'm a generalist. I don't believe in the anthropomorphic god who's just like us, up there in the heavens. There is universal divinity. We are divine. The animals we morph into are divine."

"Are you a vegan?"

Thalia laughed a monotone laugh, not without mirth, but without fluctuation. "I didn't realize this was an interview. I suppose you could say I'm a vegan witch. No animals are hurt in my rituals and I consume no animal products. The magic we create exists in our minds and isn't to be considered *real* in the physical sense. We don't make sacrifices to gods, or kill a chicken for its blood or beak or claw."

"But you just said shapeshifting is real."

"Okay, yes, shapeshifting, that's real." Thalia took on a graver tone. "It's real, but extremely rare."

"Have you ever seen it happen?" a Consumerian said.

"Let me tell you a story," she said. "A legend, a fairy tale really, from the Middle Ages. It's the kind of story that peasants told for generations, the kind that turned the people against witches, creating some of the stereotypes we're still dealing with to this day.

"It was during the Plague, so think about it. A lonely old spinster was living away from the city, away from the disease that was decimating millions. Maybe she even had warts. She lived with cats to keep the rodent population down. The plague was spread by fleas on rats in the cities, so a higher percentage of countryfolk survived than townies.

"Now, a witch like this, isolated, living alone on the edge of the forest, needed some human contact, if only to trade for goods. She needed another cauldron, for example, and access to plants and herbs she couldn't grow herself. So, she set off into town and met a lovely married couple at the market.

"The husband, a smith, could help with the cauldron. And the witch was beholden, love at first sight. He was strong, handsome, and handy. She let him have his way with her behind his stall.

"Afterward she met his wife who accompanied her to other stalls, and the witch was smitten with her, as well. Charming and artsy, the wife helped her find rare herbs and promised to make her a dress. They, too, explored each other's bodies on the banks of the creek that ran through town.

"The three of them became friends that day and promised to meet up at the market at a future date. While waiting for the day to come, all the witch could think about was them, making charms as gifts to protect them and their home.

"When she saw them, she gave them their gifts, as well as gold for the cauldron and dress, and ran off with each of them individually, expecting a repeat of their affections, and was quite spurned. Something had changed.

"She returned home feeling foolish and sad for falling for two people who cared more about business than love. She had never been lonely before, but was now utterly heartbroken. She hated these useless feelings of lust and desire. She worked herself into a rage.

"The next time she went to the market, she brought them wine she had fermented herself, telling them this was her way of thanking them for helping with her needs. Ironically, she had used those very herbs and cauldron to make the potion.

"The husband and wife drank the wine with much thankfulness and mirth, and the effects of the spell were that the husband changed into a werecat once a month during the full moon. Meanwhile, the wife became a cat who only changed into a human at the same time as the husband became a cat. They could never be human at the same time again.

"A friend came around to visit the man's smithy and the husband told him about their conditions.

"'Were you both cursed by the same witch?' the neighbor asked.

"'Yes.'

"'Then we will seek revenge.'

"And while the witch slept, just before sunrise, the two men burned down her hut. They heard laughter as the flames engulfed her and everything she owned. Something dawned on the husband, but it was too late. They had burned down the hut before retrieving her book of potions and would never learn how to cure themselves of their conditions.

"The story could have ended here, the couple cursed to spend the rest of their lives in flux. When one was human, the other was cat. When one was cat, the other human.

"There could be a moral here about how they'd both cheated on their spouse with the witch, and she levied a curse inspired by her spurned love. And many versions of the story do indeed end there. But this is an ending about hope, about how the couple experimented unsuccessfully with their own counter-potions, how they heard rumors of another book of spells existing and sent requests through traveling merchants to look for it.

"Receiving no answers, they decided to search for it themselves. The husband sold everything they owned and they traveled together, visiting many cultures, speaking with wizards, shamans, yogis, gurus, witch doctors…"

"Omniscians!" a woman added, the one Thalia had called Jessica.

"…with whomever they could find, and never found that book. Maybe the witch had had the only copy.

"But by speaking with so many experts over the years, the couple had worked out their own shapeshifting meditation, derived from a mixture of several intercultural methods. They could sit next to each other and one could project into the other's form. Or both shift into a third form, like mountain lions, for example.

"They lived long, peaceful lives, and derived a modest income teaching the practice and sleeping in their students' homes and castles as they traveled. This form of meditation is still practiced in small pockets, even today. And I'm here to teach it to you.

"So today, we're going to practice their version of ailuranthropy, which means specifically morphing from human to cat. No point practicing cat to human, right?"

Audience laughter. Gio found he wasn't laughing.

"It even works if you're allergic," Thalia joked. "Don't worry, you won't sneeze."

Phew.

MOTE:

We simply sin like sinners sin, since sinning seems like sense.

"I HAVE A QUESTION," Jessica said, holding up her hand. "These out-of-body experiences, can we do them with somebody from a distance? With them coming here, or me going there?"

"I suppose there's no reason it couldn't work, but the nearer the better."

"Like," Jessica said, sounding thoughtful, "what if one person is on the other side of the country?"

"Like on a video call? That wouldn't be easy, but theoretically..."

"What if you don't know exactly where the other person is?"

"I don't think I'm understanding." Thalia's tone changed. "Let's talk about this afterward."

Thalia dimmed the lights and played sounds of the jungle over the sound system, and walked the audience though some breathing and visualization exercises.

"Everybody good and relaxed?" she said.

She instructed groups to take turns circling the pentacle, holding hands for prayers, meditating, then imagining morphing into animals that frolicked together in the open space. They were instructed to project healing and growth, while overcoming pain and sorrow.

Then she changed the music and people danced throughout the Basil Alcove, drinking wine and other spirits they'd brought. They ate various pastries and treats, some brought from home, some bought at the Emporium.

Overall, Giovanni had found Thalia's Lodge interesting, but ultimately not very useful in finding a potion to change cats back to humans. Teaching Harper's cats to pretend they were human would be an unsatisfying wish fulfillment.

CHAPTER

TWENTY

HARPER

arper realized Cherry hadn't come by to talk, so
maybe she had left with Steve and nobody told her
yet. Maybe Cherry was angry and didn't want to
speak to her. If she had to pick one ex-partner she felt bad
for cursing, it was her. Jehri was naturally so sweet as a
human, it was almost unfair. Harper didn't deserve somebody
so thoughtful and conscientious in her life, as a partner or a
pet. She felt they could have legitimately been friends for life.

As a couple, Jehri had joked about getting cheesy BFF
pendants that children wore, the kind that fit together like a
puzzle, but as tattoos, instead. Mirrored halves of a "Best
Friends Forever" heart would be inked between their breasts
where a pendant would hang.

As a chef, Jehri worked with a lot of men who did a lot of

drugs, made lewd comments, worked sixty hours a week, and were protective of her if a customer so much as looked at her crookedly. She liked men, just didn't *like* men. She'd said the pendant tattoo would take the place of a wedding ring, something visible depending on what she wore, since she couldn't wear rings at work.

Harper hadn't felt jealousy when she was with boyfriends like Spike and Mick. She tolerated their wandering eyes. She didn't actively enjoy it, but thought of them as different creatures. A man cheated by having anonymous, or nearly anonymous, sex with another woman, but a woman cheated by emotionally attaching herself to another person, even without sexual contact.

When Jehri went to the spa with her friends, Harper lost her shit, checking her phone repeatedly for a text response about where she was, when she was coming back. Jehri only had one day off a week, and she sometimes spent it with her other friends.

A girl looking Spike up and down or giving him a hug was a compliment. A girl doing that to Jehri was a threat. Harper had been the better-looking half when she was with her boyfriends, but with Jehri, she wasn't. Jehri was stunning. It wasn't just the men ogling her, it was women. Everyone.

"You could turn a straight girl," Harper had joked with her, stroking her cheeks, admiring the natural length of her eyelashes. But she wasn't joking.

One evening when Jehri caught a late movie with a girl from work, Harper's feelings of jealousy rose to a crescendo, and it was time to concoct the potion. Harper may die single and alone, but she'd always have her kitties.

It hadn't helped that Jehri was a chef. Harper had refused to cook more than a bagel in the toaster oven around her for feelings of inadequacy, but Jehri had always complimented her garden, handpicking fresh produce to cook with. Jehri was the only other person who appreciated her Petoskey and Charlevoix stone pestle and mortar as much as she did.

And like Steve, Jehri was somewhat of a sommelier. More so, even. She would pass on a wine after noticing the nose was off. She would pour out the glass and open a new bottle. This only happened once in Harper's presence, but it *had* happened. The men had been easier. They almost took pride in drinking something awful. Real men didn't let something as petty as taste stop them. Jehri wouldn't force down a horrible wine no matter how homemade it was.

Harper's solution was to try cooking with the potion to bury the flavor. She made a red wine reduction sauce for a couple of ribeyes, mixing in items known to cover flavors, like cheap sherry, strong beef broth, and the earthiest past-their-peak mushrooms she could find. Plus, minced garlic, shallots, rosemary, and thyme from the garden, and still she suspected it wouldn't be enough.

To pull this off effectively, she needed to pretend to be a worse cook than she was. Overcook the sauce. Char the beef. Anything to create excuses for the muskiness.

With the potion reducing and the alcohol burning off, she wasn't even sure how effective any of this would be; concentrating the flavors meant she'd have to use less sauce with the entrée. So, she added the poisoned reduction to the side dish of sautéed spinach, shallots, and mushrooms, as well. Then a little butter and lemon to differentiate it from the ribeye.

She hesitated opening a bottle of uncontaminated Sangiovese for fear of comparison, but then did anyway. Why not. They could both drink something nice with their meal.

"This is a nice change of pace," Jehri said before taking her first bite. "I like seeing you spread your wings."

After each bite, Jehri took a sip of wine.

"How is it?" Harper said.

"I think the mushrooms are past their peak."

"Maybe I should have used the Sangiovese in the sauce," Harper said.

"No, no, I prefer to drink it. It's a good one."

At minimum, Jehri seemed proud of Harper's effort. Just the act of forcing that terrible food down her gullet elevated Jehri to sainthood, but if the shapeshifting hadn't occurred, Harper knew Jehri would've never let her attempt a meal that elaborate again.

That transfiguration was also the first one that bothered Harper to hear. Something about the way Jehri pleaded, confused and suffering, hit a nerve with her.

After morphing, it was like Jehri's beauty had been cast by an enchantment spell that transferred over with her. Cherry was by far the prettiest kitty.

TWENTY-ONE

GIOVANNI

D riving home from Thalia's Lodge, Gio thought about the missing cat, the one he always forgot the name of. Even though there'd been no name on the flyer, that could've been him at Emporium; the cat had fled when they locked eyes. If it was him, why would he go there? The Emporium wouldn't even have been open for business yet when the cat was still human.

When Gio opened the back door to the house, the white cat, Chico, was pacing the kitchen, upset by something, and immediately began circling Gio's feet, almost tripping him. Gio checked the food and water dishes and the two cat boxes, and everything looked fine. Then he found the bedroom door open and Harper missing. He looked under the bed, the closet, but he knew she was gone. The heavy cloud of negativity in the house had lifted.

He'd just closed the back door in case she was still in the house when Chico meowed.

"You want to go out?" Gio said.

No. Chico was still upset. Out of character, like he wanted to stomp his foot in anger. Normally the most affectionate of Harper's exes, he circled Gio several times without touching him, showing he wasn't looking to be pet.

"Don't worry, Cheeks. I'm going to look for her now."

Chico was agitated about something else, nearly pointing the way with his tail. Maybe he knew where Harper was.

"What is it? Should I follow you?"

He led Gio into the living room and circled in front of Linden's box.

Spike was lying in the head of the box on his side. Not moving. Like a taxidermy animal one might see in the Dark Arts room.

"Spike," he said. "Hey, Spike."

He placed a palm on the cat. Not breathing. This was no longer a box, but a coffin now. A viewing for Gio and the other kitties. Spike must've known he was dying and tried to find a solitary place to do so in peace. And knowing Spike had once been human made the choice of dying in a coffin more fitting. Or creepier.

Gio picked him up. He'd already stiffened and his fur was matted. Some crusts of blood were on his face, back, leg, and one ear. A cut across his nose. He was missing chunks of fur. Maybe he'd been attacked. Maybe it was Harper.

Spike had always been Gio's least favorite cat, but yet he found his death greatly unsettling. He'd died before Gio had a chance to change him back. The thought of more people dying while they were cats was one of the saddest things he could imagine.

He searched the rest of the house and property, then the

neighborhood for the next half hour. His energy was fading fast. It was late and, still not feeling a hundred percent, he had to stop for the night and continue the search in the morning.

He fished a plastic CSE bag out of the laundry room closet and put Spike's body in it. He moved some frozen fish into the refrigerator to make room. He placed Spike in the freezer. He didn't really know what else to do. He would think better tomorrow.

CHAPTER
TWENTY-TWO

HARPER

Walking west at night, avoiding people. This would take a minute. She needed answers, and she was going to the only place she could think of. What was it, six miles? As a human, that would take two hours at a leisurely pace. This would take longer, as she avoided people and brightly lit areas. Littler legs. She found that even though she could run much faster than a person, it was only for short bursts, and she tired quickly.

So many smells. Knowing a cat's sense of smell was five or ten times better than a human's was nothing like experiencing it for herself. It was almost more than she could comprehend. Every breeze had something new or interesting. She could almost see the world better with her eyes closed.

Plus, hearing higher frequencies meant there were many

high-pitched animal noises she'd never noticed before. A hunting instinct was kicking in, as if she were tracking prey.

But she had never hunted as a cat.

EARLIER TONIGHT, she'd heard Gio leave and she began pacing the bedroom. She'd been good thus far, not escaping, not making a mess of the litter box, eating neatly. Eating well, really, but that gave her more energy, and made her more restless. Too many days confined to a single room. She began moaning the lonely cry of a cat.

Spike was the one who responded.

"Harpy?"

"I want out." She hated being called Harpy. They all called her that. She'd never known that as a person. "I can't be a prisoner in my own house."

"No outside. Bobcat. Last night. Scary."

Again, she didn't really hear English when communicating with him. It was more like his impressions were pressed into her mind and in her recollection of his thoughts she placed her own words over them. "Where'd you go?" she said.

"Linden truck. Go mountains. Eat fish, birds, squirrels."

He was delusional. She didn't know cats could think like this. Could cats get dementia? Spike had always been grandiose, but now it was full-blown fantasyland. She doubted he could live in the wild for more than a few days, much less drive a truck to get there.

His mind seemed to white out. Then, "Attacked. Bobcat. Prey. Fight. Beat."

Harper doubted Spike could beat a bobcat, but he was all ego. Apparently, he was attacked when he predictably couldn't get into Linden's truck.

"Will you help me get out of here?" she said.

"Your house."

"So, you'll help me get out?"

"No outside."

"I won't." Won't go outside, or won't promise. Didn't matter.

"Bad bobcat, Harpy!"

She heard him jump and hit the doorknob. It sounded painful, as the force of the heaviest cat against the knob pushed the air out of his lungs. The door would open inward, so she moved to the side.

"Bobcat dead, Harpy!"

Another thud, but louder, and the doorknob rattled again.

"Oof!" This sound was accompanied by a thud when his body hit the floor.

Since the house had settled so much over the years, few of the doors latched properly, and some, if not fully closed, popped open on their own. That had creeped out Chico and Gio on occasion. The creepy door creaking on the other side of the house. It played into her suggestions that the house was haunted. This bedroom door would close, but barely.

Another thump and doorknob rattle.

"Aauugghh!" Spike wailed. That one had to hurt. He was wheezing. Perhaps a collapsed lung. He should stop and rest, but she also wanted out of there.

"You're jumping high enough?" Harper said. She was trying to help. Trying to keep his spirits up. His breathing was labored. He was out of shape in his old age. Overweight. He may have been arthritic, too, although he would never admit it. "Maybe you could ask Chico to help."

"No!" Spike sounded angry. The next thump included the click of the doorknob and his heavy body hitting the floor.

The door swung open a few inches. She poked her head

out, tail waving in an "S" shape. Spike was on his side, gasping for air. He really was big for a housecat. And cats were notorious for refusing to show pain, so his behavior was significant. "Oh, Mike."

"You...no..." Spike gasped for air. "Mike...years." He was in need of a veterinarian.

"Brave, stupid." She leaned over and stroked each word into him, licking his brown and gray tabby cheek like a mother would, long strokes that lifted the fur and the entire side of his face. She could smell and taste the blood in his fur. "Strong, idiotic...and old."

"Proof...I beat...bobcat."

He had somehow escaped the bobcat and made it back inside the house. Now he had helped her escape.

She left him resting in the hallway and entered the kitchen where she snacked on some chicken left out—Spike may not have eaten his portion—and lapped a little water. It was the same food she'd had in the bedroom, but she figured she should fill up while she could, in case food was hard to come by. She then hid in the laundry room by the back door waiting for Gio. She didn't want to be seen when he came home. She fell asleep. When he finally walked in, hours later, he announced his arrival.

"Kitties, I'm home!" Even hiding behind a laundry basket, she could smell the Emporium on him. Incense, tea, people, mustiness. New paint.

As was his new habit, he left the door open.

She snuck out before he noticed that the bedroom door was ajar.

〜

WALKING WEST NOW, she slowed to get her bearings. It would be a decent trek. Crossing the 5 freeway at Olive Avenue, Magnolia Boulevard, or Burbank Avenue meant a brightly lit overpass, so she chose to walk another mile or two up to Buena Vista and a less-exposed crossing under the freeway bridge there. Maybe the trek was eight miles now?

Knowing the area helped.

CHAPTER
TWENTY-THREE

GIOVANNI

Gio woke up early and walked around the neighborhood looking for Harper, this time beginning in the ravine behind the house. It got steep fast, and he couldn't go far in any one direction. Animals and real hikers could traverse this, but not him. With all the dried brush of autumn, it felt like a wildfire waiting to happen.

He hoped Harper was hungry and thirsty and ready to come home. If she and Spike had been in a fight, she was likely upset. Maybe she had calmed down by now. She was known to hold a grudge, but she would eventually settle down, even if she remained cold.

A few months ago, Harper had been convinced Gio wasn't working late at the office and waited in her car for him in front of his condo. When he saw her, he pulled up next to her and rolled down his window. "Sorry, no deliveries after five p.m.," he said.

She affected a fake smile. "Did you miss me?"

"Of course."

"I wanted to surprise you by staying over."

She ended up being distant and frigid that night, like she hadn't been missing him at all and didn't even want to be there. At the time he was confused.

The transfiguration made him realize how much her behavior was fueled by jealousy, and that she'd probably expected to see another woman in the car with him. Then she was pissed she was wrong. But it turned out she was right in a way, just a little early with that prediction.

He wondered what had happened to Spike.

MOTE:

If death is rebirth, then birth is re-death.

HARPER WAS the blackest cat Gio had ever seen, but she still had the distinctive walk she'd had as a human. And now that Gio thought about it, her strikingly green, wide-set Eurasian eyes worked well as both a kitty and woman.

He couldn't call out Harper's name, of course, as that would announce to the neighborhood that Harper the human was missing. He needed something better.

She'd always had a loose, catlike motion when she danced. Her shoulders and hips were often going in opposite directions, or making circles, or extending in unique ways. Fluid. Lithe. After seeing her move like that, he had called her Slinky for a few weeks.

"Slinky!" he presently called. Maybe Harper would respond. "Come here kitty! Slinky!"

He hadn't been allowed to call her anything but Harper in public. She wouldn't have gone for baby doll, sugar, or boo. He'd called her sweetie once, and she made a gagging sound in response. At least Slinky sounded like a cat's name.

"Don't call me Slinky," she'd finally said one day. "That's for girls who wear tight dresses." She preferred loose clothing. Like Stevie Nicks.

"Okay, Stevie." That was a great nickname. Evoked so much more of her personality.

"No." She'd known immediately to whom he referred. "I don't want to be named after somebody else."

In bed, she had moved, rolled around, and climbed on him like a cat or ferret, so he tried out Mink, which evolved to Minx. She'd been okay with that. Said it matched her seductive power. As a man beholden to it, he had to agree. But it wasn't endearing enough. So that morphed into Minxy, which was playful, and a portmanteau of the names Slinky and Minx.

It had been just under a week since their fateful anniversary, but he'd almost forgotten the Minxy nickname. After all that had happened and how differently he thought about Harper now, it was as if Minxy, that archetype or caricature, had died that night.

"Minxy! Minxy, baby! Dinner time!" he said now with more confidence. He hoped to find her. She couldn't handle being picked up by animal control, or eating garbage. Or aggressive, territorial dogs.

"Minxy!"

Linden was out walking his dog. This section of block didn't have sidewalks, so they were walking in the bike lane. Linden greeted him with his arm locked in a long wave. "Aaaayyyy! Giovanni!"

"Hey, Linden. Hey, Rudy-boy. I'm embarrassed to ask, but have you seen a cat around?" Rudy sniffed Gio's fingers and tried to lick his palms.

"He likes you better than Harper," Linden said. "Don't tell her I said that."

"I won't."

"New cat, huh? Gone already?"

"Yeah...um, Minxy."

"Minxy, Minxy, Minxy," Linden said. Harper must've named it. To each their own. Rudy's full name is Rutabaga. Good thing I didn't name him Zucchini."

Of course Linden Vowel would have a dog named Rutabaga.

"Rudy's a good name," Gio said.

"Is Minxy the same cat as escaped before?"

"No, not exactly." Gio kept scanning for movement in the distance.

"That's an odd way to put it, Nat Gio." Apparently, Linden was comfortable dishing out intimate personal modifiers. "You think you guys need another cat?"

Too late, regardless. Linden knew Gio was allergic to cats. So why would there have been a new cat in the household?

"Harper's doing, of course," Gio said. "Minxy's not acclimated yet."

"She got a new cat right before going on a trip? Huh. Where'd she go again?"

"Petoskey," Gio said, hesitating. Then, "Or was it Charlevoix?" He realized he sounded like an idiot not knowing exactly where his girlfriend was. "Could be either...or both. I know she has family in both. Yeah, she's visiting both. They're going rock hunting."

"She must trust you. I've never known her to leave the house more than a day or two."

"Yeah, we just celebrated our first anniversary."

"Well, that's a good sign. She doesn't trust people with her house, or her garden, or her cats. Sort of thought her friend Jehri would stick around and help with something like this, but I haven't seen her for a while either. Have you ever met her?"

"Yeah, kind of." Gio was getting uncomfortable with the conversation. So, what the hell. "Would you happen to have a small box? Like the size a baby would need?"

"A baby? Who died?"

"It's actually a cat. I suspect you don't get many requests for cat coffins."

"I'll admit it's a first."

"It's for Spike. The oldest one."

Linden had to know some weird shit was going on. First, he probably saw Steve leave the day he asked Gio to count the cats. Second, the new cat Minxy escaped and Gio was out looking for her. Now, Spike was dead. Gio was the worst pet-sitter known to man.

"Old man Spike, huh? Ornery as hell, but he hung in there. I think he was older than some of my students."

"Harper's going to be devastated." *Who knew, really.* "They're like little people to her."

TWENTY-FOUR

KAT

Connie was interviewing Thérèse, a potential publicist for Consumia's Spiritual Emporium. Kat had joined them in the meeting.

The office was overcrowded with stacks of merchandise, with some of the boxes open, some not. It was doubling as a storeroom. They were still renovating the new location for the grand opening, so some of its merchandise was arriving here and getting in the way. Connie and Kick had both been storing boxes at their houses, but only what could fit in their cars at the end of each day. If she so desired, Kat had several options for a seat that wasn't actually a chair.

"Oh my god, traffic was murder," Thérèse said. She sat with her knees together. Kat smelled high-end fragrance. At first she thought it was Connie, same flavor as she wore, but it was definitely Thérèse. She was wearing too much, or had just put it on in the car.

"Thanks for making the trek," Connie said. Some bosses played with a pen, a stress ball, or their glasses for effect while conducting a meeting. Connie had a brass ankh several inches long, an orphaned pendant she could fit her finger into and spin around. It wasn't graceful or intimidating, but Connie wouldn't want to give that impression anyway.

"It wasn't that far," Thérèse said. "Only from Sherman Oaks."

Kat thought she detected a bit of snark in her tone, as in, "We're busy, too. You could've come to our office, instead. Look how close it is."

Kat hadn't seen that brass ankh before, either. She may need to possess it.

"I wanted to make sure you got a feel for the Emporium," Connie said, gesturing out the door. "For the vibe here. Our members are a community, even the loners."

"Consumerians," Thérèse said. No, there was no snark. She was eager to please.

"My ego won't allow me to call them that. But outside of L.A., people mostly know us for the Omnist, so I'd like us to become more of a destination location. 'When you visit L.A., make sure to visit the Emporium,' that sort of thing. And we're opening a new location closer to downtown, in Echo Park, so the Omnist is what ties us together."

Kat nodded. That counted as participation.

"Synergy," Thérèse said, smiling. Pleased with herself. Doing and saying what she thought Connie wanted to hear.

"Yes."

"And I wanted to tell you, I love the vibe here," Thérèse said. "I just want to stay and browse. Get a tea."

"Would you like one? I can have Raine bring you one."

"Too much caffeine means *I'll be thinking in all caps*. No thanks. No, no. I'm good. I was just expressing how much I love the vibe here."

Didn't publicists think in all caps, anyway? It was the textual representation of their absolutism. *The BEST product! ALWAYS my FAVORITE!!!* Et cetera. Maybe she meant the difference between punctuating with one exclamation mark versus three.

"I *want* to stay," Thérèse continued. "I saw some herbal moisturizer out there I'd love to try."

"Would you like a sample?" Connie said.

Kat could swear Connie was toying with her. She may not have been killing her with kindness, but testing how much Thérèse could deflect before giving in.

"Oh, no, no. I don't want any freebies. I'm just expressing how I want to come back and buy stuff. I'm just saying I really get what you're doing here. I'm a Consumerian."

"That's good. I wouldn't want to work with somebody who didn't get it."

"I get it. I do. And I'm already a publicist to the stars, and frankly, Connie, you're a star."

Kat wouldn't hang out with a person like this, but then again, she had never attended a meeting with a publicist before. Maybe they were all like this. Connie had always tackled the publicity things herself.

Thérèse—whom Kat guessed to be near her own age, but who'd come off more experienced in email—seemed capable at her job. They didn't have somebody like this at CSE, somebody so eager to be compliant.

CSE employees related to the concept of the store itself, the brand, and acted accordingly. Not because Connie instructed their behavior. But it turned out, that *was* the way she wanted it done. Rather than being salespeople who worked on commission or as chaperones during Lodges, employees were Consumerians who happened to work at the place they loved.

Kat never wanted to work someplace where a boss tried to instill these feelings in the employees, claiming "We're all family here" when they weren't. And without seeming like she was trying, Connie had nurtured the right atmosphere.

"The job isn't to promote me personally," Connie said. "It's for the Emporium. And with the new location, Omnist II, we'll have twice the Lodges, twice the merch, and an app that needs ink. Or pixels, whatever. Kick—he's the one who does all the backend—is going to run the new store. He still updates the Omnist with gods and quotes and stuff, but we're too busy to promote it anymore."

"And people *want* to know what's going on here!" Thérèse said.

"Plus, another store means we'll inevitably cannibalize some of our own customers. They can't be two places at once, so we need good publicity campaigns to draw in new people from farther away."

"Then I'll be a publicist to the gods." Thérèse looked happy. "That's even better. I like that. But you're still the star, Connie. Don't go humble on me."

Connie may have actually blushed. Thérèse was breaking her down. Point, publicist.

"So, what's your take?" Connie said. "What would you do differently here?"

"That Javy thing, for one." Javy was the man found dead in the Dark Arts room seven months ago. A paranormal death, it was still legally unsolved. After a few weeks of incendiary reactions in the media and protests in front of the store, it seemed to mostly dissipate on its own. If anything, CSE was *more* mysterious to the public. "You needed to get in front of the story, Connie. Use the media attention to your advantage."

"But selling murder isn't right," Connie said.

"Neither is being blamed for that murder. Or losing your business."

Point, publicist.

"To be honest," Connie said, "after a week or two, business actually picked up."

"I followed you guys in the news. I kept kicking myself when I saw something I would've done differently. You needed a publicist. God forbid you have another crisis, but I'm used to handling these types of...surprises..." Thérèse paused, which made it appear she was trying not to sound rehearsed. As if she were talking to the media right now. "Like overdoses, arrests, extramarital affairs, all kinds of stuff."

Point, publicist.

"Well, I guess we should talk price," Connie said. She was clearly sold.

That was Kat's cue to let them haggle amongst themselves, and she excused herself. Just outside the door, she saw Steve perched on the top shelf of one of the aisles.

How the hell did he get up there? He didn't seem to have knocked anything down. A lot of cats did that; knocked things off tables and other flat surfaces for attention, but Steve was polite. Allowed things to have their space. She figured he could see much of the Emporium from up there, as well as the people walking down Lankershim through the window.

Steve was calmer today. He'd been a little worked up at Thalia's Lodge last night.

There'd been this guy; he'd hovered around the counter while she was dealing with a customer. Not checking out Kat, which men sometimes did. That hovering thing. No, this had been about Steve. The stranger had picked up a "Found Cat" flyer.

"Hey, kitty," he'd said. "I think I know you."

Steve then jumped down and hid behind the counter. She'd never seen anyone scare Steve that way. But if the man had known Steve, he would know his name. She was now glad for not revising the flyer.

Before Kat could finish with her customer, the man had left.

She hadn't thought about that until now.

CHAPTER
TWENTY-FIVE

GIOVANNI

Later that day, Gio was looking up transfiguration spells online, and finding only fantasy websites, fictional stories. Even within the people who believed in ailuranthropy, their stories were always one or two steps removed from the person who'd performed it or were victims of it. The curse of the urban legend, it was always someone who knew somebody who knew. Somebody had to know how to do this, and those who claimed to be experts seemed like charlatans.

He searched for missing people named Spike, Chico, Jagger. Cherry. Nothing. That's right, Cherry had told him when he was briefly a cat that her human name had been Jehri.

A unique name. That had to be a good sign. He found social media listings of quite a few women with that first name, more than he expected—maybe some were fake profiles—but without a last name, it was tough to narrow it down. Many of them didn't list a location, either. The few listings of a Jehri with red or auburn hair in their token photos were set to private.

He thought about the cat at the Emporium, the one that may have been one of Harper's. He couldn't recall the name, but he remembered her saying one of her exes had been a scientist. He searched for missing scientists and eventually found a story from five years ago about missing man with the name Steven Sanders, a scientist at JPL Laboratories who stopped showing up to work. He'd lived alone. His car was found parked at Union Station in downtown Los Angeles, as if he'd gone on a trip and never come back. Technically, the case was still open, but there were no leads. Authorities had questioned a friend of his, a woman named Harper, but she apparently wasn't a suspect. She hadn't seen him for a week before he disappeared, which she'd said wasn't uncommon with his long work hours. JPL had noticed something was wrong before she had.

That was him, Steve. That was her, Harper. There were many people on social media with the name Steve Sanders, but none that seemed to be him. He may not have had social media.

He looked for more clues in the house. He looked for photograph albums on her bookshelves in the front room. Many of the ancient books he found were handwritten in Latin and were somehow, magically, not falling apart. He looked through a few books of spells, but saw nothing that was obviously about transfiguration.

He checked the top of her closet in the bedroom. Under the bed. She seemed to keep no mementos at all of her exes as humans. Barely any memories of family. There was a pot she'd told him her grandmother had made. That robe, the one he'd been wearing, that had once been her mom's.

He finally found one album in a closet in the spare bedroom. It was an old one that had pictures of her great-grandparents, grandparents, parents, and her at various ages. The grandparents' early photos were of them as children standing with Harper's great-grandparents in front of the house, the first inhabitants. Then the grandparents as adults with her mom as a child, holding up a fish on a stringer. Gio remembered Harper saying her parents had been raised camping the summers, being one with the land. There were pictures here to prove it. Mountains, lakes, rivers. Even one of Harper in a makeshift swing tied to the branch of a tree. She must've been two years old.

Her mom met her dad camping one year when she was eighteen, right after graduation, he being twenty-two and recently discharged from the army. They were married a year later, and Harper was born a year after that.

Then there were no more pictures of her parents. Harper had told Gio they'd taken a private sight-seeing tour to take photographs of El Capitan while Harper and her grandpa waited at the campsite. The four-seater propeller plane crashed, and the pilot, her parents, and grandma all died.

So, at two years old, she'd moved into her grandpa's house. Her mom had only moved out three years prior. Grandpa was about fifty years older than Harper and never remarried. Twenty years later, health declining, he suffered a stroke and died in his sleep. She was the one who found him in the bedroom.

That was the extent he knew about Harper's family history. These pictures served as reminders of Harper's anecdotes, which felt cohesive enough for him to form a larger under-standing.

She used to tease Gio that the noises he heard in the house were Grandpa going down the hall to feed the fire in the front room. Of course, there'd been no fire burning at that time, but he supposed ghosts wouldn't know that. Or it'd been a ghost fire.

Now that Gio thought about it, Harper had been twenty-two when her grandpa died, the same age her mother had been when her plane crashed. The Spike relationship must've begun soon after Harper was living on her own, beginning her string of exes-as-cats.

Maybe she thought she should've been dead by twenty-two. Maybe she wanted no one to ever leave her again. Borrowed time, borrowed people.

Some things she'd said over the course of the year seemed especially ominous now:

"I'll know it when I want somebody with me for the rest of my life." He'd taken that to mean she'd just never met "The One." *Join the club.*

"People leave; that's what they do."

"Forever doesn't last forever without help." He'd taken that to mean you just had to put effort into things.

There was a picture of Linden as a young adult with Harper's mom as a teenager, arms draped over each other's shoulders, in what looked like Linden's backyard. A barbeque. But there were no photographs in the album after about eighteen years ago.

Gio had half-expected to find pictures of Harper looking the same age decades ago, as if she were a witch who didn't age. But no, the timelines seemed to work out. Things were no longer memorialized in photographs. Outside of their lives as cats, he found no other evidence of the exes' existences. He found this incredibly sad. All these people had careers, families, or aspirations. Just were like him. Probably better than him.

He rushed into the kitchen to look at the door of her refrigerator, which was much like other areas of the house: over-crowded. Magnets held up clippings of articles about new herb blends and recipes. Phases of the moon. Photos of plants and herbs, rocky seafronts, foggy swamps, and forests alive with fireflies. Wolves and cats. They were memes without the text. Until recently, there had been three photos of Harper and Gio that he knew about in the house: two on the fridge and one framed on the dresser in her bedroom. The two on the refrigerator door were gone, with other things moved into their places in the collage so there were no obvious gaps. He checked the dresser in the bedroom. That one was gone, as well.

She'd already wiped him away before they'd even sat down for their anniversary dinner.

HE WAS STARTLED by a knock at the door. He walked through the living room, past the box with its open lid, and saw Jagger tucked down by the foot. His heart skipped. He leaned down and placed a hand on the long-haired, dark-gray "ball of cat," just in case, and Jagger responded by tucking his face deeper underneath his hind legs.

It was no longer the coffin Spike had been in, but had reverted to a box again. Maybe he should put a blanket or pillows in there for the cats. This usage was better than knick-knack storage.

It was Linden at the door. Gio had never seen him upset. An awkward greeting, made more awkward by two awkward moods. Measured statements about the weather. Odd, since they'd just spoken that morning. Generic pleasantries while each of them scratched their cheeks.

"Do you want to come in?" Gio stepped aside. He could

smell dirty cat litter. Opening the door had shifted the air, announcing his next chore.

Linden stepped inside and looked into the box. "I see someone has acclimated well."

Jagger was unbothered by the visitor. He was a good cat. May have been a good boyfriend. Maybe they'd all been good partners. But Giovanni had cheated. Only once, with Hazel, but he was soiled forever. He may have deserved his punishment most, but ironically, he was the lucky one.

"They took ownership right away. It's a kitty B and B," Gio said. "Still haven't decided how I would decorate it, though."

Linden didn't seem to care. "Any sign of Minxy?"

"Not yet."

Controlled emotions belied by hands barely confined to pockets. Linden looked like he was churning ideas around in his head. "Rudy found something rather disturbing. I don't know if you've noticed yet, but there's a dead animal in my front yard. It was all I could do to keep him from putting it in his mouth. Then I remembered your missing cat."

Gio hadn't seen anything. "Let's go take a look at it," he said, not wanting to go look.

They walked to the far side of Linden's front yard, behind a tree, unseen from street view. It had definitely once been a cat, and looked to have been sawed in half. Not much blood, so the body may have been moved from where it'd been killed. He didn't recognize the fur. He had a horrible visual of Linden sawing a cat in half in his garage, and he shook it out of his head.

"It's okay," Linden said. "It's upsetting. This is someone's pet."

"It's not any of the cats I know," Gio said, deciding he was done looking at it forever.

"I'd say it's about half the size of Harper's cats." Gallows humor. Linden being Linden. "I don't know her pets that well, but I know she's had them a while. Except that new one."

"Well, it's not Minxy," Gio said.

"At first, I thought it might be Harper," Linden said.

Gio, already stunned, froze even more. Did he know she'd turned into a cat?

"You know, doing that crazy stuff she does," Linden said. "Like some kind of ritual or something, but I know she's out of town. There're always funny smells coming from the house. No offense." He didn't flat-out call her a witch, but he implied it. "Or maybe someone's sending me a message. Someone who don't approve of Coffin Club is trying to cast a spell on me."

"Could be a red-tailed hawk," Gio said.

"I didn't know they could cast spells."

"A raven?"

CHAPTER
TWENTY-SIX

HARPER

S he'd arrived at CSE too late last night and the
Emporium was already closed, so she'd prowled up and
down the alleys and backyards, surprised at the sheer
volume of rats in North Hollywood. They were loud and bold,
her hearing tuned to their high-pitched communication.

After the sun came up, she tired and found a cozy place to
sleep in a backyard planter. She slept through the morning.

It was hot and the sun had moved, heating her fur and
waking her up. The neighborhood was relatively quiet, but
bustling. The human noises were annoying, but also attractive.
She felt a desire to be around people, but not too close.

She met another female cat who, surprisingly, didn't try to
chase her away from the porch she was sitting on. Females
must not have been as territorial as Spike or Chico. This kitty
was fearless. Not in an aggressive, overconfident way, but as in

literally fear was unnecessary in her world. She wasn't afraid of people, including strangers. She smelled like she'd been recently pet by a woman with scented hand lotion, and had eaten high nutrition soft food from a can. She had been fixed.

Harper didn't tell her she was a transfiguration. It would ruin the mood. The kitty knew the neighborhood and they traveled together from yard to yard. They could communicate, but she was far less educated than her exes-as-cats. But of course, they'd gone to human school. This kitty was sweet and simple. Probably spent a lot of time on her owner's lap while watching television. An adult kitten, living in arrested development. They had fun smelling areas males had sprayed. The scents left by neutered tomcats were almost depressing, if they even meant to communicate anything at all. Their glands weren't right.

Kitty went to drink from a pool of water by a sprinkler head in someone's yard.

"Kitty, No!" Harper said, startling the sweet thing. She tried to explain to her there was a sign warning people to keep their pets off the grass due to poisonous fertilizer. Kitty couldn't read, of course. She didn't even know written language existed. Harper made her promise to remember that about this particular lawn. And to look out for signs with that shape in other yards. They found another recently run sprinkler and lapped a little there.

Harper had almost forgotten to go back to the Emporium. The two cats had spent hours together and ventured pretty far in the opposite direction. Harper said goodbye to the kitty and began to head back.

Walking slower, she realized how tired she was again. She was having trouble thinking and had only gone about a couple blocks. It was late afternoon, and she needed a nap. She knew this about her kitties at home. It was naptime. She found a house with a wooden deck in the backyard, perfect for shade, and a soft, protected place to lie down.

She woke before dusk, walked out to the street, and tried to orient herself. Buildings, roads, and other landmarks looked different from this low angle and reduced color palette. She had adjusted to seeing the world through the blue filter of cat eyes, but struggled to differentiate dark green from red.

She could see clearly from, say, two feet to a hundred feet, so things farther than that were blurry. Rather than taking a chance by cutting straight across town like she would in a car, she retraced her steps. It was safer, but took longer. She had no trouble remembering the exact yards she and the other kitty had cut through. She passed the house she was sure Kitty lived in. Her scent was strongest there.

It was getting late when she finally arrived at CSE, but at least it was still open. A Progressio Lodge had just wrapped and people were dissipating, mingling, talking outside on the sidewalk. There were too many people, so she went around to the back door where some people were smoking. She maneuvered close, behind a dumpster. She hadn't been seen.

She could smell Steve. Coming to CSE had been a shot in the dark to find somebody who understood her predicament, but she didn't expect to run into him. At minimum, he had marked here.

A couple people hugged a third person, said goodbye, and left. The employee Kat went inside. As the somewhat-broken hydraulic system pulled the door closed, Harper snuck in just behind her.

Kat continued into the Emporium. Nobody else was in the Dark Arts room. Harper jumped up on a display counter. There was a new section for O'Cult-branded potions, each aimed at a different desire. The tags said one was to attract money, another love. Most were mainstream blends, a lot of basic stuff.

One was called Own Won Now. The tag said it granted personal power, internal strength, control over your life. Be the person you want to be. A few swipes with her paw and she knocked a corked vial out of the display. It rolled off the counter to the floor, bouncing and breaking in half. She jumped down and gingerly poked through it, avoiding any sharp glass. She couldn't see what was right in front of her mouth, but her whiskers and fur made eating the herbs easier than she expected. She would find out how good O'Cult potions were.

She wandered into the Emporium area. Steve was sitting on the front counter, the furry white spot on his chest puffed out proudly. He looked well fed. He was wearing a new black collar. Most of the Consumerians were gone, and Kat and Connie were conversing.

She saw Steve's food dish on the floor and ran up to it.

"Hey!" Steve said.

"Steve!" Harper looked at him, smiling as only one cat could smile to another.

"Harpy? I thought I smelled you. How the hell did you get here?"

"Spike helped me escape, then I walked. You?"

"I stowed away in Linden's truck."

None of the people had noticed her yet. Steve gave off a presence like he owned that counter.

"I take it you'd never been here before," Harper said.

"How could I? It's only been open a couple years. But you talked about it enough times."

"You know I sell some herbs here. I can show you if you like."

He looked away as he sniffed. Well, sort of. Meeting Kitty

today had improved her feline communication skills, and that sniff said, "I don't care."

"You've found a new home then?" Harper said.

"I can't complain."

"Don't you want to change back?"

"Actually, that's not what I said." Typical Steve.

"I might want to stay a cat. I don't know," she said. If he could be nonchalant, then so could Harper.

"Back up." Steve jumped down, then went to the water dish. "This way we'll both be out of sight until one of them comes back around." He took a cursory three laps of water. "Funny how people don't know it's better to drink from running water," he said.

"Like a sprinkler or leaky hose." She'd just learned this today.

"Even though Kat changes this every day, it doesn't take long to oxidize and acquire a surface film. It's kind of gross. But she's got a drip in her bathtub. It's nice." Steve walked down an aisle, implying Harper should do the same. "You said Spike helped you escape. I just walked out when Gio opened the back door. Why didn't you?"

"Because Gio locked me in the bedroom."

"That makes sense. I'd lock you up, too." Steve had a talent for making a simple fact sound like an insult and an insult sound like a simple fact.

"You would? I thought you loved me. You used to sleep in my lap."

"For warmth, Harpy. Actually, your house is cold for cats. Just because I trusted you wouldn't kill me doesn't mean I loved you."

And sometimes facts were insults.

"Well," Harper said, "I came here to find somebody who can change me back."

"Change *us* back. I've got this place covered. There's nothing yet, and as you can see, I'm still a cat. You should go find yourself a nice family to live with. Be a good kitty."

"I don't trust people. I'll end up in a rescue and locked up against my will."

"Huh. You mean like what you did to all of us?"

Connie was walking down the aisle. "Steve!" she said. "Who's this other cat?"

"Oh, Connie, meet Harpy," Steve said.

"It's Harp*er*," Harper said. "And she can't understand you, you know."

"I know. But they respond better when you try. Something in the message seems to translate."

"Kat!" Connie said. "There's another cat in here. Do you know who this is?"

Kat came around the corner. "No."

"No collar again," Connie said, trying to pick up Harper, who escaped and ran down another aisle. "Steve's attracting strays!"

Steve jumped back to the top of the counter to watch, laughing and taking pleasure in Harper's plight.

"Elijah!" Connie called. A college-aged boy walked over from the Basil Alcove, wrapping a cable around his forearm, hand to elbow. When he saw the fracas, he set the cord down and blocked the Basil Alcove from her. He bent his knees, arms up, in his best imitation of a defensive stance, like he'd never played sports before but had seen them on television. He would succeed in a sense; she wasn't going over there anyway.

Harper attempted to go back to the Dark Arts room where she'd come in, but Connie was crouched there ready to grab her. Harper's heart rate had jumped quickly, and time had decelerated. Human reactions seemed slow.

A customer opened the front door and Harper bolted out.

Fuck Steve if he isn't doing more to help. Harper was feeling a surge from the O'Cult Own One Now potion already. It was powerful being a cat. She could hunt, fight, and be independent. She'd come to CSE to find a way back, but maybe now it wasn't needed so much. She was free of Gio, free of her bedroom prison. She didn't need anyone.

TWENTY-SEVEN

KAT

P art of Kat was proud of her little man. He wasn't just popular with Consumerians, but other cats, too. Something about him had attracted another cat to Consumia's Spiritual Emporium last night, and Connie hadn't been happy about it.

So today she left Steve at the house, the first time they'd been apart in the five days since they met. She told herself it was mainly because she wanted to run errands before work, but when she got to CSE, she felt a little exposed without him sitting on the counter. He was her little protector.

That stranger who'd been scoping Steve out at Thalia's Lodge two nights ago came up to the counter again and looked around. After they made eye contact, he walked away quickly. As if embarrassed. He was probably there for Kevin O'Culled.

Maybe witchcraft was his thing. You didn't necessarily recognize a witch by their fashion.

Both Thalia and Kevin sold branded blades and wands at the Emporium. Thalia sold witch's ladders and meditation mats. Kevin sold enchanted potions. They had complementary specialties. For all the meditation and shapeshifting projection Thalia promoted, Kevin was comparatively more materials-based.

Kevin taught potions and charms one could perform at home. Toadstools and cattails. Herbs and salts. Self-described as part chemistry teacher (without the degree), part alchemist, and part chef, his book was called *O'Cult Potion Hacking*.

Kevin was just as proud of the newly painted floor diagram as Thalia had been. He stepped off the stage and walked through the audience, who parted to allow his path around the circumference of the circle, his long robe flowing behind his feet.

"Don't you just love it?" he said, sharing his joy with the Consumerians around him. "Last time I had to take off my cingulum to measure a chalk circle on the floor."

"What's a cingulum?" a Consumerian said.

He lifted the end of his belt, which had been wrapped a couple times around his mid-section, the ends left dangling another foot and a half. "This sucker's nine feet. Same as the diameter of the circle. It's a tradition the ancients did, but one I could do without. That's what paint's for."

Several of Kevin's guests wore different colored O'Cult cingula, the colors representing a position of rank within his O'Cult, but Kat's anecdotal evidence suggested that some buyers chose colors based on fashion preference alone. Until tonight, Kat had never seen so many people wear a nine-foot belt in public before, and certainly not in a color chosen for the season. Black was a color for all seasons.

Kat realized Steve was sitting next to her at end of the counter. Not only had he gotten out of the house, but he'd come here, probably just waltzing in with another Consumerian. "Hey, you little shit!"

Steve looked at her, then back at the stage.

"I take it you like witches, huh? I guess you heard us talking about Kevin yesterday. No point asking how you got out, since you won't tell me."

She picked up one of his front paws. It was dirty and had bits of debris on it.

"That was a hell of a trek you made, like two or three miles."

Steve licked her hand, telling her to put down his paw. He was listening to Kevin, who had just expressed his disappointment in the pentacle being associated with evil, especially during the satanic panic of the 1980s.

"People are made up of the five elements represented by the five points of the pentacle," Kevin said. "The first four earth elements are the ones most people are familiar with: fire, water, earth, and air. The body creates heat, which is represented by fire. We consume water, obviously, but also food, which is earth. And we respirate air. Add a fifth element, the soul, and you have animal life. As such, all living creatures are a combination of these five elements."

Or mammals, anyway. Maybe that was the origin of the suspicion that creatures that didn't create heat, like snakes and giant squids and locusts, were evil.

"You guys know Lucador, right?" Kevin said. "He's a popular Omniscian who uses swords like toys in his presentations. He makes his own blades, which is admirable, but the problem is, he's willing to use them as weapons. Blades are meant to be tools. If someone is wounded by a blade, possibly by Lucador swinging one around the Emporium..."

He awkwardly swung his arms as if he had a sword, and paused to allow laughter.

"If someone is injured, I have an ointment to rub onto the blade afterward. It heals the wound it caused." He rubbed imaginary lotion down his extended arm, the proxy for a blade.

"Now, Thalia prefers an athame, a ceremonial blade with a black handle." He picked up a blade from the table next to him onstage. "Beautiful craftsmanship, all done by hand. She sells them here, if you're interested in acquiring one. It's not just a cool-looking letter opener."

He paused again as the audience laughed.

"Personally, I'm partial to the Druidic boline." He picked up another blade and held it above his head for the crowd to see.

Kat thought that one was captivating—sort of a silver crescent moon with a handle, eight to ten inches in length. It was deadly enough, but a larger version of it would cause a sickle a fit of jealousy.

The strange man hadn't moved far from the counter. He stood on his toes to see over people's heads. He turned to Kat. "We have one of those hanging by the back door."

He must've meant the boline. She meant to acknowledge him, but he turned away. She realized who he was. He'd bought an Organica pestle and mortar set last week. He came in once in a while, but she'd never retained a name.

She felt like she was stuck in a fishbowl behind the counter. On display. Please don't tap the glass. Normally, Paula and Derby would've been here to back her up. They mainly helped with popular events and had worked during Thalia's two Lodges, but were skipping Kevin's because they expected a misogynistic bent. They said Kevin believed men and women were put on earth with opposing traits that balanced each other out. Maybe not chauvinistic so much as overtly binary.

Kat didn't quite hear that in his talk, but still wouldn't mind missing the rest of his sermon.

At his last Lodge, Kevin recommended adding a dead loved one's ashes to your coffee grounds, brewing, and then drinking it. She'd heard of people shooting the ashes out of guns, or adding them to weed and smoking them. But the idea of drinking them literally nauseated her. Plus, it seemed an obvious elevation of the cliché about cremains being stored in a coffee can. She'd lost respect for Kevin and preferred Thalia.

Now, she wanted that new kid, Elijah, to take over the register so she could do something else. He'd left the light and sound board and was walking by, probably unsure about his next duty.

"Hey, Dr. Elijah," Kat said.

He brightened up, taking the observation as a compliment. "Maybe someday," he said. "But I'm still learning..."

"If you make a gynecologist joke, so help me," she said. She could tell he was missing the joke. "It's because you look like a dentist. A dentist-in-training."

Elijah was a skinny kid with vintage, brown corduroy pants and a short-sleeved, pearl-snap button-up shirt. Tucked in, of course. She assumed his nerdy look was ironic, but the real irony was that she liked his horn-rimmed glasses. But she couldn't tell him that, because he took compliments the wrong way. As it was, he flirted with every female he came in contact with.

Connie had said his behavior was cute, that he was harmless, but she was probably flattered because someone half her age was hitting on her. Elijah probably assumed all teasing was flirtation, and that punching a girl in the arm was an effective means of communicating you liked her.

In other words, don't allow a puppy to jump on your shins

just because you think it's cute, because when they grew older...

"Oh, I suppose that's a good thing, then" Elijah said, patting his shirt pocket is if expecting to find a pen. "Are dentists real doctors?"

"I don't know, but it's time for you to cycle back here," Kat said.

She changed places with Elijah and walked through the audience, more curious about them than what Kevin was saying. The attendees weren't as giddy as Linden's or Organica's crowds, or as celebratory as Tora's and Fomotalia's. They weren't somber either, like Yksian's or Ornatu's. Or as playful as Lucador's or inquisitive as Thalia's. They were more like students drinking it all in.

She saw their new publicist, Thérèse, beaming about the room.

"Isn't this great?" Thérèse said. "I love this!"

Kat nodded. The crowd's size had nothing to do with Thérèse. No doubt her efforts would be helpful in the future, but she'd only been employed by Connie for what, a day? Maybe she had an inflated sense of how much a couple of same-day social media posts contributed to the attendance of a Lodge.

Kat continued making her way through the Basil Alcove.

"Some say magic is only undiscovered science," Kevin said from the stage. "Which makes sense when you look at it from science's point of view. But magic existed before science, because it did. It did. And when people figured out how things worked, they called it science, and the magic seemed to go away. People love to explain the mystery out of things. But, regardless, the plants used in potions still worked to augment people's immunities, moods, and realities. Natural things like aspirin—which is a type of bark—and tobacco, aloe, magic mushrooms, alcohol, salvia."

Kevin was holding an O'Cult-branded wand and, with a clear view of the table now, Kat saw beakers and vials as if he were prepped for a chemistry demonstration. It was a potions class. "What else?" he said.

"Cocaine!" a member shouted to much laughter.

"Coca plant, right. And ayahuasca, peyote." He better not have illicit drugs up there. "What else?"

"Weed!" yelled another. That was Gremmie. He was Kick's roommate, and a surfer. He wasn't there a lot, but Kick had brought him to a couple events.

"Cannabis, of course," Kevin said. "That's legal now, too. People used it, then science killed it, and then science had to bring it back again."

She guessed Kevin was part stoner, too. The crowd had perked up when the talk turned to drugs. She half expected a jam band to break out.

"These substances were used in rituals for thousands of years before they became accepted by mainstream science. Then they became, quote-unquote, *psychedelic*. Scientists accused witches or shamans of being charlatans, as in, 'Look, see, anyone can do it. Just take this drug. So the magic must be fake.'

"But that's backward. Learning something's a psychedelic is proof that roots and leaves and seeds and flowers all work with humans to bring us closer to our gods. They provide altered states of consciousness where we learn about our place in the universe."

An older man in the front was motioning with his hands, as if splashing water onto his face. It took a second for Kat to recognize him as a Consumerian named Xavier, the X-Y-Z at Yksian's book signing. He was sweating so much it looked like water had really landed on him. Nobody else was sweating. The words Kevin spoke were the holy water with which Xavier cleansed himself. He was smiling rapturously. Was this basking? He was basking in Kevin's words. Kat predicted Xavier would be an Executive Saint by the end of the year, by the end of next month.

"Then it became corporatized," Kevin continued. "The little guy was squeezed out of business. The small farmers. Home growers. The alcohol, tobacco, and pharmaceutical corporations are some of the most powerful and richest in the world. And now cannabis.

"So those who practice magic and witchcraft have to keep searching tirelessly to remain one step ahead of science. Trying new combinations. New recipes for spells. Breeding new plants. We cut and chop, grind and powder, mix and boil. All things we learned as tribal people—which I remind you, we all were not long ago—in order to prepare our food and medicine."

"What about the words we recite?" said Alex, the Executive Saint next to Kat. Consumerians paid for the honor to wear that pin, and were rewarded with first dibs on special events and trips, house visits, store discounts. Maybe Kevin would be hosting a party soon at Alex's house.

"Oh, the incantations are absolutely part of the ceremony," Kevin said. "There are those who believe words and meaning exist independently from us in the universe. We are born without language and have to learn to use it, learn to think with it. When we speak, we harness the power of language, the power of words. But we'll get into that another time."

Kat looked back at the counter and saw Steve, still sitting in his spot, taking in every word.

TWENTY-EIGHT

HARPER

H arper had spent last night wandering North Hollywood again, and hadn't had a real meal in over two days. She was starving.

She thought about the food dish at CSE, how the kibble smelled like cardboard with a weak metallic meat broth poured over it and dried. She'd had no desire to eat it at the time, but would devour it now if someone placed it in front of her.

Her claws were bothering her. Being retracted most of the time, she found they needed to be stretched. She found a young tree and scratched at it until she set both sets of claws into the bark and pulled. She hadn't realized until now that her spine needed this, too. She sort of hung on the tree and let gravity pull her vertebrae apart. She smelled other animal markings on the tree. There was a unique mixture of domestic and urban wild animals. She could also differentiate strays from housebroken, based on their diets.

And that running water thing Steve had said. She much preferred a leaky garden faucet or hose from which to drink. She could smell fresh water from a distance, but also listened for sprinklers. She settled into a padded patio chair behind a house, away from the sun. The temperature was perfect. She felt safe. She slept.

It was afternoon when she awoke to children in the backyard. Maybe school had let out. Two loud boys were looking for critters under a decorative rock, and a girl was eating yogurt out of a plastic tube. Harper could smell the artificial strawberry flavoring.

Harper trekked toward the side of the garage.

"Black cat! Black cat!" said the smaller boy, pointing.

"It's so cute!" said the girl.

"Come here kitty, kitty," said the older boy.

Harper picked up her pace. And they didn't just chase her —they chased her with two arms out in front of them, picking her up from a distance. Overexuberant children with multimalodorous hands and flexing fingers was the nightmare she never saw coming. She'd never been maternal, disliking children as a general rule, but they'd left her alone as a human. As a cat, she was a child magnet. But they were moving half speed compared to her. She could escape easily.

She'd picked the wrong escape route, however, and was now cornered between the side of the garage and a cinder block wall too high to leap. The household's three trash bins were stored here, which she knew from experience would be blue, green, and black, and there was no point trying to hide behind something so mobile.

She leapt up onto the first one, feet cycling, claws catching no purchase, almost slipping off. She steadied herself without falling. From here, she could jump to the top of the wall and run along that for a while. As she crouched to leap again, a pair of hands shocked her, grabbing her around the torso.

"Gotchoo!" said one of the boys.

Harper wailed, legs kicking. The boy was squeezing her chest too hard. The rib compression didn't hurt, as she was relatively malleable, but her lungs couldn't fill more than halfway with air. Her machine gun heart rate punched against his squeezing fingers. She scratched and clawed his forearms best she could, finally catching skin with her back paws. It felt good, like brand-new scissors gliding through crisp wrapping paper.

"Owwww!" the boy yelled.

"Put it down!" said the girl.

"Put it in here!" The smaller boy opened a trash bin and Harper was roughly thrown into it. She splayed her limbs as far as she could to catch the lip of the bin, but missed, hitting the far wall and falling. She oriented herself and tried to leap, but the folded cardboard box under her slid so that she only hit the wall hallway up. The lid slammed closed. Cardboard meant she was in the blue bin.

She heard their animated discussion:

"That's a wildcat!"

"I think it's a bobcat."

"That's not a bobcat, that's just a regular cat."

"It didn't have no collar."

"Declan's right. That's right. That makes it wild. It's a wildcat."

"Aren't bobcats wildcats?"

"Those are mountain lions."

"That's no mountain lion."

"Nuh-HUH!"

"It scratched me! Look what it did!"

"That's cuz you grabbed it wrong."

"I bet I'm gonna need stitches."

"Stitches for what? It's barely bleeding!"

"Why do you think it's all red? Magic?"

"But there's no dripping blood."

"What do you call that?"

"Like two drops. You don't need stitches for two drops of blood."

"Three drops now. If I bleed to death cuz of you—"

"Go rinse it off."

Even though the lid was closed, she could see remarkably better than she would've predicted. There was the tiniest amount of indirect light seeping in near the crack of the lid, and that was all she needed. There were several layers of boxes already folded, trying to spring back into their original shapes. Some were vertical, hugging a wall, some were horizontal. The cardboard underneath her was unsteady, like a boat on the water.

She pawed at the boxes on the wall to get them to lie flat. She made treadmill motions, anything to get them to slide down into place. She gave up arranging the boxes. It was heating up fast in there. She would die in this bin within an hour if the sun kept beating on it. She listened to the kids talking again.

"We should give it some food and water."

"Think it'll eat my yogurt?"

"They don't eat people food."

"Nuh-HUH!"

"Well, they shouldn't."

"My mom gives our cat yogurt. The white kind."

The lid started to lift, then slammed shut, like someone slapped it closed.

"What are you doing? It's gonna escape. Or maybe attack us."

"It's just a cat. And they gotta eat, too."

"And it won't escape if it's busy eating my yogurt. Move. Watch."

The lid lifted a few inches and a squeezable yogurt container slipped in. Harper leapt and got her front legs over the upper lip of the bin just as the lid fell on the top of her head. It wasn't that heavy, pushing against her with less pressure than the boy had. She clawed and pumped with her hind legs, suddenly claustrophobic.

"What's it doing in there?"

"It's going crazy!"

"It's chasing the food."

Harper stopped moving, hanging on.

"See?" the girl said. "All quiet now. Watch."

The lid lifted again, revealing three wide-eyed faces in front of Harper. She panicked, scrambling as hard as she could, managing to get a hind leg over the edge by the time the lid fell on her, knocking her to the pavement. But she was out.

"It's attacking!"

She shot out between two of the kids, down the driveway, and across the street. Fastest she ever moved, human or feline. She didn't slow down until she was a block away.

It took a while for her to calm down. She was anxious. Every human wanted to capture her. Every set of eyes had plans for her. Every pet wanted her out of their territory.

Once she relaxed, she found she was even hungrier. People cooking in houses, the smell almost too intense. Salt, spice, garlic, preservatives, artificial flavors. They were so obvious now, especially when heated. Humans ate a lot of horrible shit. Mostly, she wanted meat. Hunting promised to be fun.

She wanted the sun to set. That's when all the dinner critters came out. Dusk and dawn.

An animal control van patrolled the street, moving at walking speed. They were looking for something. It couldn't be her. They didn't go after cats, did they? Only dogs. Or maybe raccoons and opossums trapped in attics and basements. Not cats.

She cut through a couple yards and over to the next block and continued tracking scents there, but the van pulled down that street, too. Maybe they were, indeed, looking for her. She needed out of this neighborhood.

She thought about all the critters that lived in the canyon behind her house. She knew that neighborhood better, and would feel safer. She needed to avoid Gio, who may lock her up again if he saw her, but if caught, unlike animal control, he wouldn't neuter her or put her down.

She avoided yards with dogs, some of which, no surprise, were legitimate assholes. Her cat instinct and desire for safety took her back along her original route. It was longer than a straight shot, but safer. Familiar was good. Food would be better.

It was nearly sunset when she entered her neighborhood and crossed a yard to the ravine. Much of the traffic noise was gone. She could smell and hear many unseen animals. Plants parched from the sun scratched at her fur as she went under scrub as much as over it. She was sure she looked like hell. With a little searching, she was able to find feeding routes other animals took, little tunnels through plants and bushes, easier trails to ascend steep inclines or rocky ledges. Each was a highway of scents, representing all the colors of the olfactory rainbow.

She lunged at a field mouse and missed. This was not easy. Fast little fuckers. She sensed another, and before she could strike, it ran. She chased it. It went under leaves and branches of plants, but being larger, she had to go over. She leapt farther than she may have needed to, hoping to land on the critter. It had disappeared. Maybe it found its den.

She heard something to her right. Curious, she stalked her way to look.

It was her own backyard. She could sense the faintest remnants of the spell she'd cast last spring, burning a potion in a cauldron in the backyard. It wasn't enough to steer her away anymore, but it would've been hell a few months ago.

As for food, most houses in that neighborhood had citrus, loquat, or olive trees. Things she couldn't care less about. Beyond protective potions, she'd never thought about her own garden from an animal's perspective before. The aroma was nearly overpowering. It was a sensory overload.

She wanted to sample a little from every plant, not so much as a meal, but to know it intimately. Her sense of smell had greatly improved, which meant her taste had, too. It was the wrong season for strawberries, blueberries, and boysenberries. She wished it were earlier in the year.

What sounded like a large creature wailed in pain, not twenty feet away. She froze, silent. She heard it shuffle and flop, and felt the vibrations with the pads of her paws. The animalistic noise stopped, and as long as she remained quiet, maybe she'd be okay.

Then the predator's muffled cries of pain spooked her again. They were the scariest sounds she'd ever heard. It was a monster, or, more likely, a coyote or bobcat caught in a trap.

She took a few steps toward the ravine and stopped as she encountered soft, churned earth. As if somebody had planted something there. Or buried it. Burying was a form of planting.

She sniffed the ground and pawed lightly at it. It was Spike. She could smell Spike. This was so wrong.

More muffled cries. So loud they were not really muffled at all.

She fled.

CHAPTER
TWENTY-NINE

GIOVANNI

Today had been a lot of busywork for Gio. Tending the garden. Cleaning litter boxes. Vacuuming cat dander and fur. Cooking three days' worth of meals. And aggressively ignoring the barrage of work emails and texts asking if he was still sick.

"Do you need me to bring you anything?" Hazel emailed.

"No, I'll be fine." She was just being nice, but he didn't want to lead her on, either.

"We're having a meeting today. Just a heads up. I think they're taking you off this film."

He'd expected that. They were in seven-days-a-week territory now and they couldn't afford him missing any more time. He could work now, physically, but finding a cure for the cats was his priority at the moment.

He picked up the charm he'd bought at the O'Cult Lodge

last night. He'd felt like a visitor auditing Thalia's Lodge a few nights ago, but buying an O'Cult spell felt like the first step toward becoming a witch himself.

~

GIO HAD APPROACHED Kevin last night as the Omniscian thanked Consumerians for attending his Lodge.

"Do you have a second?" Gio said. "Can I talk to you in private?"

"We're all friends here." Kevin gestured to the smiling people around him. "There's no need for secrets."

"Well, ummm..." Gio slowed, measuring his question against the company of strangers. "How do you undo a potion?"

"That depends. What was it for? Was it one of mine?"

"No, it wasn't yours, but I'd rather not say what it was for."

"You're not comfortable telling me what the spell was?" Kevin didn't seem as much skeptical as just curious.

"I'd rather not," Gio said.

"Hmmm. Did it just not work, or did it do the wrong thing?"

"No, it worked. It worked really well, but I want to undo it."

"Huh. Does this fall in the category of, 'Be careful what you wish for'?"

"My girlfriend cast it. It was originally intended for me without my knowledge, but it's inadvertently affected her now. She's the one with the uh...condition."

Kevin looked like he suddenly understood the need for privacy there. "I think I see." His voice had changed. Much more sincere. Sympathetic. He placed a hand on Gio's shoulder. "Brutal, huh?"

"You could say that."

"The spell may have gotten caught halfway and rebounded back on the witch."

"Yes! That's exactly what happened!"

"Okay, okay, we'll get through this. Your girlfriend is going to need to make the potion again, but..." Kevin gestured for Gio to follow him to a display of O'Cult merchandise. He picked out a witch's ladder. "Meditate on this charm first, and keep it on hand during the process to guarantee success."

Kevin handed the charm to Gio. He held it up. It was woven with hair and bones and hemp and leather. It looked delicate, but felt sturdy.

"The other night, Thalia said to project confidence when casting spells and charms, to envision the goal as if it's already happened," Gio said.

"That's very important, and maybe your girlfriend lost focus midway," Kevin said. "Meanings of words can change if the speaker is distracted. But this will help, too. The card has instructions for a few occasions. It should be used before any difficult spell, and in this case, it should push whatever the initial spell was the rest of the way through."

It wasn't quite what Gio had in mind, but after publicly receiving advice from Kevin and now holding one of his prescribed charms, he felt obligated to buy it. Regardless, it should help with whatever the solution turned out to be.

"It sounds like you have this under control," Kevin said, patting him on the arm. "And don't worry. Women have needs, too, and you guys will be back at it in no time."

～

PRESENTLY, Gio left food and water and one of Harper's hoodies on the back patio in case she returned when the door was closed. She could curl up in it for warmth.

He drove back to his condo to check on things and bring in the mail. He worked out his finances. Assuming he would lose his current job, he figured he would be okay for at least eight months, but then would need to find work. So, that wasn't his first concern. It was the cats. Harper.

He didn't have much in the way of clothes at Harper's—he'd been cycling between a couple sets—so he packed a travel bag and loaded an extra case of sparkling water into the car.

MOTE:

The sky has eyes and the eyes have teeth.

IT WAS twilight when he returned to Harper's house and went to the back door with his things. He thought he saw something move just off the patio where the garden began. He walked over with his phone light and looked around.

Something was wrong.

His stomach cramped intensely and he buckled over, lowering his head in pain. He was trying to be quiet, so his cry came out like a stifled whimper. Like he was trying not to vomit. Last thing he needed was Linden looking through the fence.

He was dying. Something about that potion a week ago had lingering effects and was now killing him. It was poison. He wasn't supposed to revert back to being human, and now he was reverting back to not being alive.

But dying people didn't shrink, didn't grow fur.

He was morphing into a cat again.

The nearly full moon revealed itself and a most violent throe hit Gio. He fell to his knees and dropped his phone, flashlight down.

The transfiguration didn't get any easier the second time around, but he was more aware of not making noise, and screaming into the crook of his arm. Familiarity made it less scary, but it still hurt. If he'd known this was coming, he would've gone inside the house first.

As his sense of time slowed and his hearing improved, he heard an animal scamper away into the canyon. He could smell his clothes, Linden, the cats inside. Mostly he smelled Harper. It was even more her house and garden as a cat.

The change now complete, he couldn't get inside the house or car. He had to figure out where to go. He tried to hide his clothes, but they were too bulky to move much. He bit his pants and managed to pull them back a few feet, out of sight of the back door. At least they covered his phone, and the light shining underneath it. The battery would die, but as long as nobody came back there, it should be fine.

He explored the yard with his new night vision, and some of the ravine. Smells were incredible. Light wasn't a problem. Areas that would've been completely black to him as a person were now a glowing twilight. His hearing was so attuned to his environment, he could hear the finger-tapping rhythm of a mouse heartbeat.

He heard the shuffling of a larger warm-blooded creature. He could tell it was a predatory mammal. Cats, he knew, were both predator and prey, and Gio himself had now switched from the former to the latter.

This may have been the creature who ate half a cat next door. He didn't want to be next. He had to leave, so he decided to find and talk to Harper's scientist cat. That had to have been him at the Emporium and on the flyers. If he hurried, he could get there before they closed.

The trek took several hours, and CSE was already closed. But he could smell Steve. He was sure to be back tomorrow, so he would wait. But he was tired after walking many miles. He'd been awake for eighteen hours, and cats needed more sleep than humans.

He curled up in a box in the alley behind a bar/restaurant. The cardboard smelled like broccoli. Bitter and green, but he didn't mind. Funny, he hadn't seen "morph into a cat" in his horoscope prediction today. He actually never read his horoscope, but he guaranteed it didn't say that.

AS SUNRISE APPROACHED, shapeshifting back to his human form was what woke him up. Pain was a hell of an alarm clock. The produce box was stuck over his head and shoulders. He was wedged into it, his head twisted at the neck, and he couldn't remove it. This added a new level of unexpected pain. Like a wrestler tearing off a T-shirt, he gripped the sides and pulled, used the air vents as handles.

Still nothing.

Then he worked his hands on an outside corner and was able to tear across, finally relieving some of the pressure on his neck. He was on his knees now, and pulled the remains of the box off his head.

His knees hurt, with sand and gravel having embedded into his skin. He was naked, of course. No phone. No wallet. No keys. Waiting to be arrested.

His tooth hurt more than ever. Moving his clothes with his mouth last night had aggravated it. He covered himself the best he could with unfolded boxes. Another version of him would've laughed.

THIRTY

KAT

K at was at home with Steve today, as she didn't have to work.

She'd brought him along earlier for the ride to the home and garden store. He was that rare cat who would rather go for a ride in a car than stay home. No more pet carrier. He'd walked beside her down the driveway and hopped in the car himself. But he'd stayed there while she ran inside.

She'd bought a new screen for the window above the bar in the man cave. Somehow, Steve had gotten up there. The window could lock in place when it was open just a few inches, so she didn't fear a home invasion from a small window six feet up. But it was open enough for Steve to have torn a hole in the screen and squeezed through. Then he had trekked to CSE to see Kevin's O'Cult Lodge.

The screen was now replaced, and there was a fire

murmuring and news chattering on the TV in the man cave. She had a few books spread open on the bar. One was new and designed to look ancient, with pages of thick pulp bound by leather string, but the knowledge it contained was timeless. Another book was glossy and full-colored, with illustrations of animals and chimeras, and animal archetypes within other animals. This was written by Jasmine Waters, the pet psychic Omniscian. A third book was falling apart, the binding disintegrating, the pages slipping off each other like an old deck of cards.

Steve jumped on a stool, then onto the bar top, sniffed the books, and actively sat on the first one, blocking Kat's ability to read it.

"Come on now, move. I'm reading this. You make a better cat than a...window."

Steve just stared.

"You know, the old cliché? Walls and stuff."

He was staring at the television, as in, actually watching it.

Kat was looking for commonalities between the books, threads that connected myths and magic and animal psychology. All three had been purchased or borrowed from CSE. Maybe Steve was magical. Connie sold items with magic, but instead of a corpse in a jar of formaldehyde, what if the magical animal was still alive? And if a pet psychic could get inside the mind of a pet, maybe Kat could, too.

The doorbell rang. It would be Jasmine. And rather than run away, or ignore the visitor, Steve jumped off the bar to accompany Kat to the front of the house.

"So this is the world-famous Steve I've been hearing about," Jasmine said. Her brown hair was medium length, pulled behind her ears. No makeup, no hair product. Even her fashion was unassuming: comfortable jeans, a sweatshirt, and a hiking vest. She was sturdy and peaceful. Good energy.

Steve held his head up to be pet, then followed Jasmine's fingers with his nose.

"It's like he knew you were coming," Kat said. "He heard me on the phone with you. Followed me over here like a dog."

"He probably doesn't like that comparison."

"You don't like doggies, do you?" Kat said to Steve, who was part of the conversation. "Really, he's more like a little man. I know everyone says that, but it's really true. He's a magical kitty who knew I was waiting for him at a magical store. He was just watching PBS News Hour when you rang."

"That's understandable. Pets like soothing voices."

"I gave him a bath yesterday without too much trouble. Like I told you on the phone, he escaped the house and went all the way to the Emporium while I was a work. He was so dirty when he got there. Who knows what route he took. Then he wouldn't get in the tub until I told him what I was doing; that if I didn't wash him, people were going to think he was a stray. Then he just submitted to it. Like he shrugged, 'Okay,' and wanted to be picked up and put in the tub."

"Cats don't need baths often," Jasmine said.

"I mean, he really *was* a stray, so..."

"You're right. I think he's saying something."

Steve was looking at Jasmine directly in the eyes.

"Cats don't really look people in the eye like this," Jasmine said. "Normally, they find it's too aggressive."

They took a moment to let Steve "speak."

"Then I brushed him," Kat said. "I find if he's resisting something the way cats normally do, all I have to do is explain what I'm doing and he seems to understand. I know it sounds crazy, but now I know why the ancient Egyptians worshipped cats."

"Do you mind?" Jasmine said, gesturing to the couch and

then sitting. "I just want to see if he..." Steve jumped on the couch, "...is curious about me."

He was. He walked across her lap, letting her pet him.

"He lets most anyone pet him on the counter at work, but he also sort of ignores them. In only a week he's become a cherished Consumerian. But besides me, he's only been actively interested in being held by Yksian. And now you."

"I thought you said he wanted to be with Kevin, too."

"He just wanted to hear him speak. He didn't approach him like this."

Steve made a second trip across Jasmine's lap and sat next to her.

"I love that the two of us need each other," Kat said. "I mean, we found each other when we needed someone most, but yet we're still independent. We're *interdependent*."

"He lost somebody, too," Jasmine said.

"You can tell?"

"Of course."

"He had a visitor at the store. Another cat." Kat looked at Steve. "Who was that kitty who came to see you?"

Steve looked at her.

"See?" Kat said. "He knows what I said. So, what's *he* saying?"

"Animals understand us better than we give them credit for, but we also anthropomorphize them, which causes us to further misunderstand them. It's a delicate balance."

"I mean, I learned he loves David Bowie."

"Who doesn't?"

With that, Steve leapt off the couch and walked toward the hallway.

"What do you want, Steve?" Kat said.

He turned and slowed.

"I guess we'll follow," Jasmine said, getting up. "But listen,

Kat. I know you've had a rough year, and Steve is a miracle, he really is. He's happy here, I can tell. He's telling me that. But I don't want you treating him like Jesse."

"But..."

"Not that I think you are; it's just something to watch out for."

"But what if it *is* him? What if he's actually Jesse?"

"He'll tell me. But in all my experience, whenever an owner thinks an animal is a dead loved one, it turns out it isn't someone they know."

They followed Steve into the man cave and he jumped onto the bar top.

"He found me and picked me to be his partner." Kat gestured at Steve. "Look at him. He's his own cat. This was all his idea, not mine."

"That part does happen."

Steve had one paw on a page of the faux-aged book, open to a drawing of a cloudless night sky along with the question, "Can Your Pet Read Your Mind?"

"That's not the page it was on," Kat said. "You think he's telling us something?"

"Cats can be psychic, so why not? We know animals can predict storms and earthquakes."

"Are you getting anything from him?"

Jasmine placed her palm on top of Steve's head. Rather than move away or encourage a full petting stroke, he held still and closed his eyes. Jasmine closed hers as well. "I'm not getting much...but...I think...I think he likes peanuts."

"Are cats allowed to eat peanuts?"

"Small amounts. Raw and unsalted. No shells, of course."

"I don't think he brought us back here to tell you he wants peanuts."

"Let me try some more."

Jasmine picked Steve up and they moved to the couch in front of the fire. She stroked him with her eyes closed, making a soft cooing sound.

"You're going to put him to sleep," Kat said.

"Shhhh." Jasmine seemed to hold her breath for a moment. "I was wrong," she said. "It's not a person he's missing, it's other cats. He wants you to help his friends."

"I'm not taking in a bunch of strays." Kat thought about last night. "That cat visitor he had may have been a stray. But they're gone now."

Jasmine was silent for a moment as she petted him some more. She gave up and opened her eyes. "That's it for today. I'm not getting a lot, but that's not uncommon for a first visit. He's not blocking me, and he doesn't have behavioral issues, so it may only take a couple visits to find out what he wants us to know."

"Did you bring the ladder?" Kat said.

"Oh yeah," Jasmine said, brightening. "I almost forgot."

They went out to Jasmine's SUV, Steve walking alongside them. Jasmine had brought over a five-foot carpeted cat ladder with three curved shelves for him to lie in. They brought it inside and placed it near the front door. Steve leapt up the steps to the top.

"My friend makes these," Jasmine said. "I want to sell them at the Emporium, but Connie says they're too big."

"Tell her it's a larger version of a witch's ladder," Kat said. "For cats."

"Maybe you can cast some spells into it."

"Not a bad idea," Kat said. "And I'll tell her Steve took to it immediately." He looked happy, the new perch giving him an aerial view of the house and of the front window, which would be more advantageous when the indoor lights were off.

Kat thanked her for the gift and Jasmine left.

Kat lifted Steve from the top branch and set him on the floor. "Let's do this," she said. She opened a pouch of catnip and said a few charms, sprinkling some into each of the carpeted steps as she went.

"One charm for long, healthy lives.

"One to love and be loved.

"And one to keep us safe from intruders." Hence the location near the front door.

Steve seemed to approve.

"It's all you now," she said, and Steve jumped onto the first step and rubbed his cheeks into the catnip in the carpet. She imagined Steve guarding the door from the top branch and jumping on an intruder, attacking their face.

Beware of Guard Cat. She should make a sign.

THIRTY-ONE

GIOVANNI

"Gio?" Linden said.

Giovanni was crouching in his makeshift cardboard boxer shorts, hiding along the side of Linden's truck in the parking lot of the school. He'd been moving around it to avoid being seen by people as they walked by. Fortunately, Linden had a parking spot in the shade near the backside of the building. Getting to it had been risky, and Gio wasn't about to move again. Too many watchful eyes.

Gio partially stood up. "I, um, I was..."

"Your boxers look a little worse for the wear," Linden said.

"...hoping to get a ride home." Gio also needed to go to the bathroom. He had peed behind dumpsters in an alley, but this was different.

"Were you out here all day?"

"It feels like it." He was sunburned in places he had never

burned before, and his arms and his wrists hurt from pinning the cardboard against his skin. "Took me a while to get here."

"Well, get in before I get fired."

Gio didn't want to explain anything. Finding your neighbor's nearly naked boyfriend hiding behind your truck at work waiting for a ride home wasn't a good starting point for a conversation. And actually *being* that naked man correlated with no logical, believable story.

"You know you could be arrested for this," Linden said as they drove.

Gio was happy they were in a truck, sitting them high enough so other drivers couldn't see into the car. "I'll explain later." He didn't plan to, unless something believable and non-incriminating came to mind. But as it was, he was trying to push everything as far away as possible. "When I know better."

"A naked man near a school is hard to explain."

So was turning into a cat.

"Try sitting on your cardboard, not the seat itself," Linden said. Dry. Maybe a sparkle in his eye, Gio couldn't tell.

Gio shifted self-consciously. He could smell wet cardboard from his sweat. He opened his window.

"Honestly, I don't know if I want to know." Linden's fingers waved as he spoke, his palms remaining on the wheel. "But I suppose this's better than going to jail."

"Thank you."

"When the cat's away, the mice will play."

Linden must've thought Gio was on a bender with Harper out of town. Gio laughed nervously by way of response.

They stopped at a light.

A homeless man stood on a street corner, his flattened cardboard box sign on the ground, waving his arms as if to direct Linden's plane to land. Gio wondered if the man's box was a 40-waist. The man's eyes were rapturous as he made noises that sounded close to English, but were just gibberish.

"The drugs people take these days," Linden said.

If Gio had been clothed with his phone on hand, there would've been no problem procuring a rideshare that morning. But his body and soul were naked and exposed, and to society he was the same as that man on the corner. The difference was having Linden to rescue him and a house to go back to. Now that he knew werecats were real, his doors of perception had been opened further, and maybe that man was a were-raccoon or a were-opossum. Nobody knew anybody else's plights.

"Heard some noises in your backyard last night," Linden said. "Sounded like something dying. As you know, we get a lot of coyotes in the neighborhood, but I don't know what that was. First, we find half a cat, then this. I've lost half my mind. Did you hear anything?"

"I wasn't home. I..." Gio let the statement dissipate like a wave crashing on a beach. Anything more would be a weak alibi. Wet sand. Linden probably heard his transfiguration. Saying nothing was easier than lying out of whole cloth.

Linden pulled into his driveway.

"Thank you so much for the ride, Linden. If there's anything..." This was a goes-without-saying moment.

"I'd say anytime, but," Linden said, hyucking softly, "no offense, but I hope I don't have to."

Gio was glad the driveways were next to each other. He scampered up to Harper's backyard, where he grabbed his clothes and phone. His packed carry-on was still on the patio, his keys still in his pants pockets. He went inside. His phone was dead, so he plugged it in.

MOTE:

Astrology begat Astronomy.

Relevant, he supposed, but not particularly helpful. It was less predictive than maybe taunting him.

He showered.

He returned to CSE later, dressed and human, but blistered, sore, and sunburned. According to his weather app, tonight was the real full moon, so he would likely become a werecat again. He suspected if he morphed the night before the full moon, he would the night after, too. Three nights.

He saw no sign of Steve at CSE. Well, he saw the food and water dish behind the front counter along the far wall. But no cat. And no Kat.

He asked the boy behind the counter where they were.

"That's Kat's cat," the boy said. He looked a bit like Buddy Holly. "She brings him in, but didn't work today. She should be here tomorrow."

"Great." Now what.

"You know, housecats aren't native to America," the boy said. "They were brought over from Europe."

Not really information Gio needed. He had timed his arrival so Steve could come out to the alley and watch him morph into a cat. Maybe there would be something to learn from it, then they could converse like Gio had with Cherry.

"Do you know where Kat lives?" Gio said.

"That's really messed up, man."

He was right. But if this kid only knew how fucked up it *really* was.

The streetlights had already come on, so Gio had to hurry

back to the house. He felt the first twinges of morphing as he drove and made a quick decision to reroute to his condo. It was closer than Harper's, but he still had to hurry.

He stopped at a red light, and when traffic was clear enough, he went through it. He also went through a stop sign at full speed.

He parked in a red zone and fumbled with his keys as the first full cramp hit. He could deal with a ticket. He had to get into his building while he still could. He stumbled up the front steps, holding his stomach, and collapsed in the vestibule.

Mr. and Mrs. Stavros were leaving for dinner and opened the door.

"Giovanni, you okay?" Mr. Stavros said.

"Just cramping," he forced out. "Got to get to bed."

He held up his keys as proof he lived there, but of course he did.

Mr. Stavros took that as a sign to grab his hand and help him to his feet. Gio stumbled through the door.

"Want us to take you to the hospital?" Mr. Stavros said.

"Nooo-ugh!" Gio said, halfway up the stairs, unsure what noise that was that had come out of his mouth.

"Be safe!" Mrs. Stavros said.

"Feel better!" Mr. Stavros said.

Near the top, he fell forward. He was shrinking quickly, stepping on the lengthy legs of his pants and tripping. He had to hurry. He hopped the last few feet, holding up his pants like he had with the cardboard earlier.

He was half-sized and tangled in clothes when he tried to work the lock and doorknob. He barely got it to work with hybrid hand-paws and pushed his door open. Once inside, he spasmed on the floor and painfully finished the transfiguration. When he was steady enough, he pushed the door the rest of the way closed with two paws, thankful nobody had walked by.

Night two of being a werecat would be spent at his own place. He wished he was at Harper's so he could talk to the other cats. His place was smaller. Two bedrooms, the second of which he used as his office. No dining room, just a living room with a dining table at one end. He paced, absorbing the scents and eccentricities of the human Giovanni. Finally, he curled up on the couch to think.

He could hear more of the neighbors' business than he wanted to. The walls weren't too thin; that was one of the reasons he liked this place. But they were built with human hearing range in mind. The neighbor behind the wall in the bedroom was playing a video game, and a high-frequency squealing was driving Gio crazy. This had to be above the human auditory threshold, or he would've noticed it before.

He was disturbed by a knocking at the door. It sounded invasive. An attack.

Then a second set of knocks. More impatient.

He fought the instinct to run.

Silence for a moment, then a third knock. Whoever it was must've heard him come home. Maybe they'd heard him morphing.

The door slowly opened. It was his neighbor, Henry Vellichor, from across the hall. He looked about the room. "Gio, you here?"

Keys jangled as Henry worked them out of the lock. He entered the apartment and toed the clothes a little farther from the door. "Hmmm.... Helllooo..."

Gio couldn't believe it. Henry had keys. Who knew how often he entered his place? Maybe he had a thing for Harper. Maybe for him. Gio was creeped out. Yes, a werecat was creeped out by a human. He may need to make a run for it. This fucker had keys to his condo.

"Oh, well," Henry called out, as if Gio were just in the bathroom or bedroom. "Your keys were in the lock, so I'm putting them on the shelf here."

He set the keys on top of a stack of mail, and turned the lock on the knob. He jiggled it and backed out, pulling the door closed with him.

Henry hadn't had keys, Gio had left them in the lock. The good neighbor he was, he was returning them.

In the morning, Gio changed back painfully, screaming into pillows, hopefully not too loudly. He was grateful to be home this time, with access to a shower and change of clothes.

He moved his car, which magically didn't have a ticket yet. Maybe it was still early enough in the day. It had been a horrible parking job. Crooked. His doors weren't locked, and his phone was still resting in clear view on the passenger seat. But now that he wasn't racing against the moon and his transfiguration, he was able to drive his car into the parking garage and his reserved space.

He went back inside and set his keys on the kitchen counter. He stared at them like he was expecting them to move. He poked at them. Nothing.

Swiped at them. Nothing again.

Then he slowly pushed them over the edge so they fell on the floor, crunchy-clank.

This was oddly satisfying.

Mote:

If change is constant, get ahead of it.

HE WOULD TRY to sleep more.

He felt exposed on his bed or couch. From his closet he dug out a coffin-shaped sleeping bag he had used while camping with friends a few years ago, pre-Harper. He pulled the couch away from the wall. He unrolled the sleeping bag, grabbed a pillow, and squeezed himself behind the couch where he could sleep, safe and protected.

CHAPTER
THIRTY-TWO

HARPER

Trekking. Back and forth. Harper supposed this was what animals did. They kept moving. She hadn't quite determined the bounds of her territory yet, but figured it would be influenced by food sources and how much ground she could cover comfortably in a day. She didn't want any particular human to see her more than once and recognize her, because that was the first step in getting caught. Black cats were memorable. And roaming felt good. Felt natural.

Spike was dead. He said he'd been in a fight with a bobcat near the house, the injuries of which she assumed were his cause of death. After hearing the noises in her backyard, she couldn't go home, either. Chico had told her the cats heard things at night, that the house was haunted, that there were creatures in the ravine. She'd been okay with people believing those things, but now she thought it really was more than just a bobcat roaming her property.

She hadn't fully adjusted to her new sense of time, and many hours could pass while she was focused on stalking or hunting. Her hunger shifted into something closer to the mindless creativity of honing an art or a skill. It was like fishing for a lot of people. Whiling away time, whittling it like a piece of wood.

She'd managed a kill this morning. A bird. Not a lot of meat, a lot of feathers, but feeling the crunch of the ribcage and sudden squishy silence of its warm little drum-major heart was, surprisingly, deeply satisfying. She was made for this.

Finding places to nap had been a cross between banal and fun. Routine and exciting. Sleeping in the sun felt good early in the day, but horrible in the afternoon. It was important to avoid people and regulate her temperature. She was getting the hang of it, though.

When she woke for a third time today, she was in the backyard of a house near the store L.A. Obscura in Burbank. The squirrels and birds were driving her crazy, wouldn't let her think. She wanted peace and quiet. They taunted her when she walked by, so she tried to make them uncomfortable in return. They scattered when she lowered to her haunches in a springboard pose.

The Own Won Now potion she'd taken at Consumia's Spiritual Emporium had almost completely diminished. It had helped her find endurance and shelter the last couple days, to become a more powerful cat. She was sure it helped her make her first kill. She decided to visit Dani, the tarot reader from CSE who owned L.A. Obscura. The store's name had always bothered Harper, as she wanted to change it into the contraction, L'Obscura. But Dani wanted it to be L.A., as in Los Angeles.

They were sort of sister stores, with CSE and L.A. Obscura being only a few miles apart (although Connie had nothing to do with Dani's store officially). Being a psychic, maybe Dani could communicate telepathically with Harper. It was worth a shot. Since L.A. Obscura didn't have Lodges, they weren't open as late. They closed at eight.

The secret to sneaking in a store with a customer, Harper had learned, was not to run at top speed. This attracted attention. It was to trot the same speed as the customer, just behind them. The customer never saw you. Then keep to the edges, the perimeter, when possible. Or under things. She had a new instinct for going unnoticed.

"Hi, Denkins!" Dani said, sitting on a stool behind the register eating Chinese food from a takeout box. "You're a bit early for the séance."

The man named Denkins stopped. "Wait," he said, thinking for a second. Then it dawned on him. "Oh, you're just spiking my drink. It's..."

"Tomorrow." Dani looked pleased.

"Tomorrow. Right. That makes me *really* early. I just need some colloidal silver."

"Over there," Dani said, pointing with the chopsticks.

Harper had been here a few times. It was smaller, neater, and cleaner than CSE, and even though it had been around longer, looked newer. The merchandise was better packaged: read mass-produced and distributed. No aftermarket items from estate sales repurposed with story cards containing Connie's magical tales.

Apparently that O'Cult guy was getting around. There was a display for his potion blends laid out in grid format behind sliding glass. As much as she wanted to eat more Own Won Now potion, she couldn't access it.

Dani took a took a bite of food, set down the chopsticks, dabbed her mouth with a napkin so as to not mess up her lipstick, took a sip of wine, then dabbed again. It looked like a time-consuming and annoying way to eat.

Then again, Harper rarely wore lipstick and didn't think it made people more attractive. To each their own. If lipstick made Dani, a post-op trans female, feel more like a woman, then more power to her. But Dani should've asked Harper about authoring a potion that could help her maybe round out the edges, so to speak. With a little research, Harper was sure she could've found something that encouraged a woman to blossom, no matter the starting point.

Dani set her food down to ring up Denkins. Her phone buzzed.

"Sorry," Dani said, silencing it. "They only call back when you're busy."

"Don't I know it! Or not at all!" Denkins had a hand on the black velvet L.A. Obscura box on the counter, fingers splayed, looking at his nails. "Do you think press-on nails would make a difference?"

"On you? Absolutely."

"I mean in the aura reader."

"No," Dani said. "Unless they change your mood, since that's what it measures, but the nails themselves, no. I've tried everything! Rings, polish, lotion. You should do it again. Your aura changes every day. It helps me decide what to wear in the morning."

Denkins didn't bite on the upsell. Dani rang him up.

"I'll see you tomorrow," Denkins said.

"Tomorrow," Dani said. "And wear the nails!"

After Denkins left, Dani picked up her phone. "Sorry, I was

with a customer," she said. "So, did you hear what Connie did?...

"Yes, yes, yes, she bought one. She said she wanted to support local business. Thank you, I said. I support you, too. But you know what she did with it?...

"No, I thought that, too. Maybe she'd break it out at a bridal party or something. No, she put it on their counter...yes, at the Emporium! And get this, she's not even charging for them!

"No, she's just collecting info. Like the Omnist doesn't do that already...

"Oh, you should've seen Connie. She was all smiles, so pleased to be supporting a likeminded business, she said. She didn't want the discount and insisted on paying full price...

"Because now it's like, why go to L.A. Obscura when you can get the aura pic for free at CSE? It's one-stop shopping...

"No, no, I'm not going to stop cross-promoting over there. I'm not that mad!...

"As a psychic I like to call myself an internal consultant...

"*Infernal* consultant! That's rich!...

"I'm medium. A medium medium. There's better, there's worse...

"Girl, strike that. There's no average in mediums. I'm *median*...

"I told you I'm not mad! It's just like, why's she gotta be so happy to promote me? It's just like, what a bitch!...

"No, you're right...I should just go home and drink a glass of wine and get some rest."

Dani hung up and poured herself some more wine. She poked around in the stir-fry looking for something in particular and took a last bite. It smelled delicious and complex. Chicken. Fat. Rice. Sauce. If Dani wasn't going to finish it, Harper would. But it may be dangerous for her to eat. Garlic.

Pepper. Salt. She'd have to restrain herself if it ended up in an accessible garbage.

If Harper ate anything here, it should be the O'Cult Own Won Now potion. And now that it had worn off, the human part of her was craving wine, maybe even more than the chicken.

Dani threw out her takeout boxes and walked her small wastebasket to the back of the store. Harper leapt onto the counter and began lapping at the glass of wine.

"What the hell?" Dani walked as fast as she could back toward Harper, her heels apparently slowing her down.

Harper startled and jumped off the counter.

"No, no, no, no. It's okay, kitty. I'm not mad at you." Dani slowed. "You just gave me a fright."

For the first time as a cat, maybe Harper hadn't annoyed the humans around her.

"What's your name?" Dani said. "How did you get in here? Did you smell my dinner? Are you hungry? I thought cats didn't drink wine." Dani wasn't allowing space for Harper to answer, but she did anyway.

"My name's Harper. I followed that Denkins guy in. Yeah, the chicken smelled exquisite. I'm learning cats don't need to eat three times a day, but we will if food is available. But I'm really a person, so I like wine. I took a few sommelier classes."

"You want to come back up here?" Dani patted the counter.

"Sure." Harper jumped up.

"You have the most amazing aura I've ever seen on a cat." Dani petted her. "I almost don't want to break it up with my hand. But...too late."

"I'm kind of not a cat, that's why. But I'm still a cat. You wouldn't understand."

"It's like you understand what I'm saying. And your eyes."

"That's what I'm trying to tell you."

Harper hadn't been affectionate as a human, but Dani's caresses were magic. Scratches, petting, Eskimo kisses that smelled like chicken and wine were feline divinity.

"No collar or tags. You're coming home with me. You'll like it there. There's another kitty for you to play with."

That's right, there was another cat's scent on her. She hadn't noticed through the powerful smell of chicken and perfume oil. She didn't want to deal with another cat. Another actual *cat*-cat.

"No, I don't want to go with you," Harper said. "I'm a natural loner as a person, and even more so as a cat. Can you help me change back? Or maybe crack open those O'Cult potions? Let's see what you guys got."

"Let me finish closing up." Dani petted her a little too hard, her rings grinding against Harper's vertebrae. "Then we'll go home."

Nope. Dani couldn't understand her. She may have been psychic, even good with animals, but she couldn't understand Harper.

It took Dani another ten minutes to wrap things up, then she tucked Harper under one arm and went out the door.

Harper hated being carried. When Dani shifted her from one arm to another to lock the door, Harper pumped her legs to free herself and ran away.

"Kitty! Kitty, come back! I didn't even get your name!"

THIRTY-THREE

GIOVANNI

That third evening, anticipating his werecat change, Gio found a parking spot a couple blocks down a side street from Consumia's Spiritual Emporium. He got out and hid his keys on top of his front passenger tire. Got back in the passenger side and let the door fall mostly closed, but not until it latched. He removed his wallet and placed it under the seat. He tested the door again, how much weight it would take to push himself out, whether it swung back and latched or fell open further. The interior light needed to turn off. When he felt comfortable with the results, he took off his jacket, shoes, and socks, and placed them on the floor of the backseat.

He considered but decided against removing the rest of his clothes. If a passerby saw bare skin, he'd be risking an arrest.

He thought about Thalia's tale of medieval transfiguration meditation which, short of prophesying, had somewhat described his situation. Jehri/Cherry, even though he had never met her as a human, could represent the wife, with him as the husband. He was a werecat. Cherry didn't turn human once a month, but close enough. Harper, of course, was the evil witch who cursed them all. But his life wasn't a fable or fairy tale.

He was on to something, though. He was close.

He killed time reading the news on his phone.

The first cramps hit him.

MOTE:

If it hurts, you're doing it wrong.

HE BENT FORWARD TO place his phone under the seat next to his wallet and stayed there to scream, muffling the sound between his knees and into his hands. He reminded himself to keep leaning forward as he shrunk so he and his clothes would keep to the floor.

Again, having done this before was no consolation. Each change hurt as excruciatingly as the previous. Maybe worse for expecting it. He must've been doing it wrong.

When the pain subsided and he was fully a cat, he pushed his way out the cracked door. He no longer possessed the human need for sidewalks, and cutting across lawns felt so much better on his paws. Near the Emporium, he ran underneath a car parked out front to watch the door.

He didn't have to wait long. When he saw a couple entering, a man holding the door open for a friend, he followed them through.

His olfactory sense were hit hard. The expected waft of incense, oils, and dust was met with an unexpected tsunami of human sweat, pet treats, herbal potions, jerked meats. And a familiar cat. He didn't fear Consumerians startling at a cat walking through the Emporium. There was already one there.

"Hey, Harper's friend!" he called out as he went down an aisle. He was blanking again on the name. "Here kitty, kitty." Maybe he shouldn't say that. Calling someone "Kitty" may be an insult from one cat to another. "Hey, man. JPL guy. Where are you? I can smell you."

"Giovanni, I was under the impression you were human," Steve said from high up on a shelf. Steve. He was Steve. He jumped down. It was quite a distance, like six feet. He was nonchalant about it. "I saw you change back."

"Here I am."

A loud and crackly series of firecrackers behind Gio startled him, sending him vertical. When he spun around in midair, he saw a child shaking an artisanal rattle.

"I gather you're not adjusted to feline hearing," Steve said. "That's a shamanic rattle. I heard Connie say she sells more of them when they're placed on lower shelves where children can reach them. But the chakapas are higher up."

"Am I supposed to know what those are?" His ear was itching, like the loud noise had shaken a waxy buildup loose.

"Chakapas are made from bundled leaves and twigs. They're not as loud, so not as interesting to children. Plus, they can fall apart if not handled carefully."

"She should put all of them up top." Gio imagined wiggling a claw in his ear.

"Let's go over here." Steve led them around a corner by the door to Connie's office. "So, how is it you're a cat again? What happened?"

"The moon got to me. I didn't know it was going to happen when I changed the night before last. Then it happened last night for the full moon and again tonight, so my guess is three changes per lunar cycle."

"Waxing and waning gibbous," Steve said.

"What?"

"Waxing full moon, full moon, and waning full moon. You're probably right about the three nights thing. I wonder why you morph, though. That doesn't happen to the rest of us."

"Apparently Harper turned me into a werecat. Do you think the moon affects her, too?"

"It may just be you, since you're the only one who morphed back into a human. She's still a cat. And I saw her the other day. I think she was surprised to see me. She told me she escaped from you."

"She did. I had her locked in the bedroom. How'd she know you were here?"

"She didn't. She was looking to find someone to change her back."

"So, you told her you'd help her?"

"No."

"Did she tell you Spike died?"

"He did? That ornery bastard. He left me alone, though, if I left him alone. And no, she didn't say anything. Just that he helped her escape."

"I was thinking maybe he freed her and then she killed him. Maybe they fought over who would be in charge of the colony."

"Meh. If she'd earned dominance by killing him, then why bother leaving? Or if she planned on leaving, why kill her conspirator? I don't know. I've been trying to forget that place. Her, Spike, all of it. And if I figure out how to change the rest of us back, I'll get in touch. Until then I'm comfortable camping out with Kat, the employee over there."

Steve was wearing a new black collar. Kat's sign of ownership.

"But that's why I'm here," Gio said. "To fix all this. What do you suggest I do?"

Some cats looked like they were thinking when they weren't. Take that look and add Steve's thinking brain to it. "Let's try this: When you're human again, look for a fermented grape elixir Harper keeps in a hutch in the front room. It's an old green bottle with a flip-top cap. There probably isn't much left. Then find this book of Harper's. Are you familiar with anthropodermic bibliopegy?"

Of course he wasn't.

"You're looking for a book with a cover made from human skin," Steve continued. "You can't miss the smell. It's so human. It's on the top shelf in the living room and has nothing written on the spine. Inside is the recipe for the potion."

"Out!" Connie said, suddenly, seeing Gio. "What's with all the cats in here all of a sudden? Steve, is this you? Are you attracting them?"

"Connie, don't," Kat said. "Steve's worked out just fine."

"One cat can stay. Steve! That's it. We're not an animal rescue."

Kat picked up Steve. "You're so popular, huh?"

"Before they kick me out," Gio said to Steve, "why'd you avoid me when I was here?"

"I didn't want you bringing me back to Harpy."

"I wouldn't do that. I encouraged you to leave. Then all this shit happened." Gio made the cat gesture equivalent to a human pointing at himself with both thumbs. It was a twitch of the whiskers.

Connie had retrieved a twig broom with a tag that said "Besom" and shooed Gio toward the door the way he'd seen done in cartoons growing up. If he'd been human, he'd have laughed at the ridiculousness.

"See you Gio!" Steve said.

"I'll come back!" Gio said.

Gio took the long way around the block to think, to burn off cat energy. One block turned into two, two into four. He couldn't eat; he didn't want to risk getting caught. He wandered for a couple hours, cutting through yards, making a star shape with his car as the center. A pentacle. Then he began to fear something would happen to his car with its cracked passenger door, an invitation for criminals, so he headed back.

The car seemed fine. He wedged his paw inside, then his leg, pushing until he could squeeze his entire body inside. He had a sudden vision of a person pushing the door closed and snapping a femur in two. He was amazed how tight of a space he could fit through. If his head could fit, his entire body could fit. He curled up in his clothes on the floor and tried to sleep. These last few days had been draining.

But he couldn't sleep.

His mind raced as he listened to the Doppler whooshes of cars passing by, or the footsteps and jingle of a person walking a dog, followed by the sound of wet sniffs nearby. Too close. Dogs always wanted to investigate the car. They would bark, alerting the owner to the travesty of feline presence. Mostly, this bothered him because the owner may notice a door ajar.

He should've burned off more energy before getting back in the car. He wanted to roam the neighborhood. He needed air and freedom and food, but he sucked it up. He stayed and suffered cat time displacement, where one hour felt like seven.

He heard a notification and stuck his head under the seat to look at his phone. He had forgotten to turn it off. He tapped the screen with his paw. It was blurry up close, so he pushed the phone out from under the seat. He tapped the screen again and jumped up on the seat to read the message from a distance.

MOTE:

If it feels like you're selling your soul, try selling it back to the power grid.

THAT DIDN'T EVEN MAKE sense.

THIRTY-FOUR

KAT

Connie and Kick were rarely at the Emporium these days, since setting up the Omnist II location was taking most of their time. The Omniscian Lucador was the third investor in that store, which cut into his time hosting Lodges the last few months. Therefore, tonight was a big deal.

"My first Lucadorian Lodge," Thérèse said. "Aren't you excited? We're getting so many hits on social media. This'll be my most popular event yet."

Not a difficult prediction to make, but Kat couldn't fault Thérèse for her enthusiasm.

"Even Kevin O'Culled's over there," Thérèse said. "It's got to be good when Omniscians support each other, right?"

"Might be a blade thing," Kat said. "Maybe he wants Lucador to make his bolines."

"What are those?"

"What's a boline?" Kat said. Kevin had talked about them the other night. "I think it's cow-related."

"Huh," Thérèse said. "Maybe we can make that an event. Put the two of them together!"

"Good idea!" Kat enjoyed seeing Thérèse get excited. "On a farm. With different knives and swords and farm animals."

"I love it!" Thérèse said. "Farms grow herbs for spells, too! Think I should say something?"

Kat nodded earnestly.

"Really? Think I should?"

Kat shrugged and turned away, bored, then watched Thérèse head off to interrupt Connie talking to the contrarian Consumerian, Stacy. She watched Connie's professionalism and subdued expressions while being inundated with bad ideas from an overenthusiastic publicist who may not have quite understood what CSE was about. She caught Connie looking over and Kat displayed her teeth.

"It was Kat's idea!" Thérèse said, turning to her, happy to share the glory.

Connie flagged down Lucador as he walked by and introduced Thérèse to him.

"HaHAA!" he said, slapping Thérèse on the back. "Now the public will know! The stars will shine! No one's to be left in the dark!"

Connie came to the counter, looking displeased.

"At least Thérèse loves this place," Kat said, predicting the source of Connie's concern. It was just a joke.

"You have to stop bringing Steve to work," Connie said. Steve was on the counter in his usual spot closest to the door. He didn't look over.

"Is this about Stacy?" Kat said. "She told us last week she's not that allergic."

"She heard about the other cats coming in. We don't need her posting a bad review."

"She wasn't even here when it happened."

"I know, but she's right. We can't have three cats in here if it's not a Jasmine Lodge, and if people are allergic…"

"It's not like he's going out and bringing other cats in," Kat said.

"He's doing something."

"Jasmine says he lost someone, probably his owner."

"I like Jasmine," Connie said. "She's a good pet psychic, but anyone could've made *that* prediction. I did. He's a stray. He probably lost a lot of things."

"I left him home the night of Kevin's Lodge and he escaped and came all the way over here to hear him speak."

"Try locking up the house better."

"I'm saying he likes listening to Omniscians."

Connie looked out over at the packed house of Lucadorians. "Look at the bright side. He wouldn't learn much tonight."

"What's he supposed to do at home?"

"What do you mean? What does any cat do?"

"Kill two billion birds a year? He doesn't do that. He's never outside except to get in the car. And he doesn't need a leash or a carrier. He just jumps in."

"Why don't you just take him home? Between Kick and Elijah and me, we got this covered."

TEN MINUTES LATER, they were in the car driving.

"I don't feel like cooking and I'm craving a salad from Greens Cafe," Kat said. "You?"

Steve had his head down on the passenger seat, but heavy

braking for a light made him push back with his front paws and sit up.

"Yeah, you wouldn't want vegan, would you?" She kept staring at him while they waited. "Fine, I'll heat us up some fish."

The light changed and they started moving forward again. "I don't know what's up with you, but something's going to happen, isn't it?"

Steve sat on the passenger seat, looking forward, probably only seeing the passing streetlights from that angle.

"I can feel it."

He lifted a hind leg and started licking his fur.

"Don't worry. You're still coming to work with me tomorrow."

THIRTY-FIVE

HARPER

An attempted catnapping by school kids a couple days ago, and then another by Dani today, had Harper throttled. She wanted to avoid the streets for traffic and animal control, backyards for kids and asshole dogs, and people in general who either wanted to save her or chase her away.

She was hungry and wished she had grabbed some of Dani's chicken stir fry while she had the chance, spices be damned. Although this morning's meal hadn't been filling, the catch was massively rewarding.

She was in the Rancho District at the southern end of Burbank. The wash of the L.A. River was largely paved through this area, and she knew better than to eat anything swimming in it. Other animals probably did. She wouldn't. But she followed the waterway along the top of the basin down toward Griffith Park, where she figured she'd find critters to hunt.

She crossed the basin at a dirt- and shit-covered bridge with a sign that said, "Cross Horse Bridge At Your Own Risk." She stepped her way carefully across and was surprised to smell feral humans and unfixed dogs here as well.

She went under the overpass for the 101 freeway. There was little traffic this time of day on Forest Lawn Drive or Zoo Drive near the Travel Town Museum. She cut into the park and immediately saw a clutch of rabbits grazing in an open field where she couldn't sneak up on them, and they'd be far too fast for her if she tried.

She almost caught a rat running along the edge of a trail, one of the little valley ones that looked like a mouse with round, protruding ears, but it dived down a hole to escape pursuit.

Deeper into the urban wilderness she came across three deer just up the side of the mountain. A doe and two fawns. They looked delicious and completely unattainable.

LATER, she saw at least four coyotes. They may have been hunting the deer, spread out and intimidating. They would definitely kill or eat her if they became desperate, but right now were more concerned with other game. She respected them. Their intentions were pure. This was their hunting ground. She had known for years about the famous mountain lion who lived in Griffith Park, all 4,300 acres of which was territory he had to share with the coyotes, and Harper sensed they left each other alone.

Tiring of her fruitless hunting and on the verge of giving up on food for the night, she went back underneath the 101 and over the horse bridge the way she'd come. She made her way through the equestrian area, something she'd never done before. Hay and horse manure were the primary scents quashing most human smells. The equestrian center was far larger than she'd imagined, some areas easy for a cat to traverse, others blocked with impenetrable walls.

Then, like a beacon, she smelled cooked fish in the breeze, and upon investigation discovered an overfilled dumpster behind a bar where they apparently threw away a lot of scraps. She wasn't the only one who thought this way. Her presence scattered mice and rats who had gathered beneath the dumpster. But chasing them would be too much work. She wanted the fish, the easy catch.

It was leftovers from fish tacos. Greasy, fatty sauces leaked out of the bags she clawed open. Dirty napkins were the worst. They smelled delicious but had exactly zero nutritional value.

It was humbling eating garbage from a bin. The tasty, tasty food was horrible for her, but she dug in like her life depended on it. Even when she tried to avoid people and live off the land, she couldn't escape contact with people's leftovers.

THIRTY-SIX

GIOVANNI

H e woke up lying naked in the backseat. His clothes were on the floor in front. He felt the sensation of all eyes on him as he reached between the seats, stretching out, providing a full moon for passersby. Putting on clothes in a car may have been a rite of passage in high school or college, but it represented a loss of dignity for a middle-aged professional.

Checking email on his phone, Gio saw a message from his HOA that there had been a complaint of a reported cat in his condo. No pets allowed in his building. No exceptions. This was his first warning. Bastards. But that had been him. Henry must've reported seeing him. He was allowed to be home.

When he arrived at Harper's house, he heated up pre-cooked food for everybody. He'd been out-of-pocket so much lately, no one had eaten consistently. He monologued to the three remaining cats about the events of the last few days and his experiences as a werecat. Saying these things out loud helped him straighten his thoughts out. And they needed straightening.

While the food was heating, he made a pass through the living room, looking at the shelf for the book Steve had mentioned. Many had no printing on the spine, but none were the right one. Either Steve had been mistaken, or Harper had hidden it.

"If I'm correct, I don't think I'm going to change into a cat tonight," Gio said while cutting the chicken on his plate. Chico, Jagger, and Cherry were all eating with him in the kitchen, the latter two sharing a bowl. "But I won't know for sure until after sunset."

With fewer cats now, he decided to wash all the bedding. As a cat, he'd learned how much everything around here smelled like Harper, and he imagined reducing some of that would enhance everybody's moods. He loaded the washer and thought about how Harper had told him Linden made the wooden mirror frame by the back door and the cupboard above the washer and dryer, plus the new box in the living room. The solid block of wood for the knives in the kitchen may have been him, too. How many items had he actually made in this house?

Maybe Linden knew more than he let on. Maybe he had previously been a cat or a husband. A sibling. There was that photo of him and Harper's mom as a teenager. Maybe he was the bobcat- a were-bobcat. As far as he knew, both Harper and Linden had lived their entire adult lives next door to each other. Alone but together.

∾

Gɪᴏ ᴡᴇɴᴛ next door and knocked on Linden's door.

"Nat Gio!" Linden said, suddenly sounding fake to Gio. Had he always been like this?

They arranged themselves in the living room with iced sparkling waters. A part of him expected bamboo straws. That would be so Linden.

The house was neat. It wasn't neat-freak neat, but organized. Neater than Harper's. It was apparent he'd made the coasters for the beverages. Likely the coffee table, too. His work was good.

"I assume you probably already know Harper isn't really on vacation," Gio said.

"I gathered as much." Linden looked relaxed. Pleased to have a guest.

"And you know she's a witch."

Linden swallowed, then smacked his lips. "I think seeing her bookshelves, candles, and herb garden makes that readily apparent." May as well have been talking about the weather.

"So, what else do you know?" Gio said.

"Me? I think the question is what do *you* know?" Linden knew a lot, apparently. This was no surprise. Still creepy, though.

"I don't know anything," Gio said. "And every time I learn a little bit, I realize what I didn't know just grew exponentially. I'm just trying to figure out what's going on."

"You sound afraid," Linden said, not unsympathetically. "But if you killed Harper, I'm not the one you should be worrying about."

The playful tone had left his voice. He wasn't joking. It went without saying that Giovanni had never been accused of murder before.

"She's dead?" Gio said. Why hadn't Linden led with news like that?

"Oh, no, I don't know. Oh, geez," Linden said, backpedaling. "I thought that was where you were going with this. God, I'm sorry."

"Fuck, no. Then she's around somewhere. I just don't know where."

"So that wasn't her out on the lawn?"

"The half-cat?" Then it hit Gio. "That means you *know* she changes people into cats?"

"I plead the fifth." His voice sounded like he was raising both hands in a stick up.

"Come on, man."

"Where we going?" Funny, not funny, Linden looked around as if there were witnesses listening.

"You just asked me if a dead cat was my girlfriend." Gio was done playing games. This conversation was going nowhere. Basically, Linden had admitted to knowing, but didn't seem to care.

"If it makes you feel better," Linden said. "I was afraid she'd turn *you* into a cat."

"Now, how's that supposed to make me feel better? She tried. I mean, she did turn me into a cat, but for some reason it didn't stick, and I came back and she didn't." Silence for a moment as he let that sink in. "And thanks for the help."

"Hey, I don't know how she does it. Who's going to get it next and when. And if I warned you a month ago, you think you would've believed me? Or maybe she'd turn and do it to me."

"Still."

"So if Harper's a cat now, is she the new one? What'd you call her, Minxy?"

"Yeah, but she's gone now. Escaped."

"Should we be worried, you might ask." Linden rubbed his palms on his thighs. "No, I say."

"I'm not really that worried about her. I don't care. I just want to change the others back. They don't deserve this. Me, though? I don't know. I wasn't the best boyfriend."

Rudy hopped up on the couch next to Gio, asking to be pet. He seemed older now, a mature dog in the sunset of his life. Gio scratched his ear and admired his open-mouthed grin. People always saw dogs as grinning.

"You're a good boy, Rudy," Linden said, reaching over to pet him as well. "And before you ask, no, Rutabaga's not a person."

"I wasn't going... Maybe... Yeah, I probably would've asked. When did you first suspect Harper's cat thing?"

"Mick was the first one that caught my attention. Calling a new cat Jagger right after she broke up with Mick. And they were always mature...'rescues.'" Linden made scare quotes with his fingers to emphasize the final word. "Hitting the nail a bit on the head there. The Stones, that's music from my era. She said Jagger was a replacement for Mick, to keep her company, but she already had Spike and Chico. How much good would a third cat do?"

"Not much." And Gio would've been the sixth. Even less important.

"I really liked her next boyfriend, Steve. No offense to you, of course, but he was brilliant. A literal rocket scientist. I wanted to warn him about the danger, but didn't know how. Didn't get a chance. You think he would've believed me either?

"And I didn't think a Jehri breakup was possible—they didn't seem to drive each other crazy. The way Harper talked about her, I could see them maybe staying friends if they broke up, with Harper showing her the ropes or something. Tending the garden together. At minimum, she'd have someone to help with the cats."

"But you guys stayed friends throughout all this. What about you?"

"Stayed *neighbors*. Friends is a strong word. She never knew how much I figured out about the cats."

"You wanted her to get them fixed."

"I didn't think about that stuff for a while at first. If she kept the cats in the house with no females around, eventually the people-cat lineage would've died off. But when Cherry came on board, that changed everything. Who knew what her kittens would be like? Could've been a whole new species of people-cats, I don't know."

"I don't think Cherry's ever been pregnant."

"Maybe she's fixed as a person, and that carried over. I don't know."

"So listen, I came over to ask if you knew how to help all of us," Gio said.

"All of us? You mean you, too?"

"All of us. I'm still a werecat changing with the full moon. That seems to be a lingering symptom. I changed last night and went to visit Steve at CSE. Wouldn't you have seen him there?"

"That's Steve? I'll be ding-dang-damned. Hadn't realized that. I haven't been by CSE since the last Coffin Club, but I remember Kat saying she'd found a stray that day." Linden leaned forward, hands on his knees. His hands moved less when asking questions. "Tell me something: How'd you not notice Harper's a witch?"

"Being a witch isn't an issue. Witches aren't evil."

"I'll rephrase that: How'd you not notice *she's* evil?"

"I was just trying to keep my head down," Gio said, rubbing the back of his neck. These transfigurations had been murder on his body. "Trying not to piss her off. And I was happier with her than without her."

"It's dangerous to lay your head down near someone who's trying to chop it off."

"True."

"Do you think she cast a spell to make you fall in love with her?"

Good question. He hadn't thought of that. "Despite her faults, I don't think she'd do that. Her ego wouldn't let her. Vengeance, though, is a different beast."

"So, tell me. How'd she do it?"

Gio recounted the anniversary dinner, what he knew about the potion, and what Steve said about the book. "I looked for it where Steve said it should be, but didn't see it. Could it be something you may have borrowed?"

"Good god, no. She wouldn't even let me walk out the back door with a glass of water. The glass had to stay in the house."

"Yeah, she's like that with everything."

"Well, it may not amount to much, but I'll help where I can."

They went back to Harper's house, where they looked inside every item in the front room, and on an eight-shelf unit overfilled with books, trinkets, bones, and taxidermy. They discovered other writings and drawings, much of it incomprehensible.

Jagger hopped on the back of the couch and onto the credenza. He rubbed his face on an ancient-looking clasped wooden box.

"Jagger, you want me to open that?" Gio said.

"I made that," Linden said. "Probably twenty years ago."

"It looks older."

"I used weathered wood, parts I separated from a horse-drawn harvester I found on a farm up past Bakersfield."

It was gorgeous. The wood apparently hadn't been sanded, or only roughly so, but was oiled to hold its age. The inside was laid out in a grid of compartments, eight by eight, two levels deep, most of which were filled with herbaceous powders and tinctures.

Gio picked one out and uncapped it, looking for familiarity.

"Careful, you may not want to inhale some of those," Linden said.

The vial Gio held was labeled in Harper's nearly indecipherable longhand. "I think they're alphabetized. Not all are labeled, but we can probably figure them out if we need to."

"You see one that says it's for changing a cat to a human?"

"Ha. No. But I was hoping there'd be a recipe in here or something." Gio got down on his hands and knees and looked under the couch and television bureau. "Even if Steve's directions were vague, there's no way we could've missed it. We checked everything."

They split up for smaller searches throughout the house. Gio checked the utility room closet and drawers.

"Hey Gio," Linden said, standing on a kitchen chair in front of the open hallway closet. "Come check this out."

He was holding a dark green bottle with a flip-top cap from the top shelf. It was exactly how Steve had described it.

"Can I see that?" Gio said.

Linden gently handed the bottle to Gio, who tried to flip the top. Then a little harder. He finally wrestled the cap off and was nearly knocked over by the stench. It triggered a reaction in him. He clutched, buckling over, stomach cramping, and nearly vomited. "Aauugghh!"

"Are you okay?" Linden said, still on the chair as he reached a hand down to Gio's shoulder. "Are you about to change?"

"No," Gio coughed. He stood up and pressed his fist into his kidney, stretching. "Muscle memory, I think. This is definitely it."

"That's great news! We have the potion!"

241

"It's not all of it though. There's more to it. We still need the book."

"You mean this?" Linden handed a book to Gio. "It was with the bottle up here."

This was it. He knew it before opening. Untitled, floppy but sturdy. Worn but undamaged. Its condition was too good for its apparent age. Now that he'd learned to think this way, he figured Harper or someone else had cast a preservation spell on it. *So this was what human skin looked like.* It didn't look or smell any different from common leather, but he also wasn't a cat at the moment. He wished Steve hadn't told him that; he would've assumed it was bovine.

Cherry excitedly rubbed against his legs in a figure-eight and other more complex patterns. She recognized the book, too.

The book was nearly indecipherable. Old English and words and spellings Gio didn't understand. Even the drawings didn't seem to help. Maybe Steve could understand it.

"Funny," Linden said, craning his head. "I wouldn't've taken Harper for a scholar."

"You'd have to be one to understand this. I guess it's time for me to go get Steve."

Linden went home.

Mote:

Remember, Alchemy begat Chemistry.

The Omnist was Moting confidence.

Gio brought the book to CSE, saw Steve on the counter, and browsed items down an aisle until Kat was distracted with a customer. Steve had seen him and walked to the end farthest from the register and front door, and waited there. Gio came over and laid the book down. "This is the right one, right?" he said.

Steve stuck his nose under the cover like he was trying to open it.

"Swipe the page with your paw when you want me to turn," Gio said. "Then the standard tap once for yes, two for no." He turned to what he believed to be the correct section of the book.

Steve kept backing away to read, and Gio figured out he had to tilt the book up for him read at about a two-foot distance. Steve swiped the counter for three consecutive pages to be turned. He started hopping at a page as if trying to tamp out a fire with his front paws.

"This is it? You found it?" It looked as miserable to read as the other pages.

Steve pranced back and forth on the counter. A starburst of white chest fur led the way.

"What are you doing with my cat?" Kat had finished with her customer and walked over. Gio was leaning with his elbows on the counter while Steve sat and looked at her. She was wearing a shirt that read, "Witches, Bitches." It was Thalia's brand.

"Nothing," he said. "He's remarkable. The smartest cat I've ever known."

"I agree." Kat looked at Gio in disbelief, as if he were pitching a misaligned product for the store. "He is."

"Can I borrow him for the night?" This was more of a statement than a question.

"No. Of course, not. What kind of person comes into my store and asks to take my cat? I shouldn't have dignified that with an answer."

"Did you know he can read?" He knew he sounded crazy.

His cheek itched the way a nose itched. He caught himself wiggling his cheeks so he wouldn't scratch them with his hand. He didn't have whiskers. Somehow the idea of reaching up with his paw, revealing to Kat that he was a cat, horrified him.

But he wasn't; he was human. He sniffed, then rubbed his face with the back of his wrist, safe now. She looked at him intently, like she could see whatever was bothering his face.

"You know, I've been here before..." he said.

"I know. I've seen you hovering around and freaking out Steve."

Her look could speak cat. Gio had to change gears. He wasn't begging; he was explaining an impossible situation. "I'm Gio, by the way."

"As in geothermal or geopolitical or something?"

"As in Giovanni."

"Kat." She didn't offer a hand. Her arms weren't physically crossed, but they were in her tone of voice.

"You didn't name him Steve, did you? He had a leather and twine collar with that name on it. And he showed up just over a week ago—what, nine days ago?"

This seemed to catch her off guard. "You're saying he's your cat?"

"Not exactly, but I know him. I know where he lives. Come with us. I just need him to watch me make a potion, cast a spell, make sure I'm doing it right."

Speak to the Thalia in her, like her shirt; that was his only hope. Still, it was weird asking a pretty store employee to come home with him. He could get banned from here. Or worse, have the cops called, and then banned. At least he wasn't behind the store right now, naked and covered in cardboard.

"What?" Kat said.

"You know how he listens when you talk? Understands

things even you don't? Look at him right now. He knows everything we're saying. And he can read. He can read this book better than either of us."

"Is that one of ours?"

"No, but Steve instructed me how to find it at his house and bring it here. He knows what it is. I need him to make sure I'm making the potion right."

"Let me get this straight. You're saying my cat's a witch? You're saying he knows how to make potions."

"Somewhat. He's more of a scientist, really. You'll see what I mean."

"Why not ask someone like Thalia or Kevin? You were here. Why didn't you ask them? Yeah, Kevin is a potions guy."

"I did talk to him, and he wasn't much help. If I went any further detailing the problem with him, he'd just say we took the wrong drug, or that we're moving in the wrong reality." Gio reached down and petted Steve. "I've known Steve for a year now. He's a good dude. And you can meet his other friends."

"Well, he's a stray." Kat was thinking, sounded resigned. "I figured it was only time until his owner found him."

"Oh, his owner? She's gone. And I don't think Steve would choose to stay there, anyway."

Steve was reading a page in the book.

Kat was less cold, more amenable now. "A pet psychic did tell me Steve wanted us to help his cat-friends."

"Exactly. I'll take you to them."

CHAPTER
THIRTY-SEVEN

KAT

S teve had been staring at a page in the book while Kat and Gio were talking. He swiped his paw and Gio absentmindedly flipped it to the next. Then Steve head-butted Kat's forearm. She made a gesture to pet him, and rather than duck under her hand, he jumped down and trotted toward the back of the Emporium.

"I think he wants us to follow him," she said.

In the Dark Arts room, he leapt on the counter and sniffed around the displays of potions and crushed herbs and insects.

"Which one do we need?" Kat said.

Steve stuck his nose into an empty slot on the case.

"What was there?" Gio said.

"I'm trying to remember," Kat said. "We sold so much stuff after a week of Organica, Thalia, and Kevin Lodges. We're out of a lot."

"Let's see this again," Gio said, opening the book. "Maybe we can figure it out."

As he said that, a small business card fell out of the book and fluttered to the floor.

Kat picked it up and read it. "Oh, I know these guys. They're a rare herb and curio distributor downtown." She tapped the card on the empty display slot. "It was powdered cat saber. That's what was here."

Steve rubbed against her arm.

KAT FELT COMPELLED to go with Steve and Gio. Jasmine had already warned her about believing Steve was possessed by the spirit of Jesse, but the truth was odder still: Her cat was a scientist. Or a witch-scientist.

She grabbed her jacket from the office, then consulted with the kid, Elijah, about leaving him there to run the store.

"I'd be happy to close for you tonight," Elijah said dreamily, seeming only to focus on petting Steve, as if he'd learned in a how-to book that directing your attention to a girl's pet would make her like you. Elijah did that sort of thing.

"Thank you," Kat said.

"I wish he could stay, though," Elijah said. Steve tolerated the caresses, but Kat could swear he was making a gagging face. "Your boyfriend—" in his most velvety voice— "has been so patient."

Okay. Done.

Steve jumped off the front counter and headed for the door. He walked out confidently when Gio opened it for them. He was wasting no time. Once outside, Steve ran ahead of Gio and waited by a car about a block away. He knew which car to go to. Gio opened the door and Steve jumped in without hesitation. She had to make a quick decision. Strange car, strange man. She could follow in her car, but Steve would be in another.

"Steve," she called. "Come ride with me."

Steve didn't move, but stared at her from the passenger seat.

"Go with your mommy," Gio said, then looked at Kat. "Does Steve call you Mommy?"

She could see the expression of mortal pain in Steve's eyes.

Kat opened the passenger door and leaned inside to pick up Steve, who avoided her by jumping into the back. He wasn't going to get out. Kat relented and got in the passenger seat. "I guess we're going with you."

"I promise not to be a creep," Gio said. "First, I think we should go downtown to buy the saber. Are you okay with that?"

Why not.

Traffic wasn't too bad on the 5 South. Traffic looked worse in the opposite direction, with people commuting home after work.

"So, Steve," she said, turning in her seat. "You know this guy, huh?"

"We used to have the same girlfriend," Gio said.

That's not weird. "Let him say it."

Steve said nothing.

"Not at the same time, of course," Gio said. "I don't think he ever called her Mommy, though."

There was a scratching noise on the back of Gio's seat.

"Hey!" Gio said.

Steve stopped. They rode in silence for a while.

"Steve," Gio said. "Linden brought you guys over a coffin box casket thingy to play in. You can tear that up instead of my seat."

"You know Linden?" Kat said.

"How many are there?"

"Oh, there's only one. And if you know him, you know him."

"Steve lives next door to him. Linden's helping with the potion."

If Steve hadn't already eased her mind about this impromptu journey, then Linden's involvement did.

They arrived in a section of downtown Los Angeles where there was little foot traffic. A lot of aluminum garage doors, many of which had already been closed. Multiple languages on hand-lettered signs. Gio pulled the car up to a loading zone.

"I know this place. I've waited right here when Harper ran up to ring that bell." He got out of the car, door chiming, and jogged up to a windowless steel door and pressed a button. After a moment, he rang again.

He jogged back to the car.

"Fuck. They're not there," he said when he got back in. He pulled back into traffic. "We're too late."

Kat was thinking. She knew what to do. "Turn right, right here," she said after a block. "Pull over."

Gio pulled into an alley and stopped the car.

"Give me the money," she said.

"What money?"

"For the saber. Hurry. They're cash only."

Gio gave her a hundred and she got out of the car and walked back around the block, up to the door, and rang the bell. She knew they were looking through the camera above her. Good day to wear Thalia's "Witches, Bitches" T-shirt. Kat squeezed her eyes impatiently and sighed, blowing upward at her bleached bangs.

The door buzzed.

Four minutes later, she returned to the car, handing a small, folded paper bag to Gio.

"They were there?" he said. "I thought they left for the day."

"Yeah, no, that's not how they work."

"What, they didn't like how I looked? I don't look like a gangbanger. I'm not going to hold them up."

"Worse," she said. "You look like a cop."

If cats could laugh, she heard evidence of snorting from the back seat.

As they pulled up to Steve's house, she saw Linden Vowel in the yard next door. He looked less like he was doing yardwork and more like he was holding a rake waiting for them to pull up. Steve jumped out of the car first.

"Giovanni, I see you're still bringing home cats," Linden said. "Kat."

They had that awkward greeting between work acquaintances outside of their place of employment where they didn't know if they should shake hands or hug. Or nod. She wasn't a hugger, so the compromise was that they patted each other with one arm.

"Didn't realize you had such a unique neighbor," she said, referring to Steve.

"I always imagined that's what people said about *me*," Linden said. "Hey Stevie-boy. How ya doing lil' buddy?" Steve passed under Linden's outstretched hand.

"I figured you guys all knew each other," Gio said.

"His Coffin Clubs are the bomb," Kat said.

Linden stood up straight, pleasantly surprised, taken aback.

"But I'm not decorating a box yet," she said. "I don't care what anybody says. Too soon."

"I told her it'd be a great coffee table until it's needed for its other purpose. Did she tell you about her cremains bar? A coffin would look great in there by the fireplace. It'd really tie the room together."

"I thought you said it wasn't a coffin until it was occupied," Kat said.

"Pedantic trivium. Semantics intended to encourage the crestfallen," Linden said, his eyebrows stretching with his vocabulary. "How about calling it a 'personally flaired sarcophagus serving as a temporary refectory table'? Put a piece of glass over it if you want to protect the finish."

"I'll admit, it sounds a little better now than it did seven months ago," Kat said. "Black and purple, maybe. Or black and crimson."

Steve was impatiently walking circles around them. He shoulder-butted Gio, nudging him toward the house.

"I think it's time to head inside," Linden said.

CHAPTER
THIRTY-EIGHT

HARPER

H arper sat on the hood of a car that'd recently been
parked and groomed herself with long strokes. She
liked how the warm engine felt underneath her.
Her skin was both more protected by fur than she'd
expected, yet more sensitive. Every hair provided a sensory
explosion for the skin, and in this case, it was relaxing. She
could sleep here, right now, right out in the open. She
predicted it would get hot later and the car would shift from
being a useful source of warmth to a useful source of shade.
She'd developed a better sense for weather prediction, just like
her sense of direction had improved. The clouds would burn
off soon, and the late fall sun would be blazing.

She wouldn't stay here long, anyway. She didn't feel safe
anywhere for long. She had never needed friends and could

take care of herself, but that was easier when she had a roof over her head and locks for the doors.

And she did miss the other cats—Spike, Chico, Jagger, Steve, and Cherry. Spike was gone; she'd smelled his grave. Those were her friends.

Okay, and maybe she didn't miss Steve so much. He wanted nothing to do with her, and had a decent setup with Kat and CSE. He had learned how to be happy as a cat, using his skills to his advantage, and maybe she should do that, too. Maybe Steve's implication had been correct. Inadvertently or not, his actions showed he believed that the best you could hope for as a cat was to pick your own prison, and the prison he chose was nowhere near Harper.

But most of all, she missed Cherry. Harper had briefly seen Chico and Jagger after Spike had opened the bedroom door, but not her. Maybe Cherry had been avoiding her. Harper wished she had looked for her before leaving.

She also wished she had a soft brush with which to groom. The little hairs on her tongue helped tremendously, but as a young girl it had felt so nice when her grandpa would brush her hair while they watched television. She wanted this now.

Cherry.

She wanted to brush Jehri's beautiful red hair.

She remembered their promise about the BFF pendant tattoos: A broken heart cut in half, with a different half on each of their chests. No necklace needed; a tattoo was as permanent as their love was at the time. She wondered if she'd had that tattoo, would the fur on her chest have grown out in those colors, a furry projection of their enduring love?

The original idea had been tacky and immature, spurred by the chemical high of new love, but the reasoning now was profound. Harper was feeling heartbroken, possibly for the first time in her life, as if half her heart had been ripped out in lieu of a pendant, and she wanted to look down and see that the tattoo had been real, and that they'd really said and believed those things. She wanted proof that those events had really happened.

Maybe the Own Won Now potion had been the problem, prolonging her inevitable dive into despair by overdosing her with confidence. This was the way she should've been feeling this entire time. This wasn't a potion hangover. This was how she felt.

Spending that day with a simple house cat had been the best day she'd had in as long as she could remember, probably since Jehri had been a person. But that kitty hadn't been Cherry. Not even close. Kitty had been, well, not dumb, but... naïve. Innocent. She was a true housecat, living in as close to feline nirvana as her owner could provide. She was a kitty enjoying a life of an adult kitten. And if that was the goal, good on her.

Harper had always considered herself a pet owner like that, someone who provided a soft enjoyable life for her exes, cooking their food, protecting them. She didn't force affection upon them. The spells she cast were always for their own good, and if she had known to research a spell to psychologically make them kittens, instead, like that kitty, she would've cast it.

She could return home. When Spike had been the dominant cat, he would've protected her if she returned. But that was no longer possible. It was likely either Chico or Jagger were alpha now, and both seemed to be harboring human grudges against her. If she had to guess, Chico would be top cat—reasons being that he'd been a cat longer and was more prone to hierarchical thinking as a human. Jagger was too much of a free spirit to concern himself with territory as a possession.

Gio was a question mark, as well. Would she be allowed to

roam free now like the other cats, or would he lock her in the bedroom again? There were other reasons she was returning, none because she loved him. This must have been how the other cats had felt. They didn't love her. They called her Harpy.

She likely wouldn't be welcome, but she needed to find Cherry and convince her to leave. They could handle the city better as a pair, and with Cherry's beauty, the kindness of strangers was assured.

It took all day to get home. Traffic was heavy and crossing roads was dangerous. As soon as she could, she darted into ravines, a slower but safer journey away from people and cars. She climbed up to her backyard. Spike's grave was more settled, and other, larger cat prints had trekked across it. A bobcat, possibly. They had a muskier smell. More primal.

Predictably, the back door was open, and the lights in the kitchen were on, but those in the laundry room were off. She approached slowly and carefully, ready to flee at the slightest sign of danger. She was listening with her ears, the pads of her paws, and her fur. She sensed other cats as she tip-pawed through the door. The old house smelled like home. Recent cooking. Gio. Cherry. She smelled Cherry. She was still there.

Unsure who exactly was in the kitchen, Harper darted into the darker laundry room.

She heard the landing of little feet, the trot of pads, then Cherry appeared at the door to the kitchen.

"Harper? Where have you been?" she said. They touched noses gently, both slightly inhaling, a much better Eskimo kiss than Dani's had been. Soft, tingling, cold, and damp. She smelled beautiful. She'd eaten delicious chicken much earlier. Nobody could beat Cherry.

"Long story." Harper realized how much she missed the telepathy of familiar cats.

"Are you looking for Gio? Or Steve? They're making a potion to change us back."

"Just plain old coming home. I miss you more than you could know." She caught a whiff of the human attendance. She could smell Linden, too. "Wait, Steve's here? I thought he moved to CSE."

"He did. Gio brought him over with some girl from the Emporium."

A loud noise caused Cherry and Harper to wince low to the ground as if being attacked by a flying object. The falling object in the kitchen had been small and heavy, and rolled on the floor. A pestle.

"Damn it!"

Harper knew that voice. It was Kat.

"And you heard about Spike, too?" Cherry said. "Gio buried him after you left. Did you come back to be the boss?"

The boss? That meant nobody had claimed dominance yet in the colony, if three unrelated cats could be considered a colony. Maybe with four.

"No. I came back for you," Harper said. "Just for you."

People were talking ten feet away around the corner, and certain named ingredients were catching her ear. As a cat, she realized how much more she liked Linden's voice. She'd never noticed that before. He was a natural orator with good intentions.

"Let's get out of here," Harper said. "We don't need them. There's so much out here for you to see."

"Why would I want to do that?" Cherry said.

"I don't trust Gio."

"I don't understand. It's your house and he's trying to help us."

"I'm well aware it's my house, but look at me. I don't think I'll be able to prove it in the court of law."

"I don't think he wants it. The last few days he's been gone as much as he's here taking care of us. He tells us everything he's thinking, especially when he's cooking."

"He cooks now?"

"Changes the litter every other day."

"I'm sure he's still angry. He's just going to lock me up again."

"I doubt it. You know that was my idea, right? I told him to lock you in the bedroom when I saw you guys changing."

"Why?"

"I didn't want you to leave. I was afraid I'd lose you and I wanted him to change us back first. And I was right, Harpy, you did...you did leave."

She shivered at the mention of the name Harpy. It was cold and cruel. "Call me Minxy," she said. "And I did come back."

"Minxy. Minxy. Isn't that what Gio used to call you?" Coming from Gio it had sounded obtuse and brutish. Coming from Cherry it sounded sexy and suave. "Yeah, I heard him call you that."

"It doesn't remind me of him, if that's what you're thinking," Harper said. "When you say it, I imagine you curled up on my pillow. Your fur breathes and I smell its breath. It's how I want to be. Unless you like another name better."

"No, Minxy works. And you can still call me Cherry."

The humans were getting louder in the kitchen. They had figured out another ingredient from the nearly illegible handwritten book. There was no way they could do this. *She* barely could. She imagined them turning the entire house into a giant ox.

"But why did you stay with me at all?" Harper said. "I thought you hated me."

"I never hated you, Minxy. I was confused, and you were jealous, but it was that last meal that kept me around."

The only real meal she had cooked for Jehri, made horribly on purpose to cover the flavor of the potion. Harper was positive that was the worst-tasting meal ever fed to a chef. Proof that Cherry still had her sense of humor.

"And then, I don't know," Cherry continued. "Nothing you cooked for us was ever that bad again. It's hard to be that terrible. You were trying."

And right on cue, Harper smelled the base in the kitchen. They were performing the final steps of combining the ingredients. It was far more pungent as a cat, but also more attractive.

"It was the potion," Harper said. "I was afraid you were going to leave me and I didn't want you to."

"Same," Cherry said.

They'd each tried to lock the other into their lives. That meant they were destined to be together forever. Locks weren't needed if both parties were there willingly.

"The adults in there are trying to save us kids," Harper said. "I came back because the thought of you avoiding me as a cat made me sick to my stomach, so when the potion's ready, you drink it with the others. I'll stay a cat. As my punishment. Karmic retribution."

"I don't know why you call it punishment. Being a kitty isn't as bad as you think."

"Especially if I get to have you taking care of me."

"Then maybe we should both stay kitties."

"No, we need someone to take care of us. Take care of the house. We shouldn't have to fight for food. For our space. For our peace of mind."

"This is it!" Gio said from the kitchen. "Here, smell this! Tell me it isn't the same!"

"Let's go!" Cherry said. "They have the potion."

Every hair on Harper's body went on edge. Her tummy hurt

from the greasy and spicy fish leftovers she ate last night. The exes were about to become human in the kitchen. She couldn't leave the laundry room until Jehri was back and able to protect her.

She wanted to watch the transfigurations, but if the potion didn't work, she didn't want to reveal herself, either—especially to Gio, whom she still didn't trust. Cherry wasn't lying to her about him, but she also tended to see the best in everyone. Cherry couldn't possibly see how someone could hold a grudge.

"Come on!" Cherry was bouncing like a kitten. "We can be human again!"

"I'm going to stay here," Harper said. "Come get me when it's done."

"I've never seen you look scared before."

"Just promise me you won't drink it first. Make sure it works. I couldn't handle if anything bad happened to you."

Harper stayed in the laundry room, listening intently as Cherry joined the others. This was exciting. Her heart rate was rapid-fire, but she felt like she could adjust it by will, lowering her respiration and blood pressure so she could pick up sonic details farther away. Her finely tuned hunting instincts honed by evolution were now employed for eavesdropping on humans.

"Put it in this," Gio said. The sound of liquid pouring from one vessel to another.

"Ready, Steve?" Kat said. The sound of a dish sliding across the floor, followed by cat lapping.

"Barely better than my own cooking," Linden said. A few more laps. "Don't all laugh at once; I was kidding. That's got to taste so bad."

"It does, trust me," Gio said.

The lapping stopped.

"I didn't mean for you to stop," Linden said. "That's what she s—...oh never mind."

Kat snorted.

Silence for a few moments as they were waiting for the morphing to begin.

"Well?" Kat said. "Anything, Steve?"

Another moment of silence.

"Did he drink enough?" Kat said.

"Give it a second," Gio said. "It took like a minute before I noticed something was wrong."

Silence for another few seconds.

"Feel anything?" Kat said.

Two taps of a paw on the floor.

"It's not working," Linden said.

"You think we got the directions right?" Gio said.

One tap.

"I don't get it. If we got the potion right, why didn't it work?" Kat said.

"Story of my life," Linden said. "Bad ideas that work and good ideas that don't."

THIRTY-NINE

GIOVANNI

He'd had a feeling in his bones the previous few nights, the way some people felt the weather. Something akin to barometric pressure in arthritic joints. And he hadn't felt that this evening. His tooth hurt, but that was it. He played with it with his tongue, then caught himself poking it with the tip of a finger and stopped. Mixed company didn't want to see that.

He looked outside at the moon, which proved to him the curse was effectually three nights per month. "It's official," he said. "I'm not changing tonight."

Linden was pacing. "That's good, I think. But I have to admit, I'd like to see it. What size box do you think you should decorate?"

"Seriously?" Kat said.

"He's just joking," Gio said. "I'd do both sizes, Linden, just in case."

"Two boxes. Smart," Linden said. "Good way to keep busy."

Gio sat down at the kitchen table and put his face in his hands. He didn't want to spend the next decade or more caring for cats. And they'd rather be human again. His eyes and the back of his throat were itchy, which meant the allergies were back. They had subsided for three days. He needed to stop touching his face.

A tiny paw tapped at his shin. Steve was crouching at Gio's feet, preparing to leap. Gio sat straight up to give him room to land on his lap. He thought about how, pre-anniversary, Steve had never asked for attention. Always kept a respectful distance. This was a first.

"Well, at least you have Kat," he said to Steve as he petted him. "You can be king of her house." He looked to Kat for approval. She looked worried and sad. The weight of this was affecting everyone.

Steve stood on his rear legs, front paws on Gio's shoulder, and tried to smell his mouth.

"I haven't eaten in forever. Nothing to smell, buddy."

A little paw reached up and tapped his lips once. Once for yes. Gio closed his mouth and let him do it, shaking his head, teasing him.

Steve opened his own mouth and tapped Gio's lips again.

"You said he's a scientist, but look at him," Gio said out of the side of his mouth. "He's a little dentist now."

"Do it," Linden said. "Open up and say 'Ahh.'"

"I don't want to. I actually have a toothache."

"Seriously," Kat said. "You asked me to trust Steve, now you should, too. Just open up."

Gio opened his mouth and Steve's little face got right up to it. Gio smelled the residue of the potion in the cat's mouth, so he held his breath. A paw reached in and touched the bad tooth. Gio pushed him away.

"I get it. You can smell my rotten tooth. Another thing I have to take care of."

"No, no, no! Steve's right!" Kat said. "A human tooth! For the potion!"

"Why?" Gio said. "The recipe says cat saber."

"Right. Cat teeth and cat fur changes a human to a cat."

"So human hair and teeth changes a cat to a human!" Linden said.

Gio went to the front room to retrieve the wooden potion box Linden had made. They'd found pulverized cat hair in it earlier, but there was nothing related to human teeth or hair.

"I've got an idea," Linden said. "I'll be back." He left the house.

In the meantime, Gio's tooth still hurt. He needed a proper dentist. He'd already taken a double dose of ibuprofen when they got home.

"Fuck it," he said, and took a third dose from the bottle on the counter. Six capsules in an hour. Not good for him, but neither was the pain. There were still a few bottles of unopened Bordeaux from the case Harper had bought. He opened one, but the smell made him feel ill. He was just getting over being sick from a potion that had this in it. He didn't retch like he did when he'd smelled the elixir, but it was still palpable. He recorked the bottle, then thought about his guest. He poured a glass for her.

"Wow," Kat said, receiving the glass, "treating me like a lady." That had to be sarcasm. She swirled her glass on the table with extra flair, watching the legs drift up and down the sides of the glass.

"Should we get started on pulverizing hair?" Gio said.

"We could use mine," Kat said, "but I just dyed it. I don't

know if that'll make a difference." Dyed black hair, bleached bangs. Both could have changed the hair's chemical composition.

Gio pulled out three or four strands of his own, then four more. It didn't seem like enough. Pulling out a couple hairs was one thing, but pulling out an actual quantity was another. It felt wrong. He stopped at a baker's dozen.

He saw the Organica pestle and mortar set he had bought for Harper, still in its box. He took it out and moved the pestle around the mortar. It felt nice. Smooth, with machine-cut precision. It was a quality product.

Her favorite P and M, the one made from Petoskey and Charlevoix stone, was at the end of the counter, awaiting its next job. He played around with it as well. It felt different. More friction, yet somehow smoother. She'd clearly held it the same way every time and ground with the same hand, so it was worn into a slight elliptical pattern. He hadn't thought this was possible; how many hundreds or thousands of grinding hours would this take?

"I think my arms are too long." Gio almost wished he hadn't said that. But somehow his arms really were too long to use this tool.

"That's not possible." Kat took the set and mocked a plastic, infomercial-chef smile while pulverizing imaginary herbs. "I don't know what drugs you're on, but this feels perfect."

That settled it. Kat got to work grinding and pulverizing Gio's hair in the P and M.

Linden returned with several sizes and types of pliers, all on the longer and skinnier side. Lineman, needle nose, slip joint, locking. More variety than the two pairs Gio had on the wall of his walk-in closet.

"What do you think?" Linden said, miming shoving a set

down Gio's throat. "I haven't done this before, but I think it'll work."

Gio almost gagged at the thought.

"Unless you want to do the ol' string-and-the-doorknob method," Linden said, wiping a set with a single-serve sanitizer wipe. "My mom did that to me when I was little."

"I probably need a root canal anyway. Strings, slamming doors; I'm too old for tricks like that." Gio turned a chair away from the table and sat down again.

"Oh, hush. I'm old enough to be your dad."

"Do your worst, doctor."

Linden opened his mouth, with Gio mimicking him in turn. Prelinguistic instincts. Linden inserted the pliers and twisted his hands and shoulders into odd shapes and angles. He caught hold of the tooth, which wiggled and slipped. The mouth stretching hurt terribly.

"Sorry, they keep slipping," Linden said. "Can't get a good grip on the tooth." He pulled the pliers out to adjust them.

"Want me to do it, doc?" Gio said.

"No, I got it. Head back."

"Are those clean? I taste grease or metal or something."

"I said keep your head back."

A few more moments of stabbing, sharp, intermittent pain as Linden kept rooting around, clenching on the tooth, then slipping off again. The slipping hurt more than the pliers did when actually gripping the tooth.

"I'm drooling," Gio said. This came out as a wet, muffled grunt. He reached up to wipe under his chin with the back of his paw. His wrist.

"What?" Linden said. "Quit moving."

Then a flash of white-hot pain and Gio groaned. Both he and Linden were making contorted, frustrated faces.

Foreheads. They spoke with their foreheads.

"Almost have it. Tilt your head back. Stop moving. This is
—" Linden pulled out the bad tooth with a soundless, expansive pop in Gio's head— "the one."

"Aauugghh!" Gio said, immediately pushing Linden away
and covering his mouth. He got up to spit in the kitchen sink.
Kat handed him several sheets of paper towel. The towels
helped, they did, but he hadn't prepared himself for the
draining of blood down his throat. After fifteen seconds, he
began to feel a little sick to his stomach.

"Are you okay?" Kat said.

"Yeah." As well as he could be, considering.

Linden rinsed and dried the tooth with a paper towel while
Kat poured a glass of water. Gio threw away the old towel and
rinsed out his mouth, leaving a bloody lip print on the glass.
He folded another sheet of towel to fit the new gap in his teeth
and bit down to add pressure.

Kat found a bag of cotton balls in the bathroom and gave
that to him as well.

"Before you stuff your mouth again, can I see?" Linden
said. He looked in Gio's mouth, admiring his handiwork. "I can
now officially add 'amateur dentistry' to my list of
achievements."

"I shink I'm shwelling." Gio packed cotton balls in his
cheek and put an ice cube in his mouth. He wondered how
many people choked to death during or after dental surgery.

"So how do we make this into a powder?" Kat said, looking
at the tooth on the table. "Hit it with a hammer?"

"Let's go to my place. I have a vice."

"We'll be back," Linden said to the cats: Chico, Jagger, and
Cherry.

The three humans and Steve went to Linden's garage,
where Linden placed the tooth in a desk-mounted vice grip. He
tried to hold the tooth in place as he tightened, but having no

flat sides, it kept turning from the pressure. But after a single cracking noise, it was ready, a half inch of crown extending over the top of the vice.

"Just enough," Linden said.

He placed a plastic face shield under the grip to catch errant shavings, and angled a funnel as close to the tooth as possible. He dragged a fine-grit wood file across it, slowly at first, testing for stability, then faster as a fine dust began shaving off the tooth.

"I have sensitive teeth," Linden said. "This is what regular brushing feels like."

After a few minutes of sanding, the exposed bit of crown above the vice had been ground away. He put the funnel in a cup, and tapped the face mask to deposit the residual white dust into it. "That should be enough, I think."

Kat was still trying to pulverize Gio's hair with the pestle and mortar. She was all elbows and pained expressions. "I can't get this to grind up right."

"Oh," Linden said, looking at the tiny uneven mess in the mortar. "Don't worry about that. My electric razor is full of hair dust. I'll go get it."

"Something you could have told me ten minutes go."

Linden opened the door to the house and Rudy came flying out, barking and running directly at Steve. "Rudy!" Linden said.

Steve jumped onto the workstation, too high for the dog to reach.

"He's always been jealous of the cats," Linden said.

"Hey Rudy, remember me from the store?" Kat said, petting to calm him down. "He's fine. Just greeting Steve in his own way."

Linden disappeared into the house and returned with his electric razor. He took the mortar from Kat and dumped the clumps of partially crushed hair in the garbage. He tapped the razor against the rim of the mortar, depositing hair dust from the trap. He then added the tooth dust. "Try it now."

Kat picked up the pestle and ground the hair and tooth together. "I get the feeling this stuff's grinding into the bowl itself."

"I think that'sh why she didn't want the Organica shet," Gio said out of the side of his mouth not packed with cotton. His ice cube had long ago melted. He hadn't been needed since donating his tooth, and he focused on pressing cotton between his jaws. The pressure felt good.

"Isn't granite really hard?" Kat said.

"Ish not granite." He'd finally discerned this particular P and M was probably important for the magic in her potions.

Steve, still pacing on top of the workstation, rubbed against Gio's arm, asking to be picked up.

"Shteve shahs it'sh ready."

MOTE:
The poison is in the dosage.

CHAPTER
FORTY

HARPER

While the humans were gone, Harper walked into the kitchen.

"Harpy!" Chico said.

"I know, she came back for me," Cherry said, as happy as telepathy could sound. Not quite bragging, but close. Cat pride.

"The queen returns," Jagger said flatly. "Just in time to change herself back."

"Gio might not let her," Chico said.

"I just want to make sure he gets the potion right," Harper said. "You guys can't change without it."

"Maybe he'll just let you have human smell," Jagger said. *Smart ass.*

"He's not going to let you near it," Chico said.

"I think he will," Cherry said. Her telepathy was bright and optimistic, but not delusional.

"I think he'll just lock her up," Chico said.

"I'll stay in the laundry room," Harper said. "But if you guys help me push the basket over from the dryer to the washer, I can hide inside and watch."

Chico reluctantly went with them. Jagger stayed in the kitchen, artistically brooding.

Both Harper and Cherry pushed the half-filled basket, their hind legs braced against the rim of the utility sink, and Chico bit the side of the plastic mesh and pulled. It only moved an inch or two, as the front edge of the basket got caught in the gap between the machines.

"Great," Harper said. "This doesn't help at all."

"Hold on, push on three," Chico said. He bit the lowest part of the mesh and lifted while he pulled. The basket popped up and over and past the gap. Chico jumped down and out of the way.

Harper and Cherry pushed the basket flush with the far edge of the washer. The position was decent. Not quite like being in the kitchen, but she'd be able to hide in the clothes and look through the mesh to somewhat see their activities at the counter.

Harper hid behind the hamper when she heard the humans returning, then once they were all in the kitchen, she jumped into the basket to spectate. The people sounded like they were in good spirits.

"Let's do this," Linden said, clapping his hands once.

They added herbs to the P and M according to the recipe, as Kat continued to grind.

"Oh shit," Gio said, looking where Steve was tapping his paw at the book. "That's right. There was cat feces in the other one."

"So, who's gotta poop?" Linden said.

"Do you?" Gio said, looking at Kat. "I already went today."

"Me, too," Linden said.

"We don't need much. Like the size of a pea." Gio grabbed a butter knife from a drawer and handed it to her. "Half that. You can just..."

"I know how to do it," she said. "I can't fucking believe this."

She left and was gone a long time.

While they waited, Gio held the O'Cult witch's ladder and recited some incantations off the story card.

"That spell didn't help much last time," Linden said when Gio had finished.

"I disagree." Gio swung playfully in slow motion at Steve, his open palm brushing against whiskers. "It turned him even more into a cat." Steve swiped a dismissive follow-up paw in return.

They heard a flush from the other room, and Kat came back with the knife, covering the tiny bit of substance with a cupped hand.

"I'll do it," she said, turning her back to the others as she added to the P and M and began mixing it up. "It's clumping. This could take a sec. The cat stuff last time was already dry."

"And I used to eat food ground in this thing?" Gio said.

"You never want to see how the sausage is made," Linden said.

Harper wanted to jump out and see the mix, but held back. As long as everything was broken down and combined well, having an extra drop of moisture in it shouldn't matter.

"It's almost empty," Gio said, holding up the bottle of elixir Linden had found. "There's maybe two ounces left."

It would take them months to prepare a new batch, even if

they figured out how to do it right. This would be their last shot. Gio poured the remainder into a coffee mug.

Harper had always augmented the recipe with her own details, and she feared the potion wouldn't work if they didn't perform all the rituals correctly. Maybe that had played a part in their last potion not working for Steve.

Kat was about to scrape the mixture into the mug.

Fuck it. Harper jumped down and entered the kitchen. "You guys are doing it wrong," she said.

"Who's this?" Linden said.

"Hey!" Gio said. "Harper's back. Hold on, Kat."

So Gio wasn't going to immediately lock her up. Harper jumped onto the counter.

"That's Harper?" Linden said. "Of course she'd be a black cat. Howdy neighbor."

"I think this kitty's been to CSE." Kat said. "Like a few days ago, to visit Steve. We chased her out."

"Yeah, that was me," Harper said.

"You know how I told you cats can talk to each other?" Gio said. "If she's been to CSE, then maybe she's learned something from Steve."

"I didn't learn shit from him," Harper said.

The cats understood her, of course, but Gio couldn't. Steve looked at her with an expression that would communicate a lot in both cat and human.

"We need to put the mixture in the coffeemaker," she said. "It's a brew." Harper nudged the pour-over rack with her nose, trying to edge it away from the wall.

"Harper doesn't use a regular coffeemaker," Gio said, pulling it out in front of him and grabbing a filter. "This is for pour over."

"It's always a good time for coffee," Linden said, not

completely without sarcasm. He placed an empty mug underneath the rack.

"Let's try it," Kat said. She poured the mixture into the filter.

Harper nudged the mug with the fermented base. She went back to the pour-over stand and touched it with her nose.

"You want me to pour this through?" Gio said.

She pranced in a circle, showing she agreed.

Gio poured the fermented base over the moist grounds. "This wasn't in the book."

"Can't imagine it would be," Kat said. "And you drank this shit?"

"She combined it with better wine."

"Like this?" Kat held up the bottle of Bordeaux she'd been drinking from.

"Yeah, exactly like that," Gio said.

"I doubt cats need as much as humans, though," Linden said. "Littler metabolisms."

When the dripping stopped, Kat tapped the filter for the last drops, then moved to pull the cup out.

"No!" Harper said. "Pour it through again!" Harper nudged the mug.

"We know," Gio said. "We're going to combine it with good wine."

"Do it like this," Steve said, tapping his paw twice on the counter.

"Steve's saying no," Kat said.

Steve touched the mug, then the top of the pour-over rack.

"I think he wants us to pour it through again," Kat said.

Steve tapped the table once for yes. *Smug little shit.*

Gio put the now empty mug under the filter and repeated the process, then after a third pour over had finished dripping, Harper was satisfied. She tapped her paw once.

Kat picked up the cat dish and rinsed out the old potion.

"Should I add?" Gio said, removing the cork and holding the Bordeaux over the potion.

Harper tapped the counter once. Gio slowly poured the good wine into the mug, watching Harper for his cue. When it looked right, she tapped the counter twice and he stopped. She had to admit, Steve's paw code worked.

"I still think Steve should drink first," Gio said, swishing the mixture with a delicate crystal stirrer. He must've seen her use that before. Homemade margaritas with limes from the yard, perhaps.

Harper didn't disagree. If the potion misfired, Steve was her least favorite of the cats. Collateral damage she could deal with. And she didn't plan to have any herself, anyway.

Gio poured in the final potion and Kat set down the dish.

"Cheers," Steve said. He didn't hesitate and the first five or six laps went quickly. Harper imagined the horrific taste in Steve's mouth. The next several went slower, then the last few were labored. He lapped at least a dozen times.

Steve sat straight up and looked at the ceiling.

"Oh, fuck," he said. He walked in tight, unsteady circles, clearly bothered, then shook himself like he was wet.

"Is it working?" Chico said.

"It's either that or a bad trip," Jagger said.

"Paws...sweating." Steve lowered his front legs as if supplicating. Then he began whipping his head wildly back and forth, making noises not unlike a rapid series of sneezes. He bit at the air, eating unseen flies. Then the muted choking and wailing began.

This wasn't a sound Harper could tolerate easily. She was barely able to stay in the room. It sounded like he was being tortured. For some reason, it hadn't bothered her to hear a human in pain, but as a cat hearing another cat, it was too much. Maybe she had changed.

Chico, Jagger, and Cherry backed away to give Steve a wide berth, ready to bolt at any moment.

"Poor Steve," Cherry said.

Maybe the potion had been prepared incorrectly. Steve flailed, violently fighting an invisible leash. Flying, twisting, bouncing.

"Co...co...collar!" Steve choked out in between gasps.

"Why're you all standing there?" Chico said. "Look at him!"

"Somebody help him!" Cherry said.

"He's dying!" Jagger said.

Their cries would sound like a group cat wail to the people in the room, but they didn't need to understand Steve's words to know something was wrong. Harper pounded her paw twice on the floor, then the other cats did as well.

"My poor kitty!" Kat said, leaning down to caress him. Gio held her back.

"Let him finish," Gio said. "I went through this four times already. He'll be fine."

Four cats with four sets of panicked, doubled heart beats pounded on the floor.

"Collar!" Harper yelled as loud as she'd ever yelled anything in her life.

"His collar!" Kat wrestled herself free and pinned Steve down, struggling to unlock the clasp. She finally got it and flung it away and started petting him as he gasped at air. He was already losing fur and had grown twice as big. "You're okay now. You're okay."

Linden picked up the collar. "We need to take all of these off."

"Good call," Gio said. "*Close* call."

He put his hand on Kat's shoulder. "Give him space. It's going to hurt, but let it happen."

Steve flopped on the floor, less violently now, his uncanny-valley screaming growing closer to that of a human adolescent.

"You guys have a robe or towel for him?" Kat asked, still squatting closest. "I don't know that we should be watching this."

"There's a robe in the bathroom," Gio said. "Another in the bedroom."

"I'll get them," Linden said.

"Nobody else drink until we see that Steve's all right," Harper said to the other cats.

"No problem there," Chico said.

"Complete change took about ten minutes for me," Gio said. "We should keep the other cats away from the potion until Steve says everything's okay."

"What a trip," Jagger said.

"A hero," Chico said, as Linden lay a robe over Steve. "A martyr."

Eventually Steve was complete, and he and Kat stared at each other like long-lost friends. Kat kept her eyes trained on his face while he put his arms into the robe.

"Your eyes," Kat said. "They're you, for sure, but so different."

"Objectively, I know you're the same," Steve said, the skin of his neck an irritated red ring. "But observing you with my original eyes is so different."

Gross. Harper wanted to gag. But neither of them could compare to Cherry.

"So, we're good?" Linden said. "Got all your parts? Hairy palms?"

Steve looked at his palms and smiled. He rubbed them on

his robe. "Hurt like hell, but now every muscle's tingling from the most intense workout of my life."

"That's how I felt, too," Gio said. "Do you still feel like you have a tail?"

Steve stretched, twisting his back. "Oddly, I do. Phantom tail syndrome."

"Step right up!" Linden said. "Who wants to be human again like Steve here? But funnier, I hope."

"Who's next?" Harper said.

"I'll go," Chico said. "I've been a cat second longest after Spike. It's only fair."

Nobody argued with that. Chico went to the potion dish and Linden removed his collar. There was less drama this time, both people and cats knowing what to expect. He tested the potion with the tip of his tongue.

"Eck!" He shook his head. "How did you drink this?"

"Don't hesitate, Chico," Steve said. "The faster, the better. If I can do it, you can do it."

Chico attacked the potion with gusto. Gagging noises as he powered through, lapping twice as fast as Steve had, maybe a few more total. He stopped, out of breath.

His first movement was a twisty belly jiggle. He clapped his front paws together, either catching an invisible fly or trying to pray but losing his balance.

He wailed screams of persecution as he flopped and morphed. Harper didn't think she would ever tire of witnessing these changes, if only she could plug her ears. It was like she had learned to access power over a core function of the universe. Chico had tried to introduce her to his god of the afterlife through a wafer and wine, and here she was showing him the reality of corporeal life through biomass and wine.

Transfiguration complete and ashamed of his nudity, Chico

quickly put on his robe. With help from Gio and Linden, he sat at the table. He'd gained a lot of weight since the last time Harper saw him as a person. Maybe it was the power of suggestion, but with his new receding hairline, he looked like a monk.

"You okay?" Kat asked him.

"Yeah." Chico was sweaty and out of breath.

"I think it was harder for him," Steve said, placing a hand on his shoulder. "He'd been a cat longer."

Chico pushed himself to his feet unsteadily and hugged Steve. A long hug with weak pats. He seemed a lot older than Steve.

Gio handed out ibuprofen like they were party favors at an afterhours party. He opened another bottle of wine to share with the new arrivals.

Chico lifted a hand, denying a glass. "Just a water," he said.

Jagger was next, and morphed into Mick again. His hair was long and streaked with gray. Still on his hands and knees, he threw up. Gio squatted next to him for support, placing a blanket over him, then helped him up.

"Not the first time I've thrown up at a party," Mick said weakly. "That's a hell of a drug."

"Don't worry about it," Gio said. "We'll make Harper clean it up."

"I guess it's time," Cherry said to Harper as they lightly touched noses.

Harper didn't want Cherry to morph, then she did, then she didn't. Either way, she wasn't going to fight her decision.

Cherry drank the potion. This particular transfiguration was the most painful Harper had ever seen. She couldn't watch, but couldn't leave either. Each wail forced Harper's eyes closed, then each gasp opened them again. When the flailing stopped, there was Jehri now, more beautiful than ever, curled naked in a fetal position.

"Cherry?" Chico said, placing a blanket over her.

"Wow," Gio said.

"She's beautiful," Kat said.

Those were the only two in the room that hadn't seen Jehri as a human.

Harper was first to touch her, nudging her arm. She remembered that human scent. Skin, not soap. Natural oils, not bacterial. There was no response. She approached Jehri's head, and her eyes were closed. Harper smelled in her mouth the faint essence of the chicken from earlier, but there was no breath.

Harper bunted Jehri's cheekbone, then rubbed under her chin. "Wake up, Cherry! Wake up! They're all fine now, why aren't you?"

"I don't think she's breathing," Chico said.

Gio dropped to his hands and knees and shoved Harper roughly out of the way. "Jehri, remember when you told me to change us all back? We did it. You're back."

"Hey!" Harper said, raising her fur at Gio's slight.

"So come be with us," he said. "Steve's back. Chico. Jagger."

Chico was holding Jehri's wrist. "It's hard to tell if there's a pulse."

Gio put the back of his wrist to her nostrils. "That may be breath. I can't tell either." He stood up and grabbed the empty green elixir bottle off the counter.

Harper took his spot in front of Jehri's face and touched her nose. "Cherry, it's Minxy. You did it! You're a hum—"

"Harper, move!" Gio said, pushing her out of the way again.

"Hey!" she repeated, uselessly. It escaped as a hiss.

Gio placed the end of the bottle under Jehri's nose. Nothing

279

for a moment, then her eyeballs moved beneath the lids. Her eyelids fluttered. She shook her head a little.

"I'll be damned, witches' smelling salts, huh?" Linden said.

Jehri's eyes opened and she sat up, keeping the blanket around her. Kat cheered.

Harper tried to access Jehri, standing on her hind legs and pawing. Jehri tried to stand. Gio and Linden helped her, sliding a chair under her to sit on.

"How do you feel?" Kat said.

Jehri nodded. She only sat for a moment. "Hold on," she said as she stood up unsteadily and stumbled out of the room, hunched over and blanketed.

"Maybe she's throwing up," Mick said.

Jehri returned a few moments later wearing a pair of Harper's sweatpants and a hoodie. She looked adorable, like she had just woken from a nap. She hugged Gio first. "You figured it out!" she said. "I'm so happy!"

"Not so loud," Chico said, rubbing his temple. "We still have headaches."

"You're the headache, Chico," Mick said, two fingers against his own temple. "I think I'm going to puke again."

"I wanted to change you first," Gio said to Jehri. "But I didn't want to risk it in case there was a problem."

"I know, Gio. It all worked out."

A pang of jealousy flared in Harper for a moment, as she recalled how Cherry and Gio had spoken like fast friends when he was briefly a cat. She'd missed hearing Cherry tell him to lock Harper up, so who knew what other secrets they'd shared.

But then it passed. Jehri didn't like guys. She liked Harper. They would be together for life now, with Jehri as her caretaker.

Jehri hugged Chico, Mick, and Steve.

"I'm Kat," Kat said, formally, holding out a hand to shake.

Jehri pushed her hand aside and hugged her. "Thank you, Kat, for taking care of Steve. And for feeding us all your shit."

"That wasn't all of it," Kat said.

"And Jehri's a chef, so she knows," Steve said. "She's a culinary master."

Finally, Jehri picked Harper up. "You sure this is what you want?" she said. "You don't want to change back? You'd rather be babied for the rest of your life with no responsibilities?"

"Wait, what?" Mick said. "Harper wants to stay a cat?"

"She says it's only fair since she caused so much pain to all of us. It's her penance."

"If that's what she wants," Chico said. "But we never got a choice in the matter."

"Maybe she's scared to be my equal," Jehri said. "Right Harpy? You couldn't handle a real woman after all this."

Not a fair accusation. Of course, Cherry had waited until she changed back before saying something like that. It was true, though. Would she rather be babied the rest of her life, or be Cherry's equal as lover and partner? Harper had resigned herself to remaining a cat, then to the idea of a plush exile with Cherry, both as cats, and finally to Cherry as her human caretaker.

No. They were equals. Harper jumped out of Jehri's arms and went to the cat dish.

She was wearing no collar that needed to be removed.

CHAPTER
FORTY-ONE

KAT

J ehri had just changed back to human and stumbled out of the room. While Gio and Linden were speaking with Mick and Chico, Kat focused on Steve. Steve the human. Was he going to have expectations about the two of them? It had only been seven months since Jesse's death. What she needed was a friend, not a boyfriend. As a cat, Steve was perfect. A perfect friend and companion who listened without giving unwarranted advice.

His eyes were still magnetic. She wanted to enter his brain and look around at the cat and human memories and how they intermingled.

"I hope you don't expect me to act like a cat," Steve said. His voice was amazing. Much better than his meows.

"No, I suppose not." She didn't know him at all, really. She couldn't admit she was vaguely disappointed. That equated to admitting she was selfish. She was a horrible person. "I can't tell what color your eyes are," she said. Eyes like tie-dye. Blue, gray, and rust.

"It's called heterochromia iridis," Steve said. "There are like three colors in there."

"I thought that was like one brown and one blue or something."

"Actually, that's heterochromia iridum. Two completely different eyes. Mine aren't that cool."

Chico tapped him on the shoulder, breaking their mutual stare. Steve hugged him again.

"We were all wrong," Steve said. "Beautifully wrong."

"But we were also right," Chico said.

Steve had been with these people for years as cats. Who knew what sort of ideas and theories they'd come up with for what had happened, how they'd come back. Answers to the questions of the universe. She was the real stranger in this house.

Jehri returned dressed in sweats and hugged everyone, including Steve.

Jehri's benevolence extended well beyond her physical beauty and Kat was convinced everybody in the room would do anything to be with her. The world was hers to command. She thanked Kat for feeding them her shit and forced a hug on her. They all laughed. There was no ice in the room.

Except close to the floor. Jehri lifted Harper to her chest.

"Hey, Kat," Gio said, looking at his phone. "I told you I signed up for the Omnist, right?"

"Uh, no." They had really just met today.

"Well, I just got a Mote. It says, 'Do cats really always land on their feet?' Weird, huh?"

"Totally." A random Mote meant the universe picked it for you. Even if it was something Kick wrote.

Steve was maybe an inch shorter than Kat. He turned, tilted his head, and nuzzled against her ear. This was a cat move whether he realized it or not. It wasn't sexual. He was greeting her the way that felt natural to him. Maybe it was the catlike quality that didn't creep her out.

"Do I look old, by the way?" he said.

He sounded like he was trained to do voiceover acting. "Natural pipes," as Kat's best friend Lisa would say.

"I don't know what you should look like," she said. "I just met you."

"I suppose Harper would know how old everybody should look. We'd need her opinion." Steve looked annoyed. "Or not. I'd rather just look in a mirror than talk to her."

"Harper's drinking it!" Chico said, pointing.

The room went silent as everybody watched Harper lapping the potion.

"No collar," Linden said. "I guess that means my job here is done."

They all waited for the change, but nothing happened. All the cats had become human except for Harper. Linden put the last of the potion in the dish, and she drank more.

"That's twice as much as I had, and that made me sick," Mick said.

She kept drinking frantically.

Nothing.

FORTY-TWO

HARPER

A few weeks had gone by and they'd fallen into the lifestyle Harper had expected. Cherry was Jehri again, and Harper was her pet cat.

She loved looking at Jehri's jawline. Her long neck. Elegant strength and power. She wanted to brush her hair, ask her about what she dreamed about, cook for them, lie big spoon with her in bed, all things she couldn't do now.

After turning so many humans into cats out of spite, at minimum she deserved this, a gilded prison of being with Jehri but not really being with her. She deserved worse.

"I'm glad you're here," Jehri said. "But just know, if you ever want to leave, you can. If you want to find another witch who knows the right potion to change you back, or just want to go it alone, I won't stop you."

But Harper had chosen Jehri as her partner, regardless, and she planned to stick with it. It wouldn't only be for a year this time. This was for life. Besides, she still encountered the scent of bobcat in the ravine behind the house.

She tapped her paw twice on Jehri's thigh and dragged herself under her hand to show her this was what she wanted. This was as close to content as she'd ever felt.

"I know. I love you, too, Minxy."

Jehri was a kind and thoughtful caretaker, and had recently landed a job at a restaurant, using Harper's name and social security. The long hours were to be expected, but at least she and Harper could keep the house.

Harper would watch her cook and do yoga in the living room with fascination. She wondered if Jehri's time as a cat had helped her with difficult stretches and poses.

ONE EVENING, Jehri came home beaming, extra sun in her eyes. She took off her jacket and unbuttoned her shirt. She wasn't wearing a bra.

"Look Minxy, I got it." Jehri revealed a fresh tattoo, tiny, about the size of half of a quarter on her breastplate.

Harper swelled with warmth. Then she shivered when she realized she couldn't get the matching tattoo in return.

"We used this as a template," Jehri said, removing something from her pocket. It was two halves of a BFF pendant set. She lifted one to her chest to show an exact match. Then she showed Harper the other half. "That means this one's yours."

She lightly tapped the collar around Harper's neck. Harper tilted her head so Jehri could remove it. Jehri added the pendant to it, then put it back on her.

"We finally did it," Jehri said, lifting Harper to be face to face. They touched noses, then Harper bunted affectionately under her chin.

~

ANOTHER EVENING, Jehri was petting and cooing at Harper curled up on her lap. A December wind was picking up, and leaves and twigs would occasionally hit the window.

"This is cozy, isn't it?" Jehri said. "Now I know why you want to stay a cat."

Petted, caressed, kissed, fed. Days full of naps, smelling the richness of late autumn outside. It would officially be winter this week, chilly tonight, but cozy inside. It wasn't that bad.

"I'm sure you know your property taxes are overdue. I'm legally dead, so all my old accounts are closed. We don't have the money. I don't know what to do."

Jehri wasn't currently a chef, but a line cook until she could rebuild her resumé.

"Your car payment was late, too, and I took care of that, but we have nothing to live on for the next week." Jehri usually brought food home from work for them to eat.

Jehri continued petting, thinking out loud. "I think we should open a restaurant. Maybe I can take out a loan in your name." Jehri bent down and kissed the top of Harper's head. "You make a pretty good cat. A pretty good little friend."

This felt condescending. But what could she do?

"I remember you telling me once that all your exes were great, and if they were, then why would you keep breaking up with great people and turning them into cats? They all seemed pretty okay to me. What's wrong with you?"

Jehri wouldn't have heard her answer even if she tried. So she didn't.

"And you told me another time that all your exes were

crazy. Then why did you keep dating people like that? Or pushing them to the edge of their personalities until their worst traits came out? Either way. Do you think I'm crazy? Is that why you did that to me?"

"No," Harper said. "That was the biggest mistake of my life. You're the best thing that ever happened to me. I was jealous and took a familiar but horrible path. I wish I could take it back, but maybe then I wouldn't have learned anything. I deserve to suffer."

Jehri looked at her like she could understand her. The kindest eyes. The wind whipped hard enough that a breeze fluttered the curtains through the old energy-inefficient windows that Harper had never updated. Jehri twisted around to adjust the curtains and the full moon hit her in the face.

She buckled as if to vomit.

Harper jumped off her lap, and when she hit the floor, she, too, began wailing and flailing in pain, feeling her bones breaking and shifting. She was choking from the collar as she grew, feebly pawing at it, unable to unlock the clasps. At best she could catch a claw behind it. Unlike when this had happened to Steve, there were no non-morphing humans around to save her.

Jehri tried to stand and fell to the floor next to her. Dry-heaving, she lifted herself to her knees and tried to hold Harper's flailing, choking body still. But Jehri was screaming and shrinking, and her hands, arms, and everything else were shaking.

Harper moved in all directions at once, clenched every muscle, worked every limb and claw simultaneously, faster than she had ever moved in her life. If this was how she was going to die, she would go out fighting. Her life would end mere seconds from now, nightmarishly violent and painful.

Jehri continued fumbling feebly with Harper's collar.

"Aauugghh!!" Jehri screamed in her face. Harper could feel Jehri's hands contracting and seizing, gripping her neck, her fur, her collar. Trying to focus while screaming through her own torment. She managed to get the collar unbuckled but not removed, and she fell to the side and began flailing.

Harper was still growing.

This was more than just an inability to breathe. All the blood flow had stopped through her neck, with blockage on both sides of the collar. Pressure built up in her chest and in her head, and she was about to fall unconscious. Her vision whited out. Her neck was about to snap; her head would pop off.

The pressure of growing finally pushed the collar's open clasp past the grommet it was caught on, and it fell harmlessly to the floor.

Moments later, on her hands and knees, Harper gasped for air, the closest she had ever come to death. Jehri had stopped screaming as well, and was making tiny wheezing noises next to her, once again a cat.

Wearing her own robe that now smelled like Jehri, Harper stood over the sink in the bathroom, looking in the mirror at the red line the collar had made around her neck. Just like Steve. It was a symbol of a new religion of cat-people. It hurt to touch. She could hear Cherry burning off frustrated energy, running throughout the house over chairs and couches, sliding on hardwood into walls, jumping on the counter.

Harper was still trying to work out what had happened.

Taking the potion turned a person into a cat. From one

hundred percent human to one hundred percent cat. Then reversing the spell turned a cat into a werecat. Ninety percent human and ten percent cat.

But it had been different for her. She hadn't changed back until now. Why?

Maybe it was the O'Cult Own Won Now strength and power spell she ate as a cat. Cat power. Her desire to be a strong cat had polluted her desire to be a strong human.

Plus, her frame of mind was off when she drank Gio's potion. She was doing it for the wrong reasons. Self-doubt had crept in, a desire for self-punishment. The wrong words were in her head. As a witch, she knew better. With practice, many spells never needed to be voiced out loud; they would work if the thoughts were powerful enough. Her indecision about staying a cat had affected the outcome.

Assuming Jehri was in the same situation as Gio, she would be human twenty-seven days a month, with a few nights as a cat. Mostly human, sometimes cat.

Harper was the reverse image: a cat twenty-seven days a month, with a few nights as a human. Mostly cat, sometimes human.

She heard a crash in the kitchen.

"Cherry!" Harper rushed to the kitchen to find a glass had broken in the sink. She didn't see the cat. She was a new Harper. No more scolding. She took three breaths.

"Cherry, sweetie," she said, calmer now. "Where are you? I figured out what happened."

She looked in the living room, then under and behind all the furniture. In the bedroom. No other doors were open. She went to the laundry room and saw eyes glowing from behind the clothes hamper. She was hiding in the same place Harper had hidden when she first escaped from Gio, then again when she'd returned to the house. She almost turned on the light, but didn't, remembering the discomfort it had caused her as a cat.

"You can go if you want. I won't keep you. But don't go too far because there's a bobcat out there, plus you'll become human again once the moon goes down. You're a werecat just like Gio."

Cherry took a couple steps out of the shadows.

"Here." Harper opened the back door. "See? You can go. I'll go sit in the kitchen and stay out of your way, or you can come talk to me. I think this is our new normal, so we should work out how we're going to deal with it."

Cherry walked to the edge of the doorframe and sniffed the air. Then she went to the kitchen and jumped on the table.

"Let's try something," Harper said. She dialed Gio on speakerphone so Cherry could hear, but his phone rang until going to voicemail. "It would've been weirder if he answered."

Beep.

"Gio, it's Harper. Harpy. I'm with Cherry. Yes, Cherry. You'll never believe it, but she changed back into a cat. Another were-cat, just like you, and as you can tell, I think I get to be human for a minute, too. Call us tomorrow."

THE NEXT DAY, Harper was stretching her claws out on the wood inside the box in the living room when Gio called. Jehri answered on speaker phone, setting it on the coffee table.

"I take it you got Harper's message?" Jehri said.

"Yeah, I guess we all changed. Mick was with me at my place. He wanted to take notes and pictures and stuff. We didn't expect him to morph with me, but he did. At least we were safe. Someone knocked on the door right after. Everyone in the building probably heard our screaming, but at least nobody called the police. Maybe my condo isn't the best location for future transfigurations."

"It's exhausting," Jehri said. "And Harper's lucky to be alive. Another collar mishap."

"Yeah. New rule. No more collars," Gio said. "You know what, you guys should go to Thalia's next Lodge at CSE. She teaches transfiguration meditation. Since you guys can't be cats or humans at the same time, you could learn how to do that."

"As long as Thalia's not speaking right at the moment the full moon comes out."

"Good point." Gio cleared his throat. "By the way, do you think you can give me that box Linden made?"

"Minxy's in it right now. She loves it."

"Minxy?"

"That's what she wants to be called."

"Huh."

Harper could tell this bothered him, but she derived no pleasure from that, nor was she bothered. It wasn't about him.

"What?" Jehri said.

"Nothing. Well, I'll probably see you later. We're all going to stay at Linden's tonight. I'll ask him about getting another box."

LATER THAT DAY, Jehri listened to music and danced and sang as a human, cooking for the two of them. And Harper enjoyed listening to her sing.

At twilight, Jehri took her clothes off and they held each

other on top of the bed as they morphed, which made it marginally easier. Still painful, but natural, like childbirth.

Then they went to Linden's house, where Harper brushed Cherry's hair while the male kitties frolicked. Turned out Cherry didn't seem to enjoy Harper's singing quite as much.

FORTY-THREE

GIOVANNI

Everybody went to Linden's house for two more nights of morphing. It was a two-household party and a reunion of sorts as Harper came over as a human. Linden served as traffic cop, making sure nobody got hurt or out of line. Four excitable male werecats were a handful, all chasing each other and wrestling. Rudy loved it, roughhousing gently as older dogs tended to do. Cherry mostly spent her time on Harper's lap, being groomed and receiving a month's worth of attention in one session.

~

THE GUYS—CHICO, Mick, Steve, and Gio—decided to stick together. Gio was the only one who hadn't gone missing and didn't have difficulty opening accounts, taking out loans, or signing paperwork, so he was unanimously voted to be in charge of their new business.

With Chico's ASPCA background, he suggested they open a high-end pet hotel with a day spa: Kitty B & B. They knew the ins and outs of being a cat better than anyone else. Plenty of space with a plethora of cubbyholes in which to hide. Luxurious cat trees to climb. Homemade cooking with all the necessary nutrients, like that of a true restaurant. Jehri, who now lived with Harper, was in charge of food. Harper worked on spells to aid the human-cat relationships.

Mick said he enjoyed the new career more than he thought he would, decorating the place in colors pleasing to cats. He chose soft music for certain rooms, silence for others, nature sounds like running water and distant birds for another. Correct volume was of utmost importance.

In his free time, Mick continued working on his animated project. He'd learned so many things as a cat and had so many ideas, he changed it from a movie to a long-form episodic series.

Steve began research into the field of felinology, the study of cats. He found people tended to psychologically lump cats and dogs into a similar domesticated pet category, based on familiarity as household pets, but he knew from experience that cats were as different from dogs as humans were from cats. Zoology was a different branch of science from what he'd been trained in, but as he read more about cats, he continually found errors in the research and theories, many of them due to human biases. He studied cat communication, developing tests that proved intelligence, problem solving, and communication that looked like telepathy, but were rooted in brain chemicals, scents, and gestures.

Steve saw Kat often, of course. She was literally his best friend. They may have been closer than friends, Gio couldn't tell, but if they were, it was their prerogative to say or not say.

"Kat had a far rougher go of it when she watched Jesse die on their wedding day," Steve said to Gio one day. "There are far worse things than spending a few years as someone's pet."

"At least I'm still me," Kat told Gio another time. "Death of our loved ones is something all people have to deal with, but having your literal humanity stripped away from you is much, much worse."

ONCE KITTY B & B was up and running, Gio sold his no-pets condo, and they stayed in their own house next to the building. For the full moons, they drove out to Joshua Tree, or the Sierras, or Big Sur, somewhere they could set up camp and morph, romping together in nature for a few days. There were worse things in the world.

CHAPTER

FORTY-FOUR

KAT

A few months after "potion night," Kat was attending Coffin Club with Steve and Mick. As humans.

It was packed, the largest Coffin Club Kat had seen so far. The dozen boxes-in-progress were arranged in three rows like an auto show and took up most of the Basil Alcove. Plus, there were three times as many people as boxes.

The three of them were standing on the edge of the new pentacle. Steve scuffed it with his shoe. "Mick, you see this?" There was a tiny paw print in the paint. "I did this. First day I arrived."

"I never noticed that," Kat said.

"I thought you knew," Steve said. "Actually, you had to change the water after I washed my paws."

Linden walked up, happy to see them. "You guys finally made it to one of my club nights."

"This is my first chance," Mick said.

"Linden, how could you forget?" Steve said, pointing down at the paw print. "I was here for one."

"Well, I'll be. I stand corrected," Linden said. "Or can I sit corrected? Where's my chair?" He paused as if actually waiting for a response. "That's a joke about Yksian."

"Right," Steve said. He'd sat on Yksian's lap on a throne in this very room.

"Congrats," Kat said. "Biggest crowd yet."

"That just means people are joining faster than they can die. You can thank medicine and science more than me."

"You're so goth," Kat said.

Speaking of goth, Yksian swept into the room right on cue. It was apparent Linden had been waiting for his arrival. Linden stepped on stage and held his hands up to get everyone's attention. "Everyone, can I have your attention? People, people. It's like herding cats in here."

A joke only they would get.

"I know I'm usually a bit sillier in my manner, but every so often I take a more serious tone. I thought today would be as good a day as any to ask, 'Why do we use coffins?' and 'Why do we have funerals?' And for this, I would like to hand the stage over to our favorite Omniscian, Yksian."

Yksian stepped on stage and bowed just enough so his long coat fluttered behind him.

"Greetings," he said in his trademark wet bass. "Believe it or not, the easier question to ask is, 'What is the purpose of life?'"

Steve was the only one who laughed. Philosophy made a scientist laugh. That caught a woman's attention across the Basil Alcove. It was Jessica, a customer Kat had seen a few times recently. Jessica smiled.

"I say the purpose of life is to fight entropy," Yksian said. "If you take a brilliant piece of architecture, there are nearly infinite ways for it to be demolished, different ways for the bits of rock and sand and silicon to be arranged that will be unappealing to us as aestheticians. But there are comparatively very few that we find appealing. Architecture is the constant fight against disarray, which reflects life's fight against chaos."

Steve and Kat weren't really together, not in the sense of a couple, yet that glance and smile from Jessica was bothering her. They were standing so close together their arms were touching. Kat slipped her hand into Steve's. Taking ownership. She didn't normally do this sort of thing, but wanted to nip any potential Jessica confusion in the bud.

Steve held her hand in return, but didn't otherwise acknowledge anything. Just like when he'd sat on the front counter listening to Lodges.

"So, we create rituals, the architectural details of spirituality, to defy the uncertainty of nature," Yksian said. "We always light the candles the same way. We always cast the spell with the ingredients, words, and motions ritualized."

Kat thought about all the times Steve lay on her lap as she petted him. All the times he spoke to her without needing human language. The selfishness crept in again. It'd been ten months since Jesse, but another six months of Steve as a cat would have been better.

Then again, Jessica could have been smiling at her, not Steve. Kat looked over and caught her staring again. She probably couldn't see them holding hands. Too many people. Kat wasn't going to taunt her by lifting their arms triumphantly.

"And understand what I mean by chaos: It's what we often mistake for homogenization," Yksian said. "Take a glass from your kitchen. If it shatters, it's thrown away and breaks down into smaller and smaller pieces, into infinite possible arrangements. But there was only one arrangement for those pieces when they were shaped like a glass.

"Think of the universe as a cosmic version of a beach where everything has been broken down into sand, the sand drifting and recombining into limitless arrangements. But to us, it all looks the same, white noise. Our tiny brains cannot comprehend the vastness of this. We only see one thing. Sameness."

Jessica had been explicit about needing witch's ladders and spells to look for someone from her past, someone she hadn't seen or heard from in years. Steve had been a cat for at least five years. What if they'd been hanging out on her roof talking about the vastness of the universe sometime before his transfiguration?

"So, then, religion is a type of structure, a collection of rituals," Yksian said. "A method of arranging the sand of the universe into something of value. We don't want to feel pointless, so we extrapolate our life, imagine it existing beyond our time on earth so we exist for eternity. But just as we cannot fathom the arrangements of sand on a beach, we cannot fathom the arrangement of sands of time in the universe. Our ego thinks it can, but it cannot comprehend a universe it literally cannot comprehend."

And maybe Steve had told Jessica that we were all collectively the mind of the universe, and this would mean not just people, but other thinking animals, as well. All sentient beings. Sounded just like something Steve would say.

~

"AND WHILE WE'RE ALIVE, we're fighting entropy," Yksian said. "Our body is constantly dying and renewing itself, trying to keep its shape in the face of destruction of form, before we finally succumb and return to sand."

Yksian patted the box on the stage between him and Linden.

"This box here is a structure, both a shuttle returning us to the earth, and a package in which we extend our shelf life, to hold our shape a little longer."

Jessica, as if that was her cue, began weaving through the crowd of people across the Basil Alcove.

~

"SO WHEN YOU DIE, when your body wants to naturally decompose, you'll get some choice in the manner in which it's done," Yksian said. "Not much, and not forever, but it's something. You get to determine the ritual performed after your death. You don't have to have a funeral. You don't have to be buried. But you can decorate one of these and make it personal. Make it a part of you that continues on a little while after you pass."

People applauded.

Jessica stopped in front of Kat, smiling and nervous.

"Jessica," Kat said, giving Steve's hand a squeeze.

"Hi, Kat," Jessica said. "Can I ask you an awkward question? Remember when I told you I was looking for somebody from my past?"

Steve peered at her curiously.

"Jessica?" Mick said.

"Mick! I knew it was you!" She went airborne into their embrace.

"So that's the Jessica I heard about for years," Steve said. "The one Mick said got away."

Mick lifted Jessica off her feet as they hugged.

"How long was he a cat?"

"I was five years, and he was the one right before me. I'd say eight?"

"I guess her witch's ladder and other spells must've worked," Kat said.

"Maybe, maybe not." He didn't literally lift one eyebrow when he said this, but she heard it in his voice. "Does it matter?"

This coming from a man who'd been cursed into becoming a werecat.

Jessica and Mick were making happy noises and crying. They would need a moment before all the proper introductions were made.

"Now, those two guys there, those are good men," Steve said, gesturing toward the stage. "I learned a little about Linden as a neighbor, then observed his interactions here with Consumerians. And now this, I can relate to this. He's got Yksian talking about the freakin' second law of thermo-dynamics."

Steve looked at her and slow-blinked, as if waiting for a response. He probably didn't know he was doing it. Another cat-ism.

She slowly blinked in return. Her own Kat-ism.

Kat still planned to be cremated. And the box she and Steve were about to decorate was going to make a great coffee table.

ACKNOWLEDGMENTS

I've talked the ears off too many people to acknowledge them all here, but here's a bunch of them:

Becky Abeita, Aaron Akbari-Mort, Sami Akbari-Mort, Nick Allen, Joe Armstrong, Eric Augustine, Dayan Ballweg, Jeremy Barr, Kelly Bashar, Debra Bemis, Soni Benson, Caeri Bertrand, Jackie Beville, Matt Beville, Rohan Bhagwandas, Morgan Brandon, Ashley Carlson, Rocky Castro, Stephanie Castro, Taylor Montana Catlin, Debra Clark, Michael C. Clark, Tim Clark, Caroline Concha, Adam Conner, Carmelo Conti, Eddy Contreras, Christa Cooley, Francis Corby, Jill Cordova, Claire Criswell, Christian Draheim, Kyle Dolvik, Geo Donaires, Angela Duarte, Thomas Duffy, Angi Dyste, Erik Elhert, Stephen Ellis, Tony Essa, Josh Farrell, Bryan Fetner, Josh Forge, Kiki Franklin, Ruben Garcia, Derenik Gharakhanian, Joe Glading, Ken Gombos, Bryan Graves, Mercedes Graves, Daniel Gray, Annie Green, Travis Greene, Aaron Guerra, Mike Halloran, Danielle Harrower, Ian Harrower, Anne Harting, Lee Harting, Leandra Hays, Nick Hays, Keith Hershey, Kate Holt, Ken Holt, Alexis Jones, Allyson Jones, Ryan Keleher, Richard Kent, Stefanie Kent, Amanda Kibiloski, Erin Killean, Grant Knox, Erin Kruse, Scott Kruse, Anne Lane, Kyle Lane, Nicole LaPlante, June Low, Sean MacDonald, Scott Maginnis, Joe Marchitto, Renee Marchitto, Ben Marks, Buffy Marley, Peter Marley, Erik Marshall, Nachie Marsham, Wilson Martinez, Sean Mason, Tim Mayse, Katie

Mayo, Melissa McCabe, Matt McCracken, Michelle McCracken, Sean McGoldrick, Carlos Mendiola, Uriel Mejia, Frank Merle, Nick Merrick, Allison Meyerhardt, Brittany Meyerhardt, Joe Mikan, Joe Mills, John Mitchell, Chino Moreno, Dan Murphy, Adam Murray, Antoine Murray, Bekki Newton, Dave Newton, Braulio Ochoa, Eileen O'Connell, Chris Ostray, Kat Paled, Jessica Parker, Max Pastor, Erwin Payez, Nathan Pepper, Andrew Phillip, Robert Phillips, Ken Pittenger, Denise Pleune, Jacob Plsek, Jeff Prosser, Courtney Ramshaw, Jane Asher Reany, Joy Robins, Dirk Rogers, Neza Rufuku, Chris Saksa, Dennis Scheyer, Rohner Segnitz, Scott Shiflett, Julie Smith, Molly Spear, Clay Speicher, Dustin Stanton, Helen Stanton, Jodi Tack, Phyllis Tesoro, Carl Thomas, Christy Timmons, Andrew Tippie, Christian Townsend, Joe Tsai, Trisha Velez, Mike Welchans, Azul Weldon, Ed Weldon, and Tony Yanow.

ABOUT THE AUTHOR

Rob Weldon lives in Los Angeles, CA, and works at a craft beer bar. To learn more about his books or to connect, find him online at: Facebook.com/TheOmnistSeries, Instagram @ blood.wren and Twitter @WingmanMusic.